AN EVIL MOST MEN WELCOME

Leta Serafim

coffeetownpress

Kenmore, WA

coffeetownpress

A Coffeetown Press book published by Epicenter Press

Epicenter Press
6524 NE 181st St. Suite 2
Kenmore, WA 98028.
www.Epicenterpress.com
www.Coffeetownpress.com
www.Camelpress.com

For more information go to: www.coffeetownpress.com

An Evil Most Men Welcome
Copyright © 2020 by Leta Serafim

ISBN: 9781603817226 (trade paper)
ISBN: 9781603817257 (ebook)

Printed in the United States of America

For Philip

Acknowledgements

I wish to thank my friend, Dawn Lefakis, for her help with all aspects of this book and for her encouragement and support during the forty odd years we have known each other. Also, Margaret Carayannopoulos, whose encouragement has been unwavering and my beloved sister, Merridy, whose wise counsel and boundless love I could not live without. I have been blessed with many gifts, the greatest being my family and friends both here and in Greece. I thank all of you.

Chapter 1

Hope Erikson stumbled across the beach to the cave to get her mother-in-law, Sophia, the oregano she'd demanded, cursing her every step of the way. The two of them had harvested the oregano earlier that year on a hillside in Mani, the area in Greece her husband's family called home. Empty and forbidding, the region had once been considered a portal to hell and in Hope's mind it still was.

Her mother-in-law didn't really need the oregano. The tourists would never notice if it wasn't sprinkled on their souvlakias. They'd eat, pay their bill and leave. The old woman just wanted to boss her around.

Her mother-in-law was in charge of the food preparation at the family's taverna; and she stored her supplies deep inside the cavern, the cool air serving as a make-shift refrigerator. Midday, the heat was stifling; and Hope paused to wipe her face on the hem of her dress before continuing on. The gritty sand was so hot she could feel it through the soles of her flip flops.

The taverna was located in Aghioi Anargyiou, a seaside village on Spetses, an island less than three hours away by boat from Athens. It was a ramshackle affair, tables and chairs set out on the beach, a lean-to in the back serving as a kitchen. Music was blaring from the speakers her brother-in-law had rigged up in the pine trees to draw customers. Today most of the songs he'd chosen were American and dated from Hope's college years and, hearing them, she felt a wave of homesickness.

Propped up on a crutch, the old woman cooked in the back, grilling meat over an open fire, smoke encircling her in a greasy cloud. It suited her, the smoke, Hope thought, Fire burn and caldron bubble. The rest of the family waited on tables and rented umbrellas and chaise lounges to the tourists who came to swim in the bay. Hope worked alongside them, the smell of the charcoal clinging to her skin long after she'd finished her shift. She served food from eight a.m. until midnight every day of the week and slept in a two-bedroom house the family rented, her brother-in-law, Vasilis, and his wife, Daphne, in one room, she and her husband, Thanasis, and his mother on a cot in the other. Hope shook her head. And the old bat wondered why she didn't have children. Another brother, Stavros and his wife, Chryssoula, lived in another rented house with their three children, Petros, Christos and little Zoe.

Hope had discovered early on in her marriage that there was no word for 'privacy' in Greek as the concept simply did not exist in the country. She had objected to this in the beginning, but after more than a decade here, she'd come to accept the fact that her husband's family was a fixture in her life.

She ran her fingers over her dress. It dated from the summer she'd met her husband and had been washed so many times the pattern—the little sprigs of blue flowers—had long since faded. Still she clung to it as a link to her past; to the person she'd been before she'd married Thanasis and it had all gone to hell.

A baby would fix things, she told herself, patting her swelling abdomen. A baby would be the solution to everything.

She looked around before ducking into the cave. A stiff wind was blowing and it ruffled the branches of the pine trees on the cliffs above the cove, their scent heavy on the air. She was fond of the sound they made. Like most things, the Greeks had a word for it. "*Throisma*," the rustling of trees in the wind.

A group of local boys were diving off the jetty, their dark heads as sleek as seals when they re-emerged, laughing and splashing water at their friends. No one else was swimming, the fierce wind must be keeping them away.

Little more than a cleft in the rock, the cave was small, less than thirty feet in size. There were many like it on Spetses, shadowy pockets of darkness in the eroded limestone headlands. On the far side of the cove was the Bekiris Cave, where Greeks had hidden from marauding Muslim Albanians in the eighteenth century. Miraculously all of them had survived that assault. People had also taken shelter in this cave, but unlike those in the Bekiris Cave, they had been found and slaughtered. The surrounding sea had run red that day, according to the stories; and a small memorial had been attached to a rock near the entrance to mark the site. Sometimes when the wind whistled through the rocks, Hope could almost hear the victims scream.

The cave had never been wired for electricity and it was so dark she needed a flashlight to navigate. Wooden shelves held dusty bottles of wine from the family's land holdings and cases of beer, both German and domestic. Stacked in the back were tins of olive oil, embossed with the family name, the brassy metal tins gleaming in the shadows like pirate's treasure.

Tied up with strings, the oregano was hanging in bunches from one of the shelves and she grabbed one and started back. There was a dark puddle on the floor and she ran her flashlight over it, thinking one of the bottles of wine had rolled off the shelf and broken. She followed the stream of liquid with her light, seeking its source. It was too viscous to be wine and smelled familiar, something she knew, but couldn't place. She looked around again, suddenly afraid. There was another entrance to the cave— an opening in the back—but few people knew about it, and as far as she knew, aside from the family, it hadn't been used in years. Becoming more and more frightened, she wondered if an intruder had gained access, if he was in here with her now.

She saw her husband, Thanasis, a few seconds later, lying in a pool of blood, his arms over his face as if to defend himself. He was drenched in blood and there was broken wine bottle buried his throat. Shards of glass surrounded him; the jagged pieces thick with blood. She touched his face.

"Oh, God, Thanasis, Thanasis!"

Stumbling out of the cave, she began to scream and couldn't stop. Half-falling, she clutched at strangers on the beach in an effort to remain upright.

"*Voitheia! Voitheia!* Help! Help!!"

Hearing her, her in-laws came thundering across the beach and as usual, chaos and recrimination ruled the day.

Chapter 2

Chief Officer of the Spetses Police Department, Melissa Costas, walked over to the window and stood staring out. The air conditioning in her office was no match for the heat outside; and her uniform was sticking to her, the blue polyester fabric soaked in sweat. As always, the island was quiet.

By and large, Spetses was peaceful, far more so than the slums in Athens where she'd served before. In the two long years she'd been posted here, there hadn't been a single crime worthy of the name. A few domestics, a little thievery, nothing more. There were no migrants rioting in camps, no drug running to speak of. Even the drunken tourists had departed, seeking the wilder shores of Mykonos and Paros. A normal person would have rejoiced in this. But she longed to do what she'd been trained to do—ferret out criminals and arrest them—and as far as she could see, there were no criminals here. She was marooned in paradise.

Spetses?! Even the name sounded like spitting.

Late July, it was over 38 Celsius, over 100 degrees Fahrenheit. Unwilling to leave the air conditioning, Costas' subordinates were lounging around the reception area at the front of the station. She could hear her second-in-command, Michalis Constantinos, talking excitedly to someone on the phone at the front desk. Clean-shaven and earnest, he'd joined the force at the same time she had; and the two of them had debated policing techniques when he'd first arrived, arguing about the use of force and the best way to interrogate suspects. Now he spent his days playing computer games. Like her, the idleness was ruining him.

Raising the window, she leaned her head out, breathing in the warm air of summer. The police department occupied a suite of rooms on the second floor of a yellow brick building in the Dapia, the area around the harbor.

A person had to ring a doorbell to enter just like for a private house. Costas had objected to this at first, believing the doorbell and the lax way her staff answered it gave the wrong message to the citizenry.

Her subordinates had yawned in her face; and she had eventually given up. It didn't really matter if they answered the door or not, she'd soon discovered. The citizenry had no real need of their services. The only crime that took place on Spetses as far as she could tell was tax evasion and that wasn't her problem.

She shut the window and sat back down at her desk. She'd taken care to keep her office impersonal. There were no family pictures or souvenirs, nothing that gave a hint as to who she was in her off-hours or where she'd come from. She was a cop, she told herself again. That was where she began and ended. And sadly, that was just about all she was. She was no longer anyone's daughter and she had never been anyone's wife.

Constantinos burst into her office. "Chief Officer, we've got to go! A man's been killed in Aghioi Anargyiou!"

* * *

It took Constantinos and the other three policemen a long time to get the body out of the cave, Melissa Costas supervising them as they struggled. She'd done what she could to preserve the evidence before they'd started, sealing off the area around the body and making casts of the footprints she found there.

The entrance was narrow and her men wrestled with the metal gurney, fighting to push it forward, the weight of the dead man throwing them off. It was an impossible task, one of her men complained after the third try; the entrance was too small; it was like navigating in a closet. He wanted to dispense with the stretcher altogether and carry the dead man out by his arms and legs. The others demurred, reluctant to touch the corpse, the congealed blood that covered it. Eventually, they placed the dead man in a black body bag, tied the bag to the gurney with a rope, hoisted it on their shoulders and staggered out into the light. They'd gently led Hope's mother-in-law away before they'd started the process. Not so Hope, whom they pushed aside and viewed with suspicion, Costas glancing over at her now and then as she spoke to the others in Greek.

Hope watched them with apprehension, noting how the role of chief mourner had shifted almost instantly from her, by rights the bereaved widow, to her mother-in-law. As always, she would have no place here. It had been like this ever since she'd married into her husband's family and so it would be now. She'd believed for a long time it was because she was American, but now she thought it went deeper than that. Some primordial relationship between mother and son that excluded all others.

Chapter 3

"Clear the way!!" Costas yelled, pushing her way through the crowd. "Coming through! Coming through!"

The wheels of the gurney had no traction on the sand; and they had to stop, lift the dead man up and carry him to the waiting ambulance, a journey made worse by the slipperiness of the plastic body bag.

The crowd of onlookers surged forward, snapping pictures of them with their cell phones like the paparazzi.

"*Stamata! Deixe ligo sevasmo! Feige apo edo!*" Costas yelled, shoving them out of the way. Show some respect! Get out of here! Fed up, she grabbed a phone out of a woman's hand and pocketed it.

The woman started squawking in French, flailing at Costas in an effort to get her phone back. As Costas was nearly two meters tall, it was no contest.

"Enough," Costas bellowed. "*Assez!*"

"*Quelle savage*," the woman muttered.

Costas turned back to her men. "After you finish disposing of the body, round up everyone on the beach and ask them what they saw or heard. Any information they can provide."

"What about the family of the deceased?" asked Constantinos.

"Separate them and keep them separate. Under no circumstances are they to talk to each another and compare notes. Also, and I can't stress this enough, make sure they don't throw anything away. Nothing, not even a gum wrapper or a cigarette butt. I don't want them destroying evidence."

"The old woman's pretty upset."

This coming from Constantinos, her best man.

"Obviously, she's upset." Costas fought keep her voice level. "Someone just sliced her son to ribbons."

She'd already arranged for the victim's body to be transported to the coroner's office in Athens by boat. The ambulance driver would park alongside the quay and the crew of the Flying Dolphin, one of a fleet of aging catamarans, would take it from there. With any luck they would get the victim on board without too much fuss. Her boss, Haralambos Stathis, in turn would oversee the transfer of the body from the harbor in Piraeus to the coroner's office in Athens. The autopsy was scheduled for early the next morning. Murders were rare in Greece and her supervisor was moving quickly.

Before heading into the cave, Costas approached the victim's wife, Hope Erikson. "I'm Chief Officer of the Spetses Police. I'm in charge here and I need to ask you some questions."

Nearly prostrate with grief, the woman didn't seem to hear her.

Costas faltered. Never good with people, this was her first homicide and she didn't know how to proceed, whether to console this woman or treat her as a suspect. She loathed emotional outbursts—the tears and the mucous and the noise—and always backed away when people got upset, hardly possible today, given the circumstances. She was the lead investigator on a homicide. Tears or no tears, she had a job to do.

"I need you to retrace your steps," she told Hope. "To do exactly what you did before and after you found your husband's body. I want you to remember everything you saw, no matter how insignificant."

Hope dutifully stood up and followed the same route she'd taken to the cave, Costas nipping at her heels.

Costas switched on her flashlight and ran it around the interior of the cave. "Why were you in here today?"

"My mother-in-law stores food inside and she sent me there to bring her something."

"What exactly?"

"Oregano."

"She's the one in charge here?"

The American nodded.

"And once you got inside, what did you see?"

"Thanasis." Hope gestured to patch of stained soil. "He was laying there."

"You hear anything?"

"No, just the wind. It plays tricks on you sometimes when you're in here, howls and whistles through the rocks. For a minute, I thought there was someone in there with me." She shrugged. "But it might have just been the wind."

Costas cocked her head, straining to hear what the American had described—the wind crying out like a human—but all she heard was Hope's labored breathing.

"Did you see anyone unfamiliar in the vicinity of the cave, someone who didn't belong?" She was asking about migrants, but didn't want to spell it out, afraid she'd get the American's back up. In her experience, they were funny that way, friends with the whole world.

Greece had once been one of the safest countries in the world, but that had all changed in recent years, break-ins and muggings occurring on a daily basis throughout the country. One of Costas' cousins had been assaulted and her shoulder broken after visiting an ATM machine in Athens. Spetses had been spared the onslaught so far, but that might well have changed. It was close to Athens. Anything was possible.

Many people believed the recent influx of foreigners was responsible for the upsurge in crime, but Costas wasn't convinced the newcomers were entirely responsible. No question, they had contributed to it, but there were other factors as well, drugs, for one, which were making their presence felt in Athens and throughout the countryside in Greece.

"Some local kids were swimming," Hope said. "But I didn't see anyone out of the ordinary. No migrants, if that's what you're asking."

"When was the last time you saw your husband alive?"

"Just before lunch."

"When exactly?

"I don't know. Twelve, twelve-thirty." Her voice rose. "Why are you asking me these questions? I told you, Thanasis was dead when I found him." She began to sob uncontrollably.

Costas waited for Hope to regain control of herself, but she continued to cry, falling to her knees and screaming her husband's name over and over. Again, Costa didn't know what to do and looked around for someone she could turn her over to. The victim's mother was standing nearby, but she looked away when Costas signaled her. No love lost there.

Taking pity on the American, Costas helped her up and half-carried, half-walked her back to the house and dumped her in a lawn chair in the front yard. "Try and relax," she counseled. "I'll be back as soon as I finish processing the crime scene. Do you want someone to stay with you? I could send one of my men over to keep you company."

Hope shook her head.

As with the others, Costas warned her not to enter the house, explaining the entire building was now an active crime scene. "No one is to go inside until the forensic experts arrive and go through it."

"I'm pregnant. What if I have to pee?"

"You'll have to do it at the taverna."

Again, Hope's voice rose. "I can't believe this."

Before Costas left the house, she ordered Constantinos to keep the American in view at all times. "Same rules as with the others. No talking. No throwing anything away. And she's not to go anywhere near the house."

She'd been taught at the police academy that the majority of homicide victims were killed by someone they knew and that spouses were often the guilty party which meant Hope Erikson was the prime suspect in the case. Perhaps that's all this was. A private domestic tragedy. But somehow Costas doubted it.

Returning to the cave, she started processing the crime scene, draping yellow crime scene tape around the entrance and setting up a kind of restricted, no-man's land. She then summoned the newest member of her staff, Petros Simonidis, and asked him to help her.

Studious and detail oriented, Simonidis worked hard and always did his best unlike the others men in office, Giorgos Ritsos and Alexis Pappas, who did as little as they could get away with. Constantinos had also begun slacking off, which worried her. It was almost as if laziness was contagious.

Turning on her flashlight, Costas stepped into to the cave. Her heart was pounding. This was what she'd been born to do. Whoever the killer was, there would be no escape. She was coming for him.

* * *

After setting up lights and a generator, Simonidis took photographs while Costas dusted the broken shards of glass for prints. The unmistakable smell of death, feces and blood, assaulted her as she worked and she kept gagging, fighting not to vomit all over the evidence.

Before her team removed the body, Costas had drawn a chalk outline around it and she concentrated on that area, checking the ground for footprints. She then gathered up the shards of glass, dusted them for prints and bagged them in an envelope, following the chain of evidence protocol she'd learned as a student.

After she'd gathered all the shards, she swept up samples of the bloody soil beneath them with a tiny brush and carefully funneled them into a second set of envelopes. Perhaps the killer cut himself on the glass; and the lab would find his DNA intermingled with the DNA of the victim. Along with blood, wine had formed a shallow puddle, its scent cloying and obscene under the circumstances. The two substances had co-mingled, one liquid thick and viscous, the other one thin. The forensic people would have their work cut out from them, distinguishing between the two.

She measured the angle of the victim's blood and distance it had traveled, following the trajectory of blood splatter across the walls of the cave, then entered both figures in her notebook. Blood was everywhere, even high up on the rocks, indicating the killer had nicked the jugular vein.

Both she and Simonidis were wearing protective booties over their shoes, hair nets, surgical masks and latex gloves. As there were no hazmat suits on Spetses, Costas had been forced to improvise. She'd used plastic baggies to secure the evidence on the victim's hands, securing them in place with rubber bands. Primitive, she knew, but it was all she had. Her mask was so old it had started to disintegrate, flakes of plastic filling her mouth with every breath. No matter, she told herself. She was wearing it to process a crime scene, not to protect herself from Ebola.

Forensic specialists were on their way from Athens, but they wouldn't arrive for a few hours; and she'd been in a rush to get started, afraid valuable time would be lost if she waited. Her boss in Athens had concurred, but warned her to proceed carefully.

"Just do the preliminaries," Haralambos Stathis instructed. "Take your time and bag the glass and anything else that jumps out at you, but leave the rest for the experts."

Heeding Stathis' words, Costas and Simonidis worked their way slowly and steadily out from the epicenter where the victim had fallen to the far reaches of the cave. The ground around the body had been so disturbed by the men with the gurney, Costas didn't bother taking casts there—too many people, the stretcher...it was a mess—concentrating instead on the area in front the wine rack. Discovering a faint pair of prints, she instructed Simonidis to photograph them. The floor of the cave was uneven and he had to repeat the process many times before he was able to get a clear image. The footprints were still hazy, but at least they gave an indication as to the size and weight of the person who'd been standing there. She then made casts, filling the indentations with the silicone solution and waiting for it to set.

Barrels of wine were propped up on wooden trestles along the far wall of the cave, but as they hadn't figured in the murder, Costas didn't bother dusting them, focusing instead on the bottles and dusting each one in turn, starting with the ones on the bottom shelf and working her way up. Spider webs encased the top shelf; and her presence had disturbed the inhabitants which were now everywhere, running around in a frenzy. One landed on Costas' neck and she brushed it off with a shudder. The perils of police work.

"What was the sequence?" Simonidis asked. "Did the killer surprise him or did they enter together?"

"I don't know exactly what happened. My guess is the victim was sitting on the ground and the killer was standing over him and they had a fight. The killer grabbed the bottle out of his hand and hit him with it. Or maybe the victim fell during the scuffle and hit his head on the rocks."

"Hard to break a bottle over someone's head."

"I know. Maybe they wrestled over it; and it broke and killer picked it up and came at him. The first thing we do after we get out of here is check every single person who was in the neighborhood, see if one of them has cuts on their hands they can't explain."

"You said 'he gouged out his throat.' You're saying it was a man?"

"Given the level of violence, that would be my assumption. But we can't rule anybody out at this point, male or female. All I'm sure of is it was spontaneous. No way this killing was premeditated. No one sets out to murder someone with a wine bottle."

Continuing to talk, the two of them reenacted various scenarios—the killer coming at the victim from the front, then the side and finally from the back, seeking to determine what had transpired prior to the murder, Costas playing the role of the victim and Simonidis, the assailant.

Their play-acting revealed nothing to Costas. It was as she'd told Simonidis: whoever had done this had acted in haste, clumsily slamming the victim in the head with the bottle, then slicing his throat. Either act might have killed him. Thanasis Papadopoulos might also have choked to death on his own blood. They'd have to wait for the coroner. Only he could judge the sequence of events and say exactly how the victim had died.

* * *

Costas was relieved to see her men had followed her instructions and were interviewing the people from the beach. Pappas was speaking to a group of local boys, presumably the ones Hope Erikson had said she'd seen swimming, while Ritsos was questioning a foreign woman.

"Nothing," Pappas reported when she joined him.

With a weathered face and deep, penetrating voice, he projected authority which would have been valuable in police work if the weathering had actually come from the job, not from the hours he spent on his boat. Still he was physically able, muscular and fit, and, if he was to be believed, could bench press fifty kilos at the gym. But that was all he could do. Talking to him was like talking a tree. Same build, same level of animation.

Ritsos was close to Pappas in age, but unlike his cohort, he was short, thick and ungainly—also a tree, but one that had met up with a chain saw, a stump.

It hadn't been easy being a female directing an all-male work force, even one as indolent as this one, but Costas had persevered and believed she'd won the men over, organizing a party when the youngest one got married, taking a tray of sweets to another's home for his son's name day. She'd been diligent in learning the facts of their lives and acting on them and she was convinced it had paid off. In truth, the festivities had ended the moment she had arrived. Although she was unaware of it, she tended to have that effect on people. A wet blanket didn't come close.

Tall and thin with black, penetrating eyes, she was a striking woman, although her beauty was marred by the look of disapproval that never left her face, the reproachful way she always dealt with others. Her voice was strident, that of a teacher addressing a roomful of wayward students. Let me tell you, *na sou po*, was as her favorite expression. She believed being a policewoman was a serious job, hence she must behave seriously. Unfortunately, this was true in her private life as well, her hectoring manner eventually driving away the most ardent suitor. She never conversed; she lectured, envisioning herself as a stern, but righteous teacher of humanity, men especially, who in her opinion needed a lot of supervision.

Consequently, one by one her boyfriends had all fled, the last leaving her stranded in the middle of Athens in his haste to get away. They'd been in his car and she'd made a few helpful suggestions about his driving; and he'd pulled over, put her out on the street and sped off without so much as a word of good-bye.

Her four subordinates had been intrigued when she first arrived, the consensus being while she might be a good cop; she was hell on wheels as a woman.

The oldest man in the office, Giorgos Pappas, had been a police officer for over fifteen years and seen his share of Chief Officers come and go, but he admitted he'd been thinking about retiring since Costas arrived. "It's those eyes of hers," he said. "She's like Medusa, that woman who could turn men to stone just by looking at them. I see her looking at me, I feel myself stiffening up."

"Stiffening up?" Ritsos repeated, wagging a finger at him. "Naughty, naughty."

"No, no, not like that. I'd never go near Costas. You'd get frostbite, you touch her. Icicles on your balls."

'*Vouvala*,' Costas male cousins had called her as a teen-ager—water buffalo—before she'd joined the force and slimmed down. They'd bullied her relentlessly until she'd sat on the ringleader and cracked two of his ribs.

Even as an adult, she was merciless. One unlucky tourist, drunk at eleven a.m. on the streets of Athens, had found this out the hard way. Disgusted, she'd handcuffed him and dragged him through the sweltering streets without so much as a sip of water, thinking it would be a good object lesson. Unfortunately, the man had collapsed from dehydration and had to be hospitalized; and the resulting debacle had nearly cost her job.

"You do that again," her boss, Stathis, had said. "And I'll send you to Kastellorizo." Less than seven kilometers long, Kastellorizo was the Greek equivalent of Siberia.

Costa had taken his words to heart and sought to remake herself, reading articles on anger management and practicing breathing exercises, even going so far as to invest in expensive cosmetics to pretty herself up, but she knew in her heart it was hopeless. She was what she was: a bad-tempered, judgmental shrew. There'd be no changing her. Her mother, who loved her dearly, once said, "My God, Melissa, who appointed you judge and jury of the whole human race?"

Unfortunately, her superiors in Athens felt the same way. That bit about Kastellorizo had been a joke. But she knew one more misstep and they would fire her. And if she wasn't a cop, what was she? Like a priest, it was her vocation, what she had been called by God to do.

She grabbed a black spiral notebook before leaving the station and wrote 'The Killing of Thanasis Papadopoulos" on the first page. In addition to taping the tourists, she'd take down anything pertinent they had to say and follow up on it.

Keeping an accurate log of witness testimony, the so-called 'the murder book,' was crucial, her instructors at the police academy had taught her. It was one of the cardinal rules when investigating a homicide.

As she'd anticipated, nothing came of her discussions with the tourists. Not one person she spoke to had known the cave was there until Hope Erikson had run screaming from it. "Sorry, I wish I could help you" they all said, "but I don't know anything."

Costas' English was good and the interviews proceeded quickly. The tourists were very forthcoming and readily answered her questions. Most were excited to be part of a murder investigation.

"Are you really a policewoman?" a British woman asked, looking her up and down.

"Yes, I'm in charge of the department here."

The woman continued to stare at her. Like the Parthenon, Costas would be another foreign curiosity to discuss with her friends when she returned to Manchester.

A couple of middle-aged Americans, a husband and wife from Indiana, worried the killing might have been a terrorist attack, but Costas quickly disabused them of this notion, stating emphatically that to the best of her knowledge ISIS had no presence in Spetses and its operatives had not been involved.

"Look around you," she said. "There are no terrorists here."

"There's a Pakistani working in the back. I saw him," the man said.

"He was watching us," his wife chimed in. "You should have seen the look on his face when he heard us speaking English, the hate."

They both reeked of sunscreen and goodwill, stumbling over their words in their haste to tell her their story, to warn her of the dangerous man lurking in the kitchen. The woman was dressed in a sarong covered with hibiscus blossoms and had a battered straw hat on her head, tilted at a rakish angle. Her husband was wearing shorts, white socks and sneakers.

The only other person Costas had ever seen who wore socks at the beach had been Richard Nixon and that had been in a magazine, not in real life. But then these were Americans and Americans did any number of things which mystified her, Donald Trump being only the latest.

An old woman was standing next to the couple; and Costas asked her what she'd seen.

In spite of her advanced age, she was a keen observer and carefully described where people had been sitting in the taverna, their various nationalities and what they'd eaten, even what some of them had paid. She also was very specific about who had brought them their food—three Greeks by her count, two men and a woman.

"I did hear that woman yelling," she said. "I think she was the one who found him. I didn't know why she was screaming at the time. It never crossed my mind that someone had been murdered."

Well over seventy, she was wearing a floppy hat and the kind of sunglasses they give cataract patients.

"What time was this?" Costas asked.

"One, one-thirty. I'm here from Canada with my daughter and her family and we had jusst finished lunch."

"Let's go back to the beginning," Costas said. "Was the woman who found the body there when you first sat down? Was she waiting on tables?"

"No, she was helping the Greek woman, who was grilling in back. I remember thinking she, the cook, I mean, was too old for that kind of work, standing over an open fire all day long. She asked the woman who found the body to do something for her and she didn't want to do it, you could see it on her face. If she could have, she would have spat in her eye."

"Did you see where the young woman went?"

The Canadian pointed in the direction of the cave. "Took her time about it, too, the little missy..."

It was consistent with what Hope Erikson had told them. She'd been dispatched to the cave by her mother-in-law to get oregano.

Enjoying the attention, the Canadian woman continued to talk. Her family was gathered around her and they listened with growing impatience, her grandchildren fidgeting, her son-in-law rolling his eyes.

Ignoring them, Costas spent more than a half hour with her. The old woman was obviously lonely and this was how she survived—talking to the people next to her on airplanes or the kids who bagged her groceries at the store, the random policewoman when the occasion demanded it. Watching life going on around her and pretending she was a part of it.

Costas often found herself doing the same thing, holding her staff captive long after the close of day, pretending they weren't subordinates; they were friends. She couldn't seem to help herself.

"What else do you remember?" Costas asked gently.

"Now and then a dark-skinned man would poke his head out of the kitchen window and say something to the Greek woman at the grill. He looked Arabic. I have some in my neighborhood now, so I know what they look like. I thought at the time he might be a handyman. He came out a few minutes later and emptied the trash."

Although Costas doubted the Pakistani was involved, she wrote this down and circled it. The garbage cans were close to the cave. It was the first entry she'd made in the murder book.

The woman shuddered. "As long as I live, I'll never forget the sound of that girl screaming. The woman at the grill, too. You should have seen her. She fell to knees and began tearing her hair out. I've always heard that expression—'tearing your hair out'—all my life but I that was the first time I ever say anyone actually do it."

Chapter 4

It was getting dark by the time Costas concluded the last interview, the light fading from the sky. The forensic team had arrived from Athens, strung a canvas tarpaulin up over the entrance to the cave and was busy now unloading their gear.

Costas had already turned over the evidence she'd collected, pointing out where the material in each envelope had come from and describing how she and Simonidis had gathered it, making it clear they had abided by the chain of evidence protocol. Photographs, plastic gloves, labeling, they had been meticulous.

By her count, only seven people had known the cave was there; and they were all members of the victim's family, eight if she counted the Pakistani, who worked for them, eleven if she included the oldest brother's children. As the latter were all very young, she quickly ruled them out. Seven, it was then, seven possible suspects. There was the outside chance an unknown intruder was responsible, someone who had been looting the cave and been surprised by the victim, lashed out and killed him. But Costas thought it unlikely. There'd been little of value in the cave, nothing at all that warranted the level of violence she'd seen. In her opinion, this was no random attack. It was something deeply personal. That was the only scenario that made sense.

Before releasing the tourists, she'd insisted they leave their contact information with one of her men, their home addresses and where they were staying in Greece. "I am sorry if these interviews inconvenienced you, but a man was murdered today and we view anyone who was in the vicinity at the time as a person of interest."

The group gradually dispersed, complaining about the way business was conducted in Greece and the cartoonish nature of its police force, Costas in particular.

Although the criticism stung, Costas felt it was warranted. Five hours in and she had nothing.

* * *

Costas dispatched Pappas and Ritsos to the hotels where the tourists had said they were staying. Visitors had to show valid passports or Greek identification cards when they registered—it was required by law—and she wanted copies of those documents.

"I doubt they lied to us, but we still need to verify what they said. While you're at it, see if you can learn anything about the victim and his family. Spetses is small and the hotels are at the center of it. The people who work there will know if there was bad blood between the three brothers or if the victim was cheating on his wife. Gossip is what you're after. Anything that could point us in the right direction."

Simonidis had already returned to the station and was busy running the names of everyone they'd spoken to through the databases on the computer—Greeks and foreigners alike, some fifty-five people altogether. As with the hotels, Costas doubted he'd turn anything up, but she wanted it done anyway.

He'd balked when she'd ask him to run the names of the victim's family as well. "Papadopoulos is one of the most common names in Greece. There must a hundred thousand of them if not more. I'll do my best, but I'm not promising anything."

The last person Costas questioned was the Pakistani. Barely conversant in Greek, the man acted out his job when she asked him what he did at the taverna, miming washing dishes with his hands and sweeping the floor with an invisible broom. Small and dark, he was dressed in a loose cotton shirt and frayed jeans, cheap plastic sandals on his calloused feet. He had a furtive way about him and didn't look her in the eye, hesitated far too long before giving her his name, "Zahid Korai."

"Where are you from, Mr. Korai?"

"Pakistan," he said. "Karachi."

Judging from his demeanor, he was illegal, someone who'd washed ashore here and was afraid he might be deported and sent back home.

"I stay here, I work." He claimed he'd only been on Spetses for three months and swore he had never gone near the cave during that time. "Family go, but me, never."

"Which ones in the family?" Costas asked.

"All."

Costas made a note to check when the Pakistani had arrived in Greece and what his status was. Perhaps the family had kept a record when they hired him, although she doubted it. She was sure he was being paid in cash and the arrangement between him and employer was casual. Come September when the tourists left, he would go, too.

She cautioned him about leaving the island, saying he wasn't in any trouble, but she needed to know his whereabouts at all times. "A man was killed here today, you understand."

"Mr. Thanasis, he was good fellow, all the time laughing," the Pakistani said. "Only one who say '*yeia sou, Zahid*.' Good day. "The others they do not say, they do not see Zahid."

* * *

Costas walked down to the edge of the sea, wanting a moment alone before meeting the victim's family. Perhaps it had been a mistake to interview the tourists first, but she hadn't been ready to deal with the others yet. To question a heart-broken old woman, tearing her hair out.

She was fast discovering it was one thing to study murder in a classroom and another thing entirely to deal with it firsthand. Even collecting the evidence had been hard, breathing in the metallic scent of the victim's blood, feeling it permeate her hair and skin. She'd vomited twice already outside the cave and feared she might be sick again.

Cupping her hand, she scooped up some water and splashed it on her face, swished some around her mouth and spat it out. For all her training, she was a novice at homicide, a novice at death, having experienced it only once before and that had been the end of an elderly relative, comatose for years. She'd been deeply traumatized by the sight of Thanasis Papadopoulos, lying dead at her feet in a pool of blood, his throat torn out as if by a wolf. She'd wanted to investigate a homicide her entire professional life and yet when the moment came, she'd fallen apart, staggering around and getting sick all over Simonidis, who'd rushed to help her. He'd cleaned himself off without a word and gone back to work. It had taken her far longer to recover.

If she wasn't a cop, what was she?

People had left the beach and the cove was deserted. The sun was setting and its lengthening rays played across the surface of the water. The pale limestone promontories were luminous in the fading light, the hollowed-out places where the sea had eaten into the cliffs as black as mine shafts. Above her, bats were careening like kites caught by the wind. The air was still and the only sound was the soft onrushing of the sea.

Her mother had called twilight, 'the melancholy hour' and maybe it was. But Costas had always loved it. She knew the history of the area, how the islanders had taken refuge in the cave at the end of the peninsula and escaped annihilation. But that was a different time. Tonight, all was peaceful. A stage set after the actors had left.

Taking a deep breath, she picked up her backpack and walked in the direction of the victim's house. She had three ballpoint pens in a pocket protector on her shirt, her murder book in hand. The mp3 she planned to use was her own as she didn't trust the tape recorder she'd inherited from her predecessor; and she'd checked it twice before leaving the office to make sure it worked. She was as ready as she'd ever be.

Family, first and foremost, her mentors at the academy had taught her, after that all the rest, one after another in concentrating circles; the person closest to the center, to the victim, most often was the killer.

* * *

A grove of old pine trees dominated the area in front of the victim's house. The yard, what there was of it, thickly overgrown with weeds. The house itself was shabby, the walls blistered in places by the blowing sand. Lawn chairs were set up in a circle under the trees, empty beer cans rolling around beneath them.

As a child Costas had lived in a similar place, known financial hardship first hand. Her father had supplemented his meager income by growing vegetables in pots, thinking to sell them in the open-air market, the *laiki,* in Piraeus where she'd grown up. But like so many of her father's get rich schemes, the plan had failed. The tomatoes had succumbed to blight and splattered all over on the balcony, making an unspeakable mess and drawing flies, hundreds and hundreds of flies. Her mother had been furious and complained bitterly to anyone who would listen to her about it.

Someone had made a similar effort here, she saw, vegetables planted in rows along the left side of the house. These plants hadn't fared well either. The sandy soil was too poor; and the effort looked to have been abandoned, rotting zucchinis and peppers littering the ground.

A pair of men's jeans hung on a clothesline, water dripping off of them. Clothes dried fast in the summer, usually in less than an hour, which meant the pants had been washed recently. Costas made a note to ask the forensic team to bag them and have them tested for blood.

Constantinos was waiting for her at the door.

"You talk to them yet?" she asked him.

"No. I was waiting for you."

"How are they doing?"

"About as well as can be expected. I know you wanted me to separate them, but it was impossible. Mother is a mess. They're all sitting around in the back and I took a glass of water out to her and it was like she couldn't see, like she was having a stroke or something. Her sons, Stavros and Vasilis, are with her along with Vasilis' wife, Daphne. I know you didn't want anybody to go inside, so I've kept them out there. It's better anyway. Inside is an inferno. I warned them not to talk about the case and as far as I know they haven't."

"What about the others?"

"Stavros' wife, Chryssoula, is putting the kids to bed in the other house. Widow's out there, too." He pointed to the back yard. "Hasn't spoken since I got here. Been crying off and on since I got here."

"Give me their names and describe them to me."

"Thanasis, the victim, was the youngest of three brothers and, as you know, his wife is an American woman named Hope Erikson. You've already spoken to her. She's the one with the pudgy face and blonde hair. Stavros is the oldest and he's married to a Greek woman named Chyrssoula, and they have three children, all of them far too young to have been involved in this. Chryssoula isn't as beautiful as she thinks she is, but it's not for want of trying. Frothy hair and make-up about sum her up. Vasilis is the middle brother and he's married to Daphne, who's tall and silent and wears her hair in a braid."

"They have any children?"

Constantinos shook his head. "And then, of course, there's the victim's mother, Sophia, who's a force to be reckoned with."

* * *

Bleak and uninviting, the living room smelled of cigarettes; and underfoot the floor was gritty with tracked in sand. A battered green sofa occupied most of the space. In addition, there was a table and four chairs, plastic from the looks of them. A wooden armoire stood in the far corner with its doors hanging open. The only decoration were some prints of roses on the wall, the illustrations so bleached by the sun only the thorns were visible.

The Papadopoulos family had done nothing to make the space more livable. Remnants of food littered every surface and dirty plates were piled up in the sink, a pan full of congealing fat left out on the stove. A suitcase was open on the floor in the bedroom Vasilis and his wife shared, wrinkled clothing everywhere. Pulling latex gloves on, Costas examined the clothing, searching for evidence of blood, but didn't see any. No matter, they'd still need to be tested.

There was no air conditioning; and as Constantinos had said, the interior of the house was stifling. All the windows were open and she could hear the family talking out in the yard.

"*Kourageio, mana,*" a man was saying. Courage, Mother.

His words had no effect on the old woman, who was slumped down in a plastic chair, a pair of crutches beside her; and she continued to moan, her face in her hands.

Eventually, they both fell quiet. No lights were on and the yard was deep in shadows, the man's burning cigarette the only indication anyone was there.

Suddenly, the victim's mother reared up and began to pounding the metal arms of her chair with her fists—the sound shocking in the night stillness. "Ach, Thanasis!! Thanasis!!"

"*Ela, Mama,*" the same man said. "*Iremise.* Come on, Mother, calm down."

The woman stopped for a moment and cocked her head, then started up again, the pounding growing louder and louder, a drumbeat of agony. Intermittently, she called out in a sing song voice. Gibberish, it sounded like.

"Thanasis!" the old woman yelled again.

The pattern repeated itself several more times, a long interval of silence, followed by the woman's hysterical screaming.

Listening to her, Costas thought Constantinos might be right—the old woman had sustained some kind of neurological damage. Or perhaps it was only grief she was witnessing. Mary weeping at the cross of Jesus.

In ancient times, the Spartans had been told 'to gird their loins' before going into battle. Although Costas had no loins—she was a woman, after all—she appreciated the concept. She would have preferred a to face a barrage of arrows than speak to the woman sitting there, weeping in the dark.

Chapter 5

"*Kalispera.*" Good evening, Costas said. "I'm Chief Officer Melissa Costas of the Spetses Police. I am the one who will be in charge of the investigation."

Costas had deliberately omitted the word 'homicide' when she'd introduced herself, seeking to spare the victim's family additional pain. They all knew why she was here. There was no need to torment them further.

The man who'd been consoling the old woman stood up. "Stavros Papadopoulos." Coming closer, he grabbed her hand and shook it.

"Vasilis Papadopoulos," said the second man.

"I'm his mother," the old woman bellowed from her chair. "Sophia Papadopoulos," The way she said it was clear she meant the victim.

"And you?" Costas nodded to a woman, standing off to one side.

"Daphne Papadopoulos, Vasilis wife." She spoke with an air of weariness as if she was used to being overlooked by her husband and his relatives; their conduct tonight came as no surprise.

"As is customary in such cases, I will interview each of you separately," Costas explained. "With your permission, I will tape everything you say and, when warranted, take written notes as well. This is standard police operating procedure, absolutely routine, and it's nothing to worry about. All I need from you is a truthful account of what you saw today."

Again, she avoided any reference to the murder. "With your written permission, the forensic team will then go through the house. I know this is a difficult time for you, but it would be best if they did it tonight. I will also need to fingerprint you and swab the inside of your cheek for DNA in order to eliminate you as suspects."

"Do whatever you need to do," Stavros said. "A clear sky does not fear lightning." A Greek proverb, it meant the innocent have nothing to fear.

"Stavros Papadopoulos, will you come with me?" Costas said.

After leading him into the house, she set up her tape recorder and sat down on the green sofa in the living room. She knew she should wait for the forensic team to process the house, but she didn't know where else to talk to him. If neither of them disturbed anything—just sat there on the sofa—it should be all right.

She'd assumed he would pull up a chair and sit across from her—people usually wanted to get as far away from the police as they could. But he plopped down next to her, stretching his arms out on the back of the sofa. He was so close she could smell the beer on his breath.

"Shit," she muttered. She'd neglected to tell Constantinos no alcohol; and the fool had allowed them to drink.

Dressed only in shorts and an undershirt, he made her uncomfortable; and she toyed around with the idea of asking him to put a shirt on, but gave it up. It wasn't about propriety tonight or respecting an officer of the law. It was about questioning a grieving man.

"I heard you're new to Spetses. Where are you from?" Costas asked after starting the recorder. It was irrelevant to the investigation, but if Simonidis was going to find him in the database, he'd need the information.

"Aghios Stefanos. It's a village in southern Peloponnese. My parents were both from there."

"And their names?"

"Achilles and Sophia Papadopoulos."

Stavros volunteered he was the oldest of the three brothers. "We live in Athens now, Moschato. We had two souvenir shops near the Acropolis, *Tria Adelphia* and *Grecian Summer*, but we had to sell them. Way things are, we couldn't pay the rent."

"You and your brothers?"

"That's right, and our families. You might say we came here as refugees. Fleeing the economic policies of the government."

From the way he said it, it was obvious he'd made the joke many times before. "We were doing all right and then one day we couldn't pay our rent and we had to leave."

"Were the stores in Monastiraki?" The major tourist thoroughfare, it was the most likely place.

"One was there. The other was in Gazi, at the end of the pedestrian walkway."

"Prime locations."

He nodded. "It was hard when we lost them. The government froze all the bank accounts and overnight, our customers just vanished. We knew we were in trouble as soon as the crisis hit. I wanted to hang on, but it was obvious the situation was hopeless. We had to empty out the stores and sell everything at a loss."

"After you gave up the stores, you came to Spetses. Why did you decide to come here? Do you have relatives on the island?"

"No. A friend told me about this place and said it was available for rent. My brothers and I discussed it and decided to give it a try. So far, it's been good." Hearing himself, he quickly backtracked. "I mean it *was* good before today. Now I'm sorry we ever came here."

The statement sounded perfunctory to Costas, him telling her what she expected to hear. Still there were tears in his eyes.

"You've been here for some time? And you said you're doing all right?"

"Yes. We've been making money."

And all of it hidden, she was sure. This wasn't a man who paid taxes. Thankfully, she was a cop, not an employee of the *Eforia*, the Greek IRS. Being a tax agent had become a dangerous job in Greece. An *Eforia* agent had been beaten up recently by a café owner on Patmos, a crowd of onlookers cheering him on.

Unhooking a pen from her shirt, she opened her notebook. "Tell me about today," she said.

"I don't know what there is to say. We did what we always do. My wife, Chryssoula, and I got up around five and fed the kids. We've got three—Petros, Christos and Zoe. They're all under seven, so our mornings are pretty chaotic. Then around eight, we opened the taverna and started serving breakfast to the tourists. We offer it along with lunch and dinner. Have to start early, but it brings in a lot of money. After we finished, I wiped down the tables and turned on the music and started getting ready for lunch. Everyone was there by then. Hope, Daphne and my mother were chopping vegetables for the salads and making tzatziki; and my wife, Chryssoula, was stringing chunks of pork on the skewers for souvlakia. My brother, Vasilis, was busy setting up the gyros—they take a long time to cook."

He shrugged. "Just an average day."

"What was Thanasis doing while the rest of you were peeling potatoes?"

"I think he was still asleep at that point."

"She's foreign, right? Your sister-in-law?" Costas had heard something in his voice when he spoke of her. Not tension. It went deeper than that. Loathing. "How does she get along with the rest of you?"

"I can't complain," he said.

"What are her responsibilities at the taverna?"

"Like I said, she helps my mother cook. They don't really get along. Two donkeys fighting in a third one's stall."

Another Greek proverb, this one meaning although the object in question was not theirs, they still fought over it. The remark puzzled Costas and she asked him to clarify it.

"She's American and my mother's Greek. Tough for her. Tough for my mother. Hope had no idea what she was getting into when she married my brother. It was a big mistake and we're all paying for it."

"You're saying there are cultural differences?"

He threw back his head and laughed. "Cultural differences!? Yeah, sure, call it that."

Costas entered this in her notebook. She doubted Hope's relationship with her mother-in-law would prove relevant, still it needed to be explored.

"Let's talk about the cave," she said. "None of the tourists we spoke to today knew it was there. So how did your family come to discover it?"

"The man we rented the taverna from told us about it. He said he used it to store things in it and suggested we do the same."

Therefore, twelve people had known about the cave, possibly more. Costas asked him for the man's contact information; and Stavros got up, rifled through the armoire and handed her a slip of paper. She copied down the information in her notebook and handed it back to him.

"Besides the family, who else has access?" she asked.

"All the local people knew it was there. Everyone in Aghioi Anargyiou," Stavros said. "It's a cave, for God's sakes. There's no door. You can't lock it."

"Who owns it?"

"My guess is our landlord. That is if anybody does. We just use it to store things. It doesn't belong to us."

"Who else works in the taverna?"

"We have a Pakistani who washes the dishes and does odd jobs."

"Would he have access to the cave?"

"Yes, like I said, we all do. It's no secret. Kids steal beer from us and we caught a pair of tourists once, siphoning wine out of one of the barrels."

"Why was Thanasis in there today?"

"Who knows?" Stavros said a little too casually. "Thanasis did what he wanted when he wanted to do it. He was his own man. He never denied himself anything."

"What do you mean 'he never denied himself anything?" Again, she'd heard something in his voice.

"All I meant was if he wanted a cigarette, he'd have a cigarette. He wanted a drink; he'd have a drink."

"What about women? Did he have those, too?"

"No more than rest of us." Stavros winked at Costas.

He'd touched her arm repeatedly, her knee once or twice, leaving his hand there until she brushed it off. An aging Lothario, hitting on women was a reflex for him, even on a policewoman investigating his brother's murder. No doubt he flirted with the foreign women who came to the taverna, bedded them when he got the chance. All too happy to give the tourists a thrill.

Costas had encountered such men as a cop in Athens. They weren't as plentiful as they used to be, but they were still around, preying on lonely foreign women. But unlike the character in the movie, *Shirley Valentine*, the British housewife who'd come to Greece on vacation and found love— in Costas' experience there'd been no happy ending for the majority of women in those relationships. They were taken in every sense of the word and often went back to where they came from heartbroken and humiliated, a few even ruined financially.

"In the future, you should be more careful," she had cautioned these women. "Not look to movie scripts for how to live your lives."

Not one of them had thanked her for the advice.

There being no room in the house and mom underfoot, Costas wondered how Stavros succeeded in pulling off these liaisons. As far as she could see, the family possessed only one car—a KIA sedan so dirty it looked it had been driven across the Sahara—so where did he score? Could it have been in the cave? Could the victim have been using it for a similar purpose? Was that why his brother was so reluctant to tell her why he'd been in there today? 'Girlfriend?' she wrote in big letters and drew a circle around it.

Or could Thanasis been doing something else? Smuggling came to mind. Drugs or perhaps women, young Eastern European girls bound for the streets of Athens. Stavros Papadopoulos certainly seemed to have the propensity for it. She'd assumed he was just a sexual opportunist, but maybe he was something more, a pimp perhaps. Could be the victim had been one as well.

If this were the case, that would explain Stavros' silence about Thanasis' presence in the cave.

Mentally, she quickly dismissed the idea. While Spetses might be close to Athens, it was also an island. You'd have to move the women in and out by boat without being spotted, an impossibility given the number of people working in the harbor. But drugs were a definite possibility. Easily transportable, they were slowly making their way into Greece. She'd seen heroin addicts in Athens, sleeping on the sidewalk near Victoria Station, their arms scarred with needle marks. Perhaps Spetses had become an entry point for the trade.

So far Stavros' main concern had been when his brother's body would be released so he could arrange the funeral. He had asked her this twice already, both times in the same flat monotone, as if he were inquiring about a rental car and when it would be ready to be picked up, not the conclusion of a loved one's autopsy.

A curious set of priorities. Costas drummed her pen on top of the notebook. She would have thought catching his brother's killer would have been foremost in his mind, but so far, there'd been no mention.

She had expected him to rant and rave about apprehending the killer, do unto him what had been done unto Thanasis. That was what Greek men did; they went after those who harmed their families. Avenging such a wrong was expected, a requirement for manhood here. And yet there he sat.

Costas was no expert on grief; but she wondered if that was what she was seeing—Stavros shutting down, allowing himself to neither think nor to feel. She'd read about it in textbooks; but like so much else, never witnessed it firsthand.

"Thanasis was the youngest," she said, not knowing what else to say.

"That's right," Stavros said. "Our baby brother. I'm fifty-one. Vasilis is forty-eight and Thanasis was forty-two."

"And Hope, his wife?"

"Thirty-eight."

"No kids?"

"Not yet. The first one is due in four months."

Costas asked him to sign the release form, granting the police permission to process his possessions, then fingerprinted him and swabbed his cheek for DNA.

Chapter 6

Younger than his brother, Vasilis Papadopoulos was unshaven and his eyes were bloodshot. He was heavier than Stavros and had decorative plugs in his ears and elaborate tattoos on both forearms. He had little to add to his sibling's account, volunteering only that he had followed him from Athens to Spetses the previous year and been satisfied with the life he'd found here.

"The three of us, Stavros, Thanasis and me, we always worked together. We used to call ourselves, the *Treis Somatofilakes.*" The Three Musketeers.

Again, he had omitted his wife.

The door banged open and the victim's mother hobbled into the living room on her crutches. "*Kounoupia,*" she complained, waving a gnarled hand. Mosquitoes.

Costas doubted there were many mosquitoes this close to the beach. Curiosity was what had driven the old woman inside, that and the desire to meddle and control.

She was dressed entirely in black—a shapeless black dress, black stockings, black shoes, even a black kerchief covering her hair. Costas wondered if she kept these mourning clothes on hand, if her life had been reduced to this—at her age, a succession of funerals. Her hair was dyed, a thin line of gray showing at the roots around her face; and she was bent nearly double with arthritis. Her eyes were swollen from crying and she had a distracted air about her, as if she were groping for something familiar, a way to anchor herself.

"Stavros said Thanasis wasn't working at the taverna today," Costas said. "Do you know what he was doing?"

"He was there," the old woman protested. "I saw him. He was talking to Hope. They were excited both of them."

"Excited good or excited bad?"

"I don't know. I was too far away to hear what they were saying."

"Where did this conversation take place?"

"In the parking lot. I remember because the souvlakis were done and I wanted Hope to plate them and take them out to the customers. She wasn't around and I went looking for her. 'Come help,' I said when I saw her. 'I can't do everything myself.' Thanasis was with her and he waved at me. That was the last time I saw him."

She raised her head up, tears streaming down her face. "He was a good boy. I don't care what about anybody says. He was a good boy."

"What do you mean, 'what anybody says?'" Costas asked.

"He had his problems, but so what if he did? Anyway, it was her fault, whatever was wrong with him. It was that woman who made him do the things he did."

"What things?" Costas asked.

Neither Vasilis or his mother answered for a long time.

"*Den peirazei*" Vasilis eventually said. Never mind, "My mother's upset. She doesn't know what she's saying."

Costas studied him, wondering what was going on. Given the circumstances, both brothers had been surprisingly guarded in their responses, Stavros inevitably in the lead, the other silent or close to it, deferring to him even in absentia. "If that's what Stavros said, it must be right."

They'd closed ranks when she asked about the cave, refusing point blank to discuss why Thanasis had been in there today. As a rule, Greeks did not speak ill of the dead. It was forbidden by the culture and had been since ancient times. But she had a feeling this was different. They weren't keeping silent out of respect for their dead brother; they were keeping silent because they were hiding something, a family secret they didn't want exposed.

Again, she found herself wondering about smuggling, some illicit activity involving the cave.

"What about Hope?" she asked Vasilis. The American had not shown herself since Costas had been there. She'd speak to her later in English, well away from the others. See if there were any discrepancies between the American's account and that of her in-laws.

"Besides helping your mother, what did she do?"

Coming to life, the old woman snorted at the sound of her daughter-in-law's name, began to mutter again.

"I'd prefer to let Hope speak for herself," Vasilis said.

"And your brother, Thanasis, what about him? What role did he play in the family?"

"Jester," Vasilis answered without hesitation. "He was our court jester."

* * *

Tall and slender, Vasilis' wife, Daphne, was dressed in white jeans and a blue polo shirt and had bejeweled sandals on her feet. She had a tiny silver cross around her neck, so small it was barely noticeable. With classical features—a long aquiline nose and full lips—she resembled an ancient Greek statue. Her hair reinforced that impression. Thick and curly, it was braided and woven around her head like a crown.

Of the two women, she was the prize, although her inability to produce a child would have cost her, especially with a mother-in-law like Sophia. As the mother of three, Chryssoula would have occupied the more exalted place. Costas wondered how Vasilis felt about his wife, if his reluctance to include her stemmed from that. A kind of punishment.

Daphne had hurried inside when Costas summoned her, not bothering to acknowledge her husband or mother-in-law. Like her husband, Vasilis, she didn't appear to have been crying, but her voice broke when she spoke of her brother-in-law; and her eyes took on a distant view.

In the end, Daphne's account did not differ substantial from what the others had told her. Thanasis was the family clown and everybody loved him. She went a little farther than the rest and implied it might have been a migrant who killed him. "Those people are everywhere now. Who knows what they are capable of?"

As for the cave, she hinted that her brother-in-law's living situation was less than ideal, more than a little claustrophobic, and that he liked to get away whenever he could.

"It was nothing unusual for him to disappear for a couple of hours like he did today. The three of them in that one room…They could barely turn around. And Hope was always complaining."

"About what?"

"You name it. Greece was hell on earth, and we were all servants of the devil. I got along with her better than everyone else; and sometimes she'd confide in me. I spoke to her earlier the day Thanasis was murdered and she was happier than I'd ever seen her. She was more than halfway through her pregnancy and convinced this time she'd be lucky and carry the baby to term."

Daphne hesitated for a moment. "But then I saw her later that day and she was all upset. I asked her what was the matter and she wouldn't tell me. Only that Thanasis had done something. I told her to go and talk to him, to work it out. We were standing in the parking lot and she headed off to look for him."

Whether Daphne realized it or not, she'd just implicated Hope Erikson in the murder.

* * *

Costas insisted on speaking to Chryssoula alone, convinced she'd reveal more if her husband wasn't around.

Stavros seemed determined to control the family narrative—everyone working like busy little bees and living happily ever after. Costas didn't believe a word of it, nor had Constantinos when the two of them discussed it. If all had been well in the Papadopoulos household, Thanasis would still be walking the earth, Constantinos said; and Costas agreed with him.

Seeking guidance, she called her boss in Athens.

"You're crazy," Stathis told her when she proposed the brothers might have been smuggling drugs. "You have no proof of this. These people are victims—repeat after me—victims, and, until you have proof to the contrary—real evidence, not this bullshit theory of yours—you need to treat them as such."

Stathis continued to upbraid her. "I'm going to send someone to help you. Yannis Patronas. He's solved more homicides than anyone else in the department. He'll get the job done."

"I know I don't have much experience, sir…"

"You have no experience, correct? This is your first homicide investigation."

"I can do it, sir. Trust me, I'm up to the task."

"I very much doubt that, Officer Costas."

And with that, he slammed down the phone.

* * *

Yannis Patronas was eating dinner outside on the terrace with his wife, Lydia, when his phone rang, the *Flight of the Valkyries*, the special tone he kept for his boss.

An old friend of Patronas, an elderly priest named Papa Michalis, had joined them that night; and he perked up when he heard the phone.

"A new case?" he asked, all ears.

Patronas had met Papa Michalis on his first murder case and subsequently hired him to work as a counselor for the police department, his job being to minister to the wayward, the drunks and wife beaters, and help them change their ways and avoid jail time. The priest's success had been marginal at best—he talked far more than he listened—and Patronas often thought about firing him, but held off, not wanting to break the old man's heart.

The priest's work for the police gave purpose to his days, he'd told Patronas on numerous occasions. "At my age, it's hard to feel useful and I thank you for the opportunity you've given me to be of service to the community."

"You're a priest. You've spent your whole life in service."

"Policework is a bigger challenge. Far more dedicated sinners."

Unfortunately, Patronas' new wife, Lydia, had taken it upon herself to encourage the relationship and often invited the old man to dine at their house, a situation Patronas found increasingly intolerable as Papa Michalis never wanted to leave and frequently slept over. The last three weekends in a row, he'd camped out in their living room. It might have been all right if he'd brought a pair of pajamas with him when he came, but he never did and would sleep in his voluminous drawers and an undershirt on the sofa in the living room. He was a disturbing sight in repose, his beard fluttering. A primordial animal that whistled and gibbered and drooled.

Worse, Lydia wouldn't allow Patronas to watch television when the old man was asleep which was most of the time. Afternoon, evening, it didn't matter, there he lay, sprawled in the best seat in the house.

Patronas' phone continued to ring. It wouldn't be good, he knew. Stathis never called with anything good, not once in the twenty-odd years Patronas had known him. A murder, most likely, somewhere in Greece.

"Good evening, sir."

As always, Stathis started right in. "You might have to go to Spetses, Patronas. A man was murdered there last night and the officer in charge, Melissa Costas, has no experience, never worked a homicide before. What makes it tricky is the main suspect is the victim's wife, an American named Hope Erikson. By her own admission, she was the last person to see him alive. We'll see how Costas does, but I don't want any trouble with the embassy. I want you to stand by and be ready to take over for her at a moment's notice. I'll keep you posted."

And with that, he was gone.

Patronas was relieved. At least for now, he was safe. Summer was coming to an end; and he didn't want to spent the rest of it reading autopsy reports on Spetses. He wanted to swim and lay on the beach and bask like a turtle.

Papa Michalis had been eavesdropping unashamedly. "I'd wager the wife did it. As a society, we underestimate the malice in women, what they are capable of when provoked. In other species, spiders come to mind, the female uses her mate to fertilize her eggs, then eats him."

"Father, we're talking homicide here. This isn't about spiders."

But Papa Michalis refused to be silenced. "Not to mention, the spouse is American in this case and Americans are a very, violent group of people. They absolutely worship guns."

Having spent most of her adult life in the states, Lydia took issue with both of these statements and the two began to fight.

Patronas couldn't understand what drew Papa Michalis to their house night after night. He had nothing in common with Lydia. A potter by trade, she was fiercely liberal, while he was not. A true believer, he had memorized the entire Bible and could quote portions of it in its entirety, never questioning a word of it, not even the story of Jonah and the whale or Noah, who lived nine hundred years.

Patronas, a robust atheist, didn't understand such piety, but then he didn't understand much about Papa Michalis, his choice of professions for starters. To willingly spend one's life as a clergyman in the company of other clergymen, a group not known for its lightheartedness, it was a form of suicide. How could one live without laughter? Not to mention, women?

Again, he wondered why Papa Michalis had visited them that night. He doubted it was the food that brought him to their doorstep as Lydia's idea of what constituted a meal was questionable at best. Vegetables were always at the center of the stage at her table, eggplants and zucchinis cooked to an olive-drab mush, then garnished with chia seeds and other horrors. Worse was when she threw beets in, which colored the whole thing red and made it look like entrails.

"He's lonely," Lydia had said when Patronas and she discussed the priest in the past. "He's given his life to God and I'm not sure God is always the best company."

"I don't know, Lydia," Patronas had answered. "From what I've seen, I think God must have a pretty good sense of humor."

And he did think that. No question about it, God was a joker. The only problem was it took Him way too long to get to the punchline.

The priest kept talking about the phone call from Stathis. "Are we going to Spetses? he asked Patronas excitedly. "Do I need to go home and pack my bag?"

"If Stathis says 'go,' we go, but not until he says so."

Intrusive as he was, Papa Michalis did serve one useful purpose in Patronas' opinion. He could elicit a confession from even the most intractable suspect. He'd sit with them and speak of the afterlife and they'd confess. Patronas had no idea how the old man did it. A kind of voodoo, he supposed, the priest waving the Bible around instead of waving rattles or chicken bones. The tool might be Christian, but, in his opinion, it was still sorcery.

Chapter 7

Chryssoula had already put the children to bed and was in the process of opening a bottle of wine when Costas knocked on the door. She poured some into a glass and held it out to her.

"Can't," Costas said. "I'm on duty."

"That's okay," Chryssoula said and gulped down the wine.

Much younger than her husband, she was dressed in a strapless, floor-length sundress with an elasticized top and sandals with huge cork heels.

A pretty woman, she had almond shaped brown eyes and a mane of artfully tousled, bleached blonde hair. Her fingernails were long and perfectly manicured, painted the color of pearls. Seeing them, Costas doubted she had spent a single moment of her life peeling potatoes. Perhaps Stavros had lied about what his wife did at the taverna. It might be a small lie, but a lie nevertheless. Perhaps he'd told others.

The rest of the family had been exhausted when Costas spoke to them—reeking of fried food and sweat—worn out from serving customers all day, but not the woman standing in front of her. Perhaps there was a hierarchy of sorts within the family, an unequal distribution of income and labor.

Costas had left Constantinos behind, telling him to keep Stavros there until she finished interviewing the man's wife. She'd also checked in by phone with Ritsos, Pappas and Simonidis.

"Family hasn't been here long enough," Ritsos said. "No one knows them."

Simonidis had taken down the information she'd given him and said he'd try again, but so far, had found no entries for the family in any of the police databases.

Chryssoula also proved unhelpful, telling Costas virtually the same thing her husband had. It had been a routine day. Too much work, but that was how it was in the summer, work, work, work. Their lives were the reverse of most people's; they were busy June, July and August and took the rest of the year off. Her words were so similar, Costas was convinced she'd somehow escaped Constantinos' scrutiny and compared notes with her husband, Stavros.

She seemed sad, but not overly so, and said the usual things. "Poor Thanasis! I can't believe it…who could have done such a thing?" Weeping off and on, a wadded tissue in her hand.

"What was your relationship with the family?" Costas asked.

"*Etsi kai etsi*" Chryssoula said. Not good, not bad. "They're all from a village in Mani and you know the reputation of *Maniates,* they'd rather fight than breathe."

"Do they fight?"

She immediately backtracked. "No, no. I didn't mean it like that. We all get along great." As with everything she said, the words sounded contrived, rehearsed.

"Are you from Peloponnese, too?"

"No, I'm from Thrace in northern Greece. I went to school in Athens and studied pharmacology. I was planning to take over my father's store when I graduated, but then I met Stavros."

"And you lived in Athens?"

"Yes. He and his brothers owned two stores. That's how I met him; I was working in the store in Gazi for the summer. We were in Athens for over ten years. Our three children were born there."

"Do you mind if we talk about the victim? Your sister in-law didn't seem to have much use for him." Costas was fishing. Daphne had said nothing of the kind.

"Thanasis was a lot of things, some good, some bad, just like the rest of us."

"Did he pull his weight?"

"Not as much as he should have. He was the baby of the family and his mother doted on him, spoiled him rotten. Consequently, he didn't feel like he needed to contribute anything, not in the stores, not in life. His presence was gift enough. Charming, though. Absolutely charming. And a rogue. *Panagia mou,* Mother of God, the way he drank and the things he got up to."

Stirred by the memory, she began to cry harder. "The children absolutely adored him. He'd get down on the floor and play with them, gallop around like a horse with the three of them on his back, do whatever they wanted him to do."

"Vasilis said he was the family jester," Costas said.

"Yes, yes. He loved to make people laugh."

Again, Costas had the sense of something left unsaid.

Chryssoula claimed her mother-in-law was responsible for Thanasis' failings, that he never had a chance. "She's a very backward woman, a real *vlacha*, peasant. When my son was born, she came into my room at the hospital and pinched one of my breasts, then went out in the hallway and shouted to Stavros, 'your wife can't nurse, she has no teats. Can you imagine?"

Costas had heard worse about mothers-in-law. It was a common complaint in Greece, the husbands and their mothers singing a domestic duet, a chorus of insults and abuse, directed against those interlopers in their midst, the poor women who had dared try and come between them.

Chyssoula said nothing more of substance, her focus having shifted from the victim to herself. Most of her complaints against her mother-in-law were petty and Costas began to tune her out.

"I'm surprised to hear they're from Mani. They told me they were from Athens," she said.

"*Now*, they're from Athens."

"If you—a Greek—never fit in, how did Hope manage"

Chryssoula hesitated, a cat deciding whether or not to show its claws. "Hope made no effort to get along with them. But it wasn't their fault, not really, it was hers. She didn't even try. Everything was better in the States. Nothing was any good here. She's been here for ten years and she still cannot speak a word of Greek, not a *single* word. That just about says it all."

Her dress kept slipping down and she tugged at it, pulling the elasticized portion back up over her chest. The maneuver grated on Costas. Save it for your husband, she felt like saying. All that wiggling around, it's wasted on me.

"Anything else you want to tell me?" she asked.

Chryssoula shook her head. "Until Hope came out of the cave screaming, it was just another day."

Before leaving, Costas asked Chryssoula to walk her through the house. It was a twin of the other and looked to have been constructed at the same time. The three children were fast asleep in one of the bedrooms—

the youngest, Zoe, in a crib, the other two, Petros and Christos sharing a twin bed.

As she had before in the other house, Costas took numerous pictures and asked Chryssoula to sign a release form so that the forensic team could go through it.

"Do not discard anything you think might incriminate you or your husband," Costas warned. "I have a record of what was here tonight and if anything goes missing, you will be arrested for obstruction of justice and destroying evidence."

"Surely you don't think we had anything to do with this," Chyrssoula wailed. "We loved Thanasis."

She complained even more when Costas sought to fingerprint her and swab her cheek. "I can't believe it. Did you do this to Hope, too?"

"Not yet, but I will."

"What about Daphne and Vasilis?"

"Yes. Everyone."

Reluctantly, Chryssoula consented and Costas printed her, pressing her fingers down hard on the ink pad and rolling them across the card.

She put the fingerprinting kit back in her satchel. "If Hope had problems in her marriage, would she have confided in you?"

"No, never. She wasn't close to me or anyone else here. She stayed a stranger."

"You don't like her much, do you?"

"It's not that. She's…she's like having a fourth child. Hope? Her name should be 'hopeless.'"

* * *

Switching on her flashlight, Costas walked from the house to the cave, timing the length of time it took. Six minutes, no more. Someone could easily have walked there and back from either of the two houses before anyone realized they were gone. The forensic team, four men and a woman, had finished processing the scene and were packing up their gear.

"Heading to the victim's house?" Costas asked them.

The lead investigator, an older man with a moustache, nodded. "Going to be here all night. Stathis' orders."

"There's a pair of pants hanging on the clothesline. I don't know who they belong to, but they need to be tested for blood."

"Besides blood, any idea of what we're looking for?" the man asked.

"That's the main thing: blood on clothing, blood in the bathroom sink and the drain, the walls and ceiling of the shower. You saw that cave. There's blood splatter everywhere. There's no way the killer escaped without getting drenched in it."

"What about a computer? iPads, iPhones?"

"Seize everything. We'll sort it out later."

Costas accompanied the team back to the house and watched as they went through it. They were very systematic. Going from room to room, they opened drawers with gloved hands and emptied out closets, gathering up clothing and bagging it, shoes and other items. They focused on the drains in the bathroom and kitchen, undoing the pipes and swabbing the residue inside, and sprayed luminol on every surface.

The victim's family was still sitting outside in the dark, waiting for the forensic team to finish. The old woman went off again a short time later, howling and screaming, keening as the ancients must have done, the paid mourners who had once sung, *moirologia*, dirges, for the dead.

The ancients believed the ferryman of Hades, Charon, carried the souls of the dead across the Styx, the river that divided the world of the living from that of the dead. Mourners placed a coin in the mouth of the deceased to pay for the voyage and wailed as they did so, wailed their terrible poetry.

The sound of the old woman's grieving reminded Costas of those legends. Listening to her crying out for her son, she could almost see the ferryman coming toward them and hear the splash of his oars.

Chapter 8

Hope Erikson was dressed in a baggy, green shift with red embroidery across the top. Costas had already fingerprinted her and her hands were smudged with ink. Unlike her sister-in-law, Chyrssoula, the American's hands were poorly cared for, her nails bitten down to the quick.

Soft and fleshy, she was laying curled up on the bed. Her eyes were blue, her eyelashes and eyebrows so pale as to be virtually nonexistent. They made her face appear unfinished, somehow incomplete. She was too plump for real beauty, although she was appealing in the same way a baby was. Round and full and pink.

Her manner, too, was infantile.

"Oops," Hope said at one point, covering her mouth with her hand. "Shouldn't have said that." It was grotesque under the circumstances.

She also wasn't very clean. Her hair hadn't been washed in some time; and Costas could see lines of grime in the creases of her neck. Projecting a kind of willed helplessness, she hadn't moved since she'd appeared, just stayed where she was, smelling faintly of sweat.

Costas had been briefed at the Police Academy on how to recognize when a suspect is lying, the various facial tics that come into play—the blinking and the swallowing, the refusal to look a person in the eye—but so far Hope Erickson had done none of these things. All she'd done was lay there and cry.

The room they were in was long and rectangular. Two twin beds were pushed together under a window in the back, a third bed perpendicular at the foot. The latter was clearly the old woman's bed and it was neatly made, her clothes neatly folded on a shelf nearby, her slippers lined up side by side on the floor. In contrast, the area Hope and her husband had occupied was a mess, dirty clothes cast off and thrown on the floor, gear strewn everywhere. Hope had made a kind of wall between her bed and her mother-in-law's, lining up suitcases to form a kind of barrier. Although the window was open, it was still very hot inside the room.

Hell, Costas thought, looking around. *This is hell.*

There was so little space the three occupants could have held hands while they slept.

As Hope was the one who had found the body, the forensic technicians had been especially thorough in here, taking all the personal items and clothing away and stripping the sheets off the bed. They'd sprayed the entire space with luminal and shone a UV light over it, an eerie ghost-like specter in the darkened room.

The dress Hope had been wearing when she found her husband had lit up and was one of the first things the team had seized. Weeping, Hope said she'd knelt down beside her husband's body and touched his face and that's how the blood had found its way onto the dress.

"I knew it was wrong, but I couldn't help it."

She hadn't wanted to part with the dress and fought to keep it, babbling on about how her mother had told her about Jacqueline Kennedy and how she hadn't wanted to change out of the pink suit she'd been wearing in Dallas the day her husband was shot, claiming she had wanted everyone 'to see what they'd done to him,'

"I want to do the same," Hope wailed. "I want everyone to know what they did."

She lost the battle, of course, and been forced to surrender the dress.

She and Costas were sitting across from one another now, Hope on the bare mattress, Costas in a chair she'd dragged in from the living room. The American had stood paralyzed when Costas turned the light back on after the forensic people left, blinking rapidly like a mole, leaving its burrow, its kingdom of night.

Hope told basically the same story Stavros and the rest of the family had. Everyone worked hard and got along. Her husband, Thanasis, was the love of her life and she was his. He would have laid down his life for her.

Interesting choice of words, Costas noted, given what had happened.

A *soupia*, cuttlefish. Hiding in a cloud of ink.

"You're a foreigner living in a Greek household," she said. "I understand there was tension between you and your mother-in-law. What did your husband have to say about that? Did he support you?"

"Oh, yes, always. He would step in whenever she started and put an end to it."

"What did you fight about? You and your mother-in-law?"

Hope shrugged. "Money mostly."

"Someone told me your husband drank too much," Costas said, seeking to provoke her. "They said he was lazy and irresponsible and didn't do his share of the work."

Tears filled her eyes. "He was that, too. It was all mixed up in him."

"Did he frequent the bars in the port?

"He didn't pick up women if that's what you're implying. My husband wasn't like Stavros. He was no *kamaki*."

Kamaki was the Greek word for spear gun, a slang expression in the 1960s that referred to men who pursued women and bedded them. Their targets were mainly foreign tourists, Greek women, being immune to their charms. Such conquests were never taken seriously. For the men at least, it was always recreational, a kind of sport.

A breach in the walls, it was the first admission of wrong doing Costas had heard tonight. "Obviously he liked foreign women. You're foreign, aren't you?"

Hope nodded. "American. Born and bred."

"Where are you from in the States?"

"Short Hills, New Jersey." She said the name as if it meant something. "We had a big house that overlooked a golf course. It was very private, nothing but trees and grass as far as the eye could see. Nothing like here."

"What did your father do?"

"He was vice president of a bank."

"And yet you ended up here." It was a statement, not a question.

"Where I lived was never important. All that mattered to me was Thanasis. He was my life. If I had to live in a slum to be with him, I would have lived in a slum. Anywhere to be with him."

She went on like this for some time, extolling her husband's virtues and the perfect life they'd shared. Theirs had been a legendary romance. From start to finish, nothing but love, love, love. "Like in the storybooks."

Costas didn't believe a word of it. Greeks called naïve people, 'Americanakia, but Hope went far beyond that. It was a wonder she didn't break into song when she spoke of her dead husband, one of those blood-soaked arias by Puccini.

Embroidering the truth to deflect suspicion. Either that or she was delusional. Not naïve, crazy.

"He was the most beautiful man I ever saw," Hope said. "I remember the first time I saw him. He just took my breath away. Everyone on the beach was looking at him. You could see them, the women especially. And from that moment on, all I ever wanted was to be with him. After we got married, I gave him everything I had. I'd inherited some money from my father and I signed it over to him. I would have done anything to make him happy. I would have walked through fire for him."

She'd changed tenses somewhere in the middle of her soliloquy, Costas noticed, gone from 'is' to 'was' when describing her relationship with her husband.

"My maiden name is Erikson," Hope added as an afterthought. "Sometimes people spell it with a 'c,' but that's wrong. E-r-i-k-s-o-n. You have to go by your maiden name in Greece. It's the law here."

Nothing Costas liked more than foreigners lecturing her about her country. They'd started the conversation in Greek, but she'd reverted to English almost immediately, Hope's grasp of the language being that of a toddler. Her sister-in-law had said Hope didn't speak Greek and it was true. The American's grasp of the language was very limited, verb tenses in particular giving her trouble.

The American took a long, shuddery breath. "Thanasis wasn't around as much as he'd been in the beginning and I thought things would change if I had a child. I thought that was what was wrong with us." She paused and seemed to draw herself up. "I'm pregnant. After all these years. I'm finally pregnant. I thought, I thought…."

"You thought it would get better." Costas impatiently finished the sentence for her.

"My name is Hope. My sister-in-law, Chryssoula, always makes fun of that. She says I should have been called 'Hopeless.'"

Starting to sob again, she repeated this, her voice going up an octave. "Hopeless, Hopeless…Hopeless."

It was pathetic the first time she said it, worse when she kept it up. Like her mother-in-law, she probably needed to be sedated.

"You thought things would improve?" Costas tried to get her back on track. "You hadn't given up on your marriage?"

"Of course, not. I loved him and he loved me. It was just everybody else. All those people around us day in and day out." She gestured to the room. "I mean, look at this place! The three of us in here, night after night...I couldn't breathe. I felt like I was suffocating."

"Were the brothers engaged in anything illegal that you know of? Drugs, for example?"

"If they were, they would never have told *me*." Her voice was petulant.

"How did your husband get along with them?"

"They laughed, they fought, they laughed some more." She shrugged again. "You know, Greek."

"Did your husband go to the cave often?"

The American nodded. "He'd get a bottle of wine off the shelves in the afternoon and stay in there and drink it. He liked *ProPo,* too, those Greek soccer cards and he'd play that, too, sometimes. Stavros used to yell at him for wasting money, but Thanasis did what he wanted. He didn't listen."

"Do you still have family in New Jersey?"

"My brother lives there. He bought out my share of the house after my mother died. We fought about how much he should pay and he got mad and stopped speaking to me. Thanasis and his brothers thought I was richer than I was and they kept bugging me to get more money out of him. There wasn't any, but they didn't believe me. I wish I'd stood up to them. At least then I'd have a brother. Now I have nobody."

Again, Costas had the sense the American was play acting, performing in some private drama all her own. She seemed distraught, yet at the same time lethargic as if her fate was out of her hands. Costas had always sought to be taken seriously, to command respect in every aspect of her life; and Hope Erikson disturbed her. The way this woman was acting, she would command nothing

"My mother objected to us being together," Hope went on. "She didn't want me live in Greece. She said the Greeks would never accept me. It was hard. Thanasis and me, we were like Romeo and Juliet."

"What about Thanasis' family?"

"My mother-in-law was polite at first, but then after we got married, she showed her true colors. I wanted to get wall-to-wall carpeting for the apartment and you should have heard her. Carrying on like I wanted a yacht or something. I mean, it was only a rug. How much would it have cost? 'What are you thinking?' she kept saying. 'This isn't America.'" Hope imitated her mother-in-law, mocking the old woman's Greek accent. "After that it was war. The car I wanted, the clothes I wanted. Everything was a fight."

Costas kept hearing the same note in every word she said. Although nearly forty-years old, it was the whine of an adolescent. As for the wall-to-wall carpeting, her mother-in-law had been right. Like most Greeks today, the family was struggling financially and here comes this American wanting to replicate her childhood, live the way she had in her country. She'd probably wanted a second car and an oversized refrigerator, too, the kind that consumed electricity like it was starving.

She closed the notebook. She'd let the tape do the work, listen to it later and see if she'd missed anything.

"One final question," she said. "Where did you meet Thanasis? Was it in the States?"

"No, no, in Vouliagmeni. It's a beach in Athens."

"I know where Vouliagmeni is," Costas snapped. A peninsula near Athens, it was where wealthy Athenians hung out and those who wished they were. No doubt Thanasis had been in the latter category.

Hope stared off into space. "I was finishing graduate school and wanted to take some time off before I started my thesis. I was getting a PhD in anthropology. But, of course, after I met Thanasis, that all went out the window."

"What were you planning to do with your degree after you graduated?" Costas was genuinely curious. No one study anthropology in Greece. You'd be laughed at. The study of human behavior? Life would teach you what you needed to know about people, her countrymen believed, and if you didn't learn it, you'd perish at their hand.

"I didn't know what I was going to do when I graduated. I hadn't really thought about it."

So, it hadn't started in Greece. Hope Erikson, with no 'c,' had been this way forever. And her foolishness hadn't ended with her choice of majors in graduate school. No, she'd picked up a man on a beach in a foreign country and married him.

"I tried to get along with his family, I really did," Hope said. "But like I said it was hopeless. Everything in my life was hopeless." She started to cry again. "I'm all alone. My father and mother and now Thanasis. I don't have anyone anymore. Who's going to help me when the baby comes?"

"Do you have any friends here?" In spite of herself, Costas felt sorry for her.

"Yes, yes. I have a friend," Hope said, brightening up. "Margaret Vouros. There's a group of us here. 'Lifers,' we call ourselves. Foreign women married to Greeks."

"You might want to call her. Friends are useful when you're in trouble."

And definitely Hope was. Once the report came back from the coroner, there was a good chance she would be charged with murder.

Although Costas' words were a warning, Hope chose not to heed them. Instead, she continued to complain about how crappy Greece was—she actually used the word, 'crappy.' Nothing worked here. As for the Greeks themselves, they were lazy and boorish, untrustworthy and greedy. People you couldn't turn your back on. Everything in the country was filthy and chaotic. It was quite a speech.

Evidently, she believed because Costas spoke English, she was the same as she was and would agree with her assessment of Greece, however, damning it might be.

Stunned, Costas just stared at her. She was in uniform, obviously on duty, working for the *Greek* police. There was nothing even remotely American about her. But still Hope blundered on, spewing invective about her husband's homeland and looking to Costas for support.

Since joining the force, Costas had encountered others like her, people who'd swallowed their anger and kept silent for years, then when the chance finally came to tell their stories, had unloaded a lifetime's worth of rancor and bitterness. Still Greeks rarely spoke to outsiders about what went on in their marriages, let alone criticized their in-laws the way Hope was doing, violating these rules with a vengeance, fundamental ones in Greek society. She called her husband's family 'parasites' and 'vipers', spoke of them the way a Hutu in Rwanda might have a Tutsi, a Gestapo agent, a Jew. Used terms usually reserved for animals.

Pregnant or not, she was seething, alive with hatred. Her tears meant nothing. Perhaps the story wasn't Romeo and Juliet after all. Maybe it was Clytemnestra, the Spartan queen who murdered her husband, Agamemnon.

Chapter 9

Vasilis' wife, Daphne, made Costas a cup of tea before she left the house that night and they talked in the kitchen. As before, the woman was very guarded in what she said, giving voice to the usual sentiments in cases of violence—shock and horror—but revealing nothing personal about herself. This reticence did not extend to Hope Erikson, however, whom she seemed to view with a mixture of pity and contempt.

"Do you think she did it?" Costas asked her at one point.

"I don't know," Daphne said. "They were having problems; I do know that. Given that his mother was sleeping in the same room with them, it's a miracle something didn't happen sooner. I always thought she'd leave him and go back to the states, but she never did."

"How did you get along with her?"

"Better than the rest of them. I spoke to her around eight a.m. the day he got killed and she was so happy. She'd made it past the halfway point, she told me, and it looked like she was going to carry the baby to term. But then I saw her a few hours later, just before the noontime rush; and she was all upset, crying hysterically in the parking lot. I was afraid for the baby and I asked her if she wanted me to find Thanasis. But she just shook her head."

"Did she say what was wrong?"

"No. She wouldn't have confided in me. We weren't that close."

Daphne looked back toward the bedroom where Hope was sleeping. "In order to understand Hope, you had to know Thanasis, the cat and mouse games he played. As the saying goes, 'he could get milk from a ram.' A real *gois*, handsome and charismatic, very appealing to women. His mother adored him. 'You bring light into the world' she always said.

Like he was Jesus or something." Her tone was openly contemptuous. "Hope wasn't much better."

"What about you? What did you think of him?"

"At first, I thought he was wonderful, but then I started to notice things. You couldn't count on him, for one thing. One day, he'd be there for you, your best friend. The next, he'd ignore you or act like you were bothering him. Hope never knew where she stood with him. Whether he'd be nice to her or start screaming."

Finally, a motive. "Did he hit her?"

"No, never. That wasn't his way. He'd just go off somewhere. Once he went to Crete and came waltzing back three weeks later like nothing happened.

"Opening a drawer in the cabinet, Daphne pulled out a folded piece of paper. "Here," she said, handing it to Costas. "This will give you an idea. It's a letter she wrote him. I found it one day when I was cleaning up."

She offered no explanation for why she'd kept it.

Costas put the letter in her backpack, intending to read it later when she was alone. Daphne had surprised her. There had been little flickers of malice in every word she'd said. Costas could feel the antipathy, emanating from her in toxic waves.

It was sometimes like that with women, but never without cause; and she wondered what the cause was in this case. Daphne had no children, perhaps it was only that. Jealousy over Hope's pregnancy.

* * *

It was close to two a.m. when Costas climbed up the stairs to her apartment. On the third floor, it overlooked an old private school on the northern coast of Spetses. Founded in 1923, the school had been modeled on Eton and Harrow, but had ceased to exist in the 1980s. Owned now by a private foundation, the grounds remained magnificent, a forest of olive and cypress trees; and they were the main reason Costas had chosen to live there, that and the sweeping view of the sea.

She slid open the glass door and stepped out onto the balcony, savoring the smell of flowers in the garden below. Overhead, a new moon was rising, a sliver of light in the darkness.

'Touch gold when you see a new moon,' her grandmother had advised, some ancient practice that lingered into the modern age. You also wished people 'kalo mina,' good month, on the first day of each month and took care never to praise or admire in excess, be it a person or a thing, as it was sure to bring the evil eye. There were hundreds of such practices in Greece, designed to protect you and bring you good fortune, to hold in check the dark forces in the universe.

Priding herself on her modernity, for the most part Costas ignored them. Remnants of a darker age, they dated from the time men sacrificed bulls and studied their bloody entrails to predict the future. Much to her grandmother's horror, she also had little use for the church. Thanasis Papadopoulos had been wearing his baptismal cross when he'd been murdered and what good had it done him? Evil had triumphed as it so often did. There was no defense against it, save for the law and its vigilant application. If God was indeed benevolent as she'd been taught as a child, she also knew He often chose to be absent.

She stayed outside on the balcony a few more minutes, then went back inside and got ready for bed, stripping off her clothes and collapsing face down on the mattress. She fell into a restless sleep, her dreams uneasy. A scorpion figured prominently in one. Crawling up her leg, it suddenly transformed itself into a man, who stabbed her savagely in the throat with a knife. She tried to scream, but her voice was gone.

Costas woke up with a start, her heart pounding.

Pulling on a bathrobe, she walked back out on the balcony. Across the channel, the lights of the villages in Peloponnese were glimmering and the sea was very calm, so still she could see reflections of the buildings on its surface, glowing like an underwater city, undulating now and then on the current.

Sometimes she talked to herself when she was alone, discussed the affairs of the day with the walls of her apartment. Other nights, she drank. But even ouzo couldn't ease her troubled mind tonight. Although she downed a half bottle of it, the remnants of the nightmare stayed with her; she couldn't shake it.

At the beginning of the summer, she'd purchased a little orange tree and set it out on the balcony. But she'd forgotten to water it and it had died a few weeks later, its dry leaves curled up and brown. She pulled off one of its leaves and crumbled it in her hand, thinking she was fast becoming like that tree. Withering from neglect. No one to notice or care at her passing.

* * *

Costas' crew stumbled into the police station at six a.m. and took seats around the table in the conference room. Like Costas, they had been up most of the night.

The top of the table was littered with paper coffee cups and napkins; and Costas shoved them aside and took a seat. She'd read the letter Daphne had given her before coming into work, but there wasn't anything in it. Just a lot of school girl mush. Folding the letter back up, Costas felt embarrassed for Hope. PhD, be damned. She was a fool.

"What have we got on the family?" Costas asked her impatiently, looking around the table at her staff. She had a ferocious hangover and was struggling not to show it. Respect, she told herself. You must command respect. And no one respected a drunk.

"Not much," Simonidis said. "No arrests. Not even so much as an unpaid bill. They are even up to date on their taxes. It was just like they told us. One day they had two stores, then the economy collapsed and they lost them." He made an abracadabra motion with his hand.

Constantinos spoke next. "I'm still waiting on the Pakistani," he said. "From what I could tell, he slipped in under the wire in 2015 when the migrants first began arriving on Lesbos and has been moving around ever since. Three islands in the last two years."

"Before that?"

"Trail goes cold."

"That's it?" Costas asked. "Nothing personal on the victim or his family?"

"Nothing," Constantinos said. "According to the people I talked to, they kept to themselves and minded their own business."

Ritsos and Pappas were in Aghioi Anargyiou, keeping watch on the family. When Costas had checked in with them, they'd reported everyone was still asleep, even Hope, curled up on the bare mattress. The old woman had refused to share the bedroom with her and was camped out on the green sofa, her snores audible throughout the house.

"Save for the old lady, not a peep out of any of them," reported Pappas.

"When they wake up, make sure they don't leave the premises," Costas ordered. "Anybody tries, arrest them. I'll take over for you at noon. We'll work the surveillance in shifts. Constantinos, I want you to visit the bars near the harbor. See if you can't pick up the trail of Thanasis Papadopoulos. According to his wife, he liked to drink."

She turned to Simonidis. "I think the family is hiding something and I want you to find out what it is. They told me they're originally from a village called Aghios Stefanos in Mani, parents' names, Achilles and Sophia Papadopoulos. Maybe there was a reason they left the village and moved to Athens; maybe they had to. "

"Sure, there is," Simonidis said flatly. "It's called poverty. Biggest tree in Mani is a cabbage."

It was an old joke, but everyone laughed. Mani was known for both the ferociousness of its inhabitants and its unforgiving landscape.

"Also see what you can find out about Hope Erikson. She claims she's from Short Hills, New Jersey and that her father worked in a bank there. He died years ago, but her mother died recently. The local papers should have an obituary."

"My English isn't that good," Simonidis said.

"Print out whatever you find and I'll take it from there. I had the feeling she was lying about her background and I want to know why."

"You think *she* did it?" he asked.

"Maybe," Costas said. "From what I saw, that little piglet is capable of anything."

* * *

Before returning to Aghioi Anargyiou, Costas paid a visit on Hope Erikson's friend, Margaret Vouros. Something had been off with Hope the previous night, but Costas hadn't been able to put her finger on it. Foreigners sometimes reinvented themselves when they came to Greece; she'd met plenty of them during her career as a policewoman, bogus playwrights and film producers, would-be composers and artists. Worse were the college students, who roamed the countryside seeking inspiration from pagan sources, living in caves in Crete or sleeping outside on the coast of Attica. Some of the kids had been high when she spoke to them, drunk on the experience and God knows what else. One young man had dropped acid during a thunderstorm on the Acropolis and had to be rushed to the hospital as a result.

Part of the appeal of being abroad was you could be act out your fantasies and no one would call you out on it. You wanted to talk to Zeus in the middle of Athens with bolts of lightning flashing, you could talk to Zeus.

Perhaps that was all Hope had been doing, reinventing herself. Passing herself off as the daughter of a wealthy American, when in fact she was a child of the middle class. And now she was an orphan, a slave of her husband's family. Rootless in the most profound sense of the word.

Aware that if Margaret Vouros said anything significant—a crucial fact Hope had shared with her—it would be hearsay; and, as such, inadmissible in court, Costas planned to keep the interview informal. No taping or writing in the murder book. They would just have a little talk, Vouros and she, two women gossiping about a third.

Margaret Vouros lived in the old harbor, nearly two kilometers away. It would be a long walk in the sun, but Costas started off on foot anyway. The exertion would do her good, sweat off the lingering effects of the ouzo.

The walk proved to be a pleasant one. Occasionally, a horse drawn carriage, *amaksaki*, would pass her—tourists on their way to a hotel—but for the most part, she had the road to herself.

Shaped like the claw of a lobster, the old harbor was wide at the mouth and gradually narrowed. A bronze mermaid stood watch on the northern shore, the trident in her hand raised in welcome.

In the past, the area had been a major ship building center. Bouboulina, the heroine of the Greek War of Independence, had sheltered her fleet there. Although boats were still constructed there, their number had dwindled in recent years. Costas saw only one, the unfinished keel propped up in the sand like the ribs of a prehistoric beast. A *varka* from the looks of it, the traditional fishing boat of the Aegean, it had probably been commissioned by a local family.

Shielding her eyes from the sun, Costas searched for Margaret Vouros' house. Protected by high walls, the old estates had no visible doorways; and it took her some time find the right one. Vouros' house stood at the apex of a hill, overlooking the harbor, the only approach, a stone stairway behind the church of Aghios Nikolaos, the patron saint of seamen.

Costas found Vouros in a shed in the back of the house, working at a potter's wheel. Dipping her hands in water, she continued to work while Costas stood there, shaping the mound of gray clay on the wheel into a bowl. As soon as it was finished, she lifted her foot off the pedal, cut it loose with a string and set it down on the ground.

"Just give me a minute," she said. "I need to wash my hands."

A sturdy woman with wooly white hair, she had a gap between her two front teeth and a cheerful, open manner. Her face was streaked with clay and her clothes were stiff with it. Grabbing a bar of soap, she scrubbed herself off in the sink in the back.

"There," she said, shaking off her wet hands. "That's better."

She led Costas back outside and gestured for her to take a seat in the garden. "I'm Margaret by the way."

Costas frowned. Americans and their informality. They practically jumped in your lap the first time you met them.

"Melissa Costas," she said. "Chief Officer of the Spetses police."

Vouros studied her with open curiosity. "I remember when you were appointed, reading about it in the newspaper. I was amazed. A woman police chief, that's a novelty you don't often see here."

Costas bridled at the word 'novelty.' Her appointment hadn't been a 'novelty.' It had been the result of years of hard work and suffering at the hands of the men in charge, completing on one miserable assignment after another without complaint. She'd earned her stripes. Even though Vouros couldn't see them, they were cut into her flesh.

"I need to talk to you about Hope Erikson," Costas said.

"I suspected as much when you called. Did Hope give you my name?"

"Yes, she said the two of you were friends."

Vouros was reluctant to discuss the relationship. "Hope's lost her husband. I don't want to make things more difficult for her."

"This is a homicide investigation," Costas insisted. "You can either discuss your relationship with me now or later in court. But discuss it, you will."

The potter raised a placating hand. "Fine, fine. I'll talk to you although I don't know what good it will do. I wouldn't say we were friends exactly, more like acquaintances. That's about the extent of it."

"How long have you known her?"

"I met her ten years ago. I was teaching a ceramics course in Athens and she was in the class. I'd get together with her once a week, drink wine and listen to her talk about how homesick she was. She seemed lost and I felt sorry for her. I didn't know at the time 'lost' was her defining characteristic, that awareness came later."

"Was she married then?"

Vouros nodded. "They had a curious courtship, she and her husband. I don't know if she told you about it."

"She said they met in Vouliagmeni."

"That's right. Her father was working in a bank and one of his customers was a Greek shipowner. As a favor, he invited Hope and a friend of hers to spend a week on his yacht. It was anchored in Vouliagmeni; and she met Thanasis there. He saw the yacht and assumed she was rich; and she saw his Rolex and BMW—it wasn't his. He'd borrowed it from a friend—and thought the same. Neither one of them got what they wanted. In a sense, they were both frauds."

"How did they end up on Spetses?" Costas knew the brothers' version, but Hope might have confided something different to her friend.

"Supposedly her family had money, but if they did, she never managed to get her hands on it. After they left Athens, they leased the taverna here and the two of them ended up working in it. They couldn't afford to rent their own house, so they stayed with his mother in that place in Aghioi Anargyiou, the three of them all sleeping in one room. I always thought there was something unsavory about the arrangement."

"I heard they had two stores and lost them in the economic downturn."

"I never believed that story. I always thought there was some other reason they pulled up stakes and came here, that something happened to them in Athens."

Costas nodded. She'd had the same feeling. "You have any idea what it was?"

"No. Hope always changed the subject when I brought it up."

Costas' hair had worked its way loose and she moved to pin it back up.

"Leave it," Vouros said. "It's beautiful."

Surprised at herself, Costas left it down. "I supervise a roomful of men," she said by way of explanation. "I don't have a lot of choices when it comes to my appearance."

Vouros nodded. "Hard to strike the right balance. The English have an expression, 'to let your hair down,' and you obviously can't."

They chatted amicably a few more minutes.

"The victim's brothers were reluctant to speak about the cave when I interviewed them," Costas said.

"Who knows what they were up to in there."

"Drugs?"

Vouros shrugged. "With those three, anything was possible."

"Would Hope have been involved?"

"No, but Thanasis certainly would have. Everything those three did, they did together." She hesitated for a moment. "That said, I doubt that they were dealing drugs. Too dangerous. Women would be my guess. Meeting up with girlfriends without their wives' knowledge, that kind of thing. Certainly nothing that would have landed them in jail or gotten them killed."

"What can you tell me about Hope's relationship with her husband?"

"He was a beautiful man and he thought as many beautiful people do that his looks gave him special privileges, that nothing was required of him, save for the gift of his presence. He had a kind of animal magnetism and would stride into a room like he owned it. And a kind of grace. He moved like a panther. If you were a woman and he came after you, down you went. You didn't stand a chance."

"Hope is nothing like that."

"No, she isn't and I think that was part of the problem. She always talked about their grand romance, but, truthfully, I always thought it was a little tawdry. The two of them locked in a passionate embrace, like the cover of a cheap romance novel, when in fact, I don't believe that man ever loved her. He married her for her money, pure and simple. She'd bought him body and soul."

"With her inheritance?"

"The *promise* of her inheritance. The way she talked, you would have thought she was a Rockefeller, but she wasn't, not even close."

"Did she ever complain about him?"

"No more than most women. She'd say he came home late or didn't pay enough attention to her. That kind of thing. She wasn't happy here. I don't know if you know the expression, 'a one note song,' but that was Hope, only in her case, it was a two-note song, America the good versus Greece the bad. It never varied."

The garden was full of Vouros' work, ceramic birdhouses in the trees, hand-painted tiles underfoot. There was even artistry evident in the plantings, the way the colors of the bushes and flowers complemented each another. It seemed a million miles from the place where Hope lived.

"You seem at home here," Costas commented. "Do you return to the States often?"

"I used to when my parents were alive. Not anymore. I missed my country at first, but after a while, you get used to being in a different place. You get on with it. I was a student at the Rhode Island School of Design when I met my husband, Petros. He was a medical student and we got married after he graduated. I was going to be a painter, a great one like Picasso, but I had to give up the idea once I had kids. We had four of them, all boys, and they were into everything, squeezing the tubes of paint or tipping over the cans of turpentine, so I took up the wheel instead."

She smiled her crooked smile. "I didn't plan on living in Greece either. Things just happened."

From the way she spoke, it was obvious she had embraced her husband's homeland with far more enthusiasm than her counterpart had. She was fluent in Greek for one thing, although she'd switched to English at the beginning of the interview.

"You're here to talk about a murder," she'd told Costas, "My grasp of the language doesn't extend to homicide."

Costas continued to question her, seeking to further the connection, the sharing of confidences, a difficult thing for her to do in the best of times. One of her instructors at the police academy had noted her social inadequacies and given her an article on 'overcoming autism.' Costas had cried off and on for two weeks after reading it, not because of the man's cruelty, but because it was true. She was exactly as the author described, a social cripple. It was like the world used a different language, one she didn't understand or know how to speak.

Vouros had requested Costas call her by her first name; and she had complied, although it felt like a bone stuck in her throat. "Do you like it here, Margaret?"

"I don't ask myself that question anymore," Vouros replied, "not in the way I used to. My kids were born here and grew up under the trees in this garden. I planted every bush you see, every flower. Part of me has taken root and belongs to this place. Like or dislike? Who says that about their home?"

Not all Americans were created equal, Costas concluded. Margaret Vouros and Hope Erikson could have come from two separate planets, they were so different.

They talked a few more minutes. "At the end of the day, Hope's a sad case," Vouros said. "She treats Greeks like they've got a disease she doesn't want to catch. I told her they'd engrave that on her headstone: 'Hope Erikson, she died of Greece.' But she didn't get it. We all have our challenges. It's how you respond to them that defines you as a human being."

"And Hope, how did she define herself?"

"She didn't. She just quit. A lot of foreign wives are like her, especially the Americans. They don't realize that their fate is up to them, no matter where they are or who they are with. Greece isn't Saudi Arabia, for God's sakes. You have some say in what happens to you here. It might be hard, but you can adjust."

Vouros kept looking back at the shed, obviously wanting to get back to work. Costas had the sense she was never still, that idleness grated on her. Not a drone like Hope, a worker bee.

"You're probably wondering why I put up with her," Vouros said.

"It did occur to me," Costas said.

"I don't know if she told you and I'm probably talking out of school, but she had four miscarriages, one right after another. Boom, boom, boom. I did what I could for her. We all did, but she was grief-stricken. There's a lot of mourning that goes on when you have a miscarriage, but Hope took it to a whole other level. There was no sadness like her sadness, no grief equal to hers.

"You don't have to admire people in order to help them. You just do it. Acts of kindness should be freely given. Thrown into the wind, as the Greeks say. Anyway, I didn't see her that often, two or three times a month on average. I couldn't take much more than that. She just wore me out. I kept at it though; visited her every time I was in the neighborhood. Ordered gifts for her from the States, books mostly; she is a prodigious reader. I thought I could turn her around, show her how she could live in Greece, thrive while she was here. But in the end, I don't think I did her much good. I wasn't really a friend. I was just as a shoulder to cry on."

"Why do you think she's had such a hard time adjusting?"

"I don't know. Maybe there's some kind of pathology at work. Borderline personality disorder maybe. Those people thrive on chaos and misery. They create it wherever they go. I often thought if she didn't have Greece to blame for her unhappiness, she would have invented it."

"Mentally ill?"

"Maybe." Vouros hesitated for a moment. "Yes, maybe a little."

She went on to say she and her husband owned an art gallery on Spetses.

"I offered Hope a job there at one point. She was always complaining about how they didn't have any money and I wanted to help. But she turned me down. Worse, was the way she did it. Acting like she was some kind o aristocrat and the job was beneath her. That's when I finally lost patience with her."

"How far do you think she'd go to change her situation?"

Vouros flicked some clay off her pants. "You want to know if I think she killed him."

"Do you?"

"I've known her forever and always despaired at her passivity. She never initiated anything, never actually *did* anything. I don't know what she was like in the United States, but here in Greece, she had to be taken care of, have someone drive her places and translate for her. A trip to the grocery store was a major undertaking. I swear she couldn't buy a kilo of apples without help. Some part of her had just shut down."

She paused. "So, no, Melissa, in answer to your question. I don't think Hope killed him. Not because it was wrong, but because it would have taken too much effort."

"What about her relationship with in-laws? Do you think her grievances were justified?"

"Not really. I remember once there were a group of us here and she imitated her mother-in-law getting out of her wheelchair, how long it took her and how slow she was. When Hope didn't get the laugh she was expecting, she stopped, but I was appalled. Another time there was a death in the family. In Mani, I think it was, and she picked a fight with her husband's relatives outside the church because they didn't call her. They were up in the mountains and the phone reception was poor, but she didn't realize it and blamed them, saying they were intentionally excluding her. Mind you, this was at a funeral. And that wasn't the only time. She collects grievances and holds onto them. Always feels slighted, like everyone's at a party she wasn't invited to. This really comes into play in her relationship with her in-laws. She was always pointing out their sins to Thanasis, forcing him to choose between them and her."

After glancing at her watch, Costas stood up to go. "I've got to get back to the office. I appreciate you talking to me today. You've been very helpful."

"The person you should really talk to is Hope's mother-in-law, get her side of the story. I'll bet that old woman has some tales to tell. Hope may act like a child, but my feeling is that if you cross her, she'll come after you with everything she's got. She'll scratch your eyes out."

The two statements—that Hope was too passive to kill and that she'd scratch your eyes out—contradicted one another. Whether she'd realized it or not, Vouros had just fingered Hope Erikson for murder.

Chapter 10

Costas reviewed what Vouros had said as she drove back to Aghioi Anargyiou on her moped. She wasn't convinced Hope Erikson was the killer—what the potter said about her passivity rang true—but still she was the most likely candidate.

Costas had left her hair down after leaving Vouros' house. Curly and unruly, it reached the middle of her back and took on a life of its own, fluttering like a curtain as she roared down the road.

Huge estates now occupied the hills overlooking the sea in this part of Spetses; and heavily forested island of Spetsopoula was so close, she could count the kayaks lying out on the beach. The history of the family that owned the island was a sad one, drug overdoses and rumors the founder of the dynasty had beaten one of his wives to death. Her mother often said money can't buy happiness, citing them as an example. Costas felt differently. Money might not buy happiness, but it sure could buy a lot of other things; and she, for one, was tired of not having any.

A municipal bus was inching around the curve ahead, and she lifted her foot off the gas and let the moped drift back, in no hurry to return to Aghioi Anargyiou.

She found Ritsos sitting out in the yard with the victim's mother. The two brothers and their wives were at the taverna, he reported, hard at work serving lunch to the tourists. As per her instructions, Pappas had accompanied them.

"And the widow?" Costas asked.

"She's shut up in the bedroom. Last time I checked, she was still lying on the mattress, staring at the ceiling."

Ritsos was clearly dumbfounded by Costa's appearance and kept sneaking peeks at her hair. Let him wonder, she told herself, flicking it with a hand She was a free woman.

Overcome by the midday heat, the old woman had been dozing in her chair, but awoke when she heard them talking

"You, woman police chief." Sophia pointed an arthritic finger to Costas, "Have you found out who killed my boy?"

Costas shook her head. "I need to talk to you."

Sophia eyed her suspiciously. "What about?"

"Your daughter-in-law, Hope, the foreigner." Costas spat the word. While most Greeks were hospitable to foreigners, there was an undercurrent of xenophobia in many of them, especially elderly women from the village. Costas had used the word, 'foreigner,' deliberately, hoping to exploit this, Sophia's 'us' versus 'them mentality.

"Thanasis' wife, you mean?" Sophia mumbled. "What is it you want to know about her?"

The pouches under her eyes were so dark, she looked like she'd been beaten. The kerchief was gone from her head; and there was a line of black dye visible near the part. The old woman shifted uncomfortably as she sat there, inching first this way, then that.

"How do you get along with her?" Costas asked.

"Not good. When she first came, I tried to make her feel at home here. When we went to a restaurant, I'd keep the receipt and check off what she'd like and cook it for her. I even learned to make pancakes." Her tone was self-mocking, bitter.

"Nothing mattered. She always found something to complain about. If my friends came over and didn't fuss over her, she'd say I shouldn't be friends with them. People I have known all my life. It was like she wanted Thanasis to hate me, me, to hate me, me, his mother, his mother."

"Did she fight with you in front of her husband?"

"No, she was quiet about it, always speaking against me in English."

Costas wondered if the old woman was being entirely truthful. The relationship between mothers-in-law and the women their sons married was fraught with peril in Greece, often a minefield. Sophia might be old and crippled, but Costas was willing to bet she gave as good as she got.

The old woman kept rubbing her hands together. The knuckles of her fingers were swollen, nearly twice the normal size, and twisted with arthritis. Costas imagined they ached and that the rubbing brought her a measure of relief.

"Thanasis is soft. Was soft," the old woman said. It grieved her switching to the past tense and a shadow passed over her face. "Weak. Thanasis was weak. He couldn't stand up to her."

She closed her eyes for a moment. "She lost a baby and I offered to help her and she said, 'sure, like Nurse Ratched.' She thought because I was Greek, I was stupid and would not understand. But I asked someone I knew who this woman, this 'Nurse Ratched' was and she told me she was an evil woman in a movie, a nurse who forced this man, Jack Nicholson, to have surgery, surgery she knew would destroy him. And this, this is what Hope says to me that day. Always, always she acts like I am her enemy."

Costas was expecting rage, but all she saw was sadness.

The old woman's voice was plaintive. "We were one family before she came and I thought we could be one family again. I wanted Thanasis to have a good life with her, to have love in his life. What could I do? She was the one he'd chosen."

She asked Costas to help her inside, saying she was worn out and wanted to lie down. Putting an arm around her waist, Costas eased her out of the chair and handed her the crutches. Her body so thin Costas could feel her ribs, pressing against her.

She followed her into the house and helped her down onto the sofa. "What happened in Athens?" she asked before she left. "I need to know. What's the real reason you moved here?"

Sophia's eyes filled with tears. "My family has suffered much loss. Too much loss. We are cursed."

And with that, she fell silent and refused to say another word.

* * *

Stavros was busy seating people at a table in the taverna, bantering cheerfully as he recited the menu. Vasilis had taken over for his mother at the grill, Daphne at his side, while Chryssoula dished up portions of *moussaka* and *pastitsio*. Short-staffed, they'd enlisted the Pakistani to take the plates they'd prepared out to the waiting customers.

Wiping her hands on her apron, Daphne greeted Costas warmly. The whites of her eyes were bloodshot, probably from the smoke of the grill;

Costas doubted Daphne had cried herself to sleep the previous night. Of all of them, she'd seemed the least affected by the murder.

"Any news," Daphne asked.

Costas shook her head. "Still waiting on the lab work."

One by one the others approached her, too, none of them referring directly to the murder, only asking if there'd been any developments in the case.

"No, nothing," Costas told them.

She ordered two gyros to go and waited while Stavros prepared them.

"Given what happened, I'm surprised you decided to open today," she said. "Brother's been murdered and here you are flipping souvlakis on the grill."

"We have no choice. We need the money. It's as simple as that."

"So, business as usual."

"I repeat: we don't have a choice."

* * *

The crime scene tape was still in place, but beyond that, there was no trace of Thanasis Papadopoulos or hint of what had befallen him in the cave. He might never have existed, so little did his dying leave behind.

Sitting outside the cave, Costas ate the gyros, dabbing at the tzatziki with a napkin. It made her uneasy being so close to where the body had been found, yet she lingered there long after she finished, reviewing the facts of the case.

There were four possible reasons for the murder, she concluded. The first, because the victim had been part of some illicit or immoral activity in the cave. Smuggling, adultery, drunkenness, whatever it was, judging by their reactions, both brothers knew of it and chose to remain silent, implicating themselves to a degree in the crime. The second possibility was the killing was rooted in the past, in an event that had occurred long before, a secret buried deep in their shared history. If it were indeed a vengeance killing, again there was a good chance someone in the family had been involved.

Siblings in Greece often fought over their inheritance, but there'd been so little to inherit, she doubted that was the case here. No, if the killer was a member of the immediate family, there had to be another reason.

Whatever loss the old lady had spoken of, it had altered the course their lives and predated their coming to Spetses.

And then, of course, there was the victim's erstwhile spouse, Hope Erikson, the most obvious candidate, who might have killed him in a fit of rage.

Or worse, the fourth and final possibility, a migrant was responsible. A stranger, who had wandered into the cave, looking to steal, and been caught by Thanasis. If this were the case, a political fire storm would undoubtedly ensue once the facts of the crime came to light, the party of the far right, the Golden Dawn, using the killing as a pretext to wage war on the refugees now flooding Greece. Of all the scenarios, this was the one she feared the most.

Costas yearned for her days as a student in the academy, when everything had been laid out for her by her instructor, the motive for the murder obvious, the killer looming large on the horizon, impossible to miss.

Today, all she had were theories. The family dynamic was slowly revealing itself to her—mom and her boys in charge, their wives pushed off to the side—and she had her suspicions as to who the perpetrator might be, but suspicion alone wouldn't count for much in court.

* * *

In the end, it was Hope Erikson who resolved the dilemma for her. Making a run for it, she crawled out the window of her bedroom and fled in the family car.

Costas had been standing in the front of the house when she heard the engine start up; and she ran after the car, waving her arms and yelling for Hope to stop, but the American just kept going.

The incline was very steep and the gears of the KIA were giving her trouble—Costas could hear them grinding—and for a moment she thought the car would stall out, but then it lurched forward and began to pick up speed.

Hearing the commotion, Hope's mother-in-law staggered out of the house. Her hair wild from sleep, she shook her fist in the direction her daughter-in-law had taken and damned her for all eternity.

"She did it! She's the one who killed my boy!"

* * *

Costas' moped was no match for a car; and Hope was traveling fast. Although Spetses had only one road, there was a warren of side streets; and Hope quickly disappeared down one of them and was gone.

Worried, Costas called Stathis and told him what happened.

"Well done, Officer Costas," Stathis said. "You lost suspect in a murder case. Do you have any idea what this means? If she makes it to the United States, we will fucking have to extradite her."

"What should I do?" Costas struggled to keep her voice steady.

"Seal off the harbor. There's only one way she can get off Spetses and that's by boat."

"And when I find her?

"Lock her up. For God's sakes, Costas. Do your job. She's a witness in a murder case."

"On what grounds, sir? On what grounds do I lock her up? According to *aftoforo*, citizens' rights, you can only hold a suspect for twenty-four hours without charging them with a crime. After that you have to let them go, which means tomorrow at this time we'll have to let her go and we'll be right back where we started from."

"How dare you lecture me on the law!"

"I just thought…"

"Don't think. You're no good at it. Just do what I said. Find her and lock her up. As for her rights, let me worry about them."

"But, sir…"

"You heard me."

Deeply discouraged, Costas hung up the phone. Climbing back on the moped, she continued to search for the KIA, driving up and down the streets of the town. She eventually found it abandoned in the back of a hotel. There was no sign of Hope.

The truth was Costas was in no hurry to find her, afraid if she followed Stathis' orders and arrested her, she'd be setting something in motion she could never undo. There'd be hell to pay if it came out that Hope was innocent; and Stathis would make sure she was the one who paid it. He'd never admit the error was his.

* * *

Constantinos was equally pessimistic when Costas told him about the conversation.

"God, what a mess," he said. "You're not careful, this could go down like the Amanda Knox case in Italy. She was American, too; and the police framed her for murdering her roommate. The Supreme Court of Italy overturned the conviction. Last I read, she's suing for damages."

"Out with it, Constantinos. What are you trying to say?"

"I'm saying that case contaminated everyone who touched it like radioactive waste and if you're not careful, this one will do the same. The American government likes to throw its weight around, especially now that Trump's in power. You're not careful, you could be charged with false arrest or even worse, a human rights violation."

Costas tried to make light of it. "You mean like Idi Amin?"

"Pol Pot. Saddam Hussein. Kim-Yong-Un. There's a lot of them. Nobody you'd want to be associated with."

* * *

"Wife's flown the coop," Stathis told Patronas on the phone. "She made a run for it in the family car. Took off right under Costas' nose. Worst display of police incompetence I've seen since you mistook those goats for a murder suspect and shot them to death. I still don't know what you were thinking. Human beings walk on two feet, goats on four and yet…"

Patronas wondered where his boss was going. Stathis' bullying usually preceded some impossible request.

"I'm forwarding the information to you on that case in Spetses," continued Stathis. "I want you read it and familiarize yourself with the facts of the case, then make some calls and see what you can find out. As I told you before, the prime suspect is an American, so you'll need to proceed carefully. You can't afford to antagonize Washington. You do that and the whole thing could blow up in your face."

Patronas swore under his breath, aware now of where his boss was going.

Melissa Costas wasn't going to be the fall guy here. It was going to be him.

Chapter 11

Hope was halfway up the ramp when Simonidis spotted her. "There she is," he yelled to Costas. "She's coming toward you. She's thirty feet away and moving fast."

Costas and Constantinos leapt onto the ramp and quickly boxed the American in.

"Hope Erikson," Costas said. "You need to come with us."

"Back off," Hope shouted. "Leave me alone!"

When Costas moved to take her arm, Hope raked her face across with her nails, then picked up her backpack and swung it at Constantinos, hitting him squarely in the face.

Costas heard the cartilage splinter and saw the center of Constantinos' face collapse. Within seconds, all three of them were splattered with blood, blood the onlookers assumed was Hope's.

An angry murmur arose from the crowd. "Let her go!" a man shouted in English. "Fucking pigs!"

Hope was now sobbing hysterically, well aware of the trouble she was in. It was textbook law enforcement. Someone dies; the first person the police look at is the spouse; and she was that spouse. It was the same the world over. Once they got her in custody, they'd never let her go.

Costas grabbed Hope's arms, yanked them behind her and snapped handcuffs on. But the move knocked Hope off balance and she stumbled, tumbling head over heels off the ramp. Whimpering, she lay on the ground and didn't move.

"Oh, my God, she's pregnant," a person cried.

Holding cellphones aloft, the mob surged forward and began taking pictures of Hope's prostrate form.

As gently as they could, Costas and Simonidis raised Hope to her feet and lead her away, Constantinos trailing after them with a bloody handkerchief pressed to his nose. People hurled abuse at them as they made their way to the squad car, spitting on them and screaming obscenities.

Costas settled Hope into the back seat and slammed the door. "Don't move," she said angrily. "Don't you dare move."

After Simonidis and Constantinos got in, Costas hurriedly started the car.

But before she could pull out, a group of drunken Australians engulfed them. Rocking the cruiser back and forth, they yelled obscenities and poured a can of beer through one of the open windows, then climbed up on the hood of the car and began to jump up and down, laughing like maniacs at the sound they made. The fenders were next; and after they'd succeeded in tearing them off, they went back to work, trying to flip the car over.

"Turn her loose, cuntstable!" one shouted at Costas.

Immediately, the others picked up the cry. "Cuntstable, cuntstable!"

Gritting her teeth, Costas gunned the engine.

Startled, the Australians fell back and scattered in all directions, only to regroup a moment later and come running after the car, pelting it with rocks. One came flying through the windshield, shattering it and spraying those inside with glass. Other rocks followed in quick succession, boom, boom, boom.

"*Panagia mou*," Constantinos wailed. Mother of God. "Will it never end?"

Costas hauled Hope out the car as fast as she could as soon as she reached the station, dragged her up the stairs and locked her in. After the others were safely inside, she and Simonidis shoved the sofa in front of the door, afraid the Australians would return and storm the place like the Bastille.

Only then did Costas call Stathis. "We found Hope Erikson," she said, working to keep her voice level. "And I am happy to report, we now have her in custody."

She was careful not to volunteer anything else. With any luck, he'd never find out what had happened at the harbor. It would be the end of her if he did. He'd demand her head the way Salome had John the Baptist's.

Nor did she mention that Hope Erikson was pregnant, a far more serious omission.

Stathis ordered Costas to hold Hope Erikson indefinitely, not transport her to Piraeus as they'd previously discussed, making it clear he intended to distance himself from the case.

Again, Costas thought of John the Baptist, Stathis waltzing around his office in Piraeus, doing the dance of the seven veils.

* * *

After a cursory examination, the physician said Hope Erikson and the baby were fine. "She's a little hysterical," he told Costas. "But, given what happened, that's to be expected. I painted her knees with mercurochrome and bandaged them, also the palms of her hands where she scraped them on the pavement."

Afraid Hope would miscarry, Costas had summoned the doctor to the police station. Hearing his assessment, she breathed a sigh of relief. Proof positive the American had sustained no lasting damage at the hands of the police.

Costas hadn't searched Hope's backpack; and Hope called the American Embassy with her cell phone the minute she was alone. "I'm almost six months pregnant and the police on Spetses knocked me down and beat me up. I have bruises all over my body."

The duty officer on the other end requested photographs and Hope quickly supplied him with them, taking multiple photos of her injuries and forwarding them to him.

After viewing them, the man told her he'd look into it. "Where are you now?"

"Locked up in a room at the police station."

"Why are they holding you? On what grounds?"

"I don't know. So far, they haven't charged me with anything."

"I can't believe this," he said. "Give me an hour. I'll get you out of there."

* * *

Fearing Hope would hang herself, as a precautionary measure Costas had taken the sheets off the bed before locking her in for the night. It hadn't been an act of kindness, Hope thought bitterly, looking around the squalid space. There'd been no kindness shown to her since that first day in the cave.

It wasn't a proper jail cell, only a closet-like room with a cot in it that was stuffy and hot. She tried to pry open a window to get some fresh air, only to find it had been nailed shut.

She nearly lost it then, but held back, afraid if she started to cry, she'd never to stop. "Oh, God! Why is this happening to me?"

Using the sleeve of her shirt, she rubbed at the pane of glass, but was unable to get it clean. She didn't know how many hours had passed since she'd been locked in here, whether it was night or day.

A single, naked bulb hung from the ceiling. Providing scant light, it buzzed like an insect and went out a few minutes later.

Hope gave into tears then. She felt as if she'd been buried alive, walled up in a grave so deep, no one would ever find her again.

* * *

Constantino was sporting a metal splint on his nose and the beginnings of two massive black eyes. He'd have to have surgery; he told Costas when he returned from the clinic. The doctor said they'd need to rebuild the bridge of his nose.

"I'm thinking of resigning. What happened at the harbor wasn't what I was expecting when I signed up to be a cop. I assumed people would welcome my presence in their lives, the protection I offered, not spit on me and break my fucking nose."

"What are you going to do?

"Maybe join the Coast Guard. They seem a lot happier than we are."

"Go home and get some rest."

Costas completed an incidence report and emailed it to Stathis, attaching the doctor's notes and x-rays Constantinos had given her, carefully documenting what Hope Erikson had done to him. She'd taken headshots of Constantinos' face and she forwarded them to Stathis as well. She might not have enough to charge Hope Erikson with murder, but she had her for assaulting a police officer, no question about it. The American wouldn't be leaving Greece anytime soon.

She labored to make the attack appear unprovoked. "Hope was hysterical and out of control..." The cruiser was another story. No way she could pass that off if her boss came calling. She'd have to think of something.

Simonidis had been checking the computer; and he reported the fiasco at the harbor was already working its way through cyberspace, the image of Hope Erikson, her head bloody but unbowed, going viral and getting countless hits per minute.

* * *

"Hope's mother-in-law really went to town," Pappas said, collapsing in a chair in Costas' office. "She packed up everything Hope owned, stuffed it in a suitcase and threw it at me. You should have seen her. She couldn't get rid of it fast enough."

"Appears they've abandoned her," Costas said.

"That was my impression. '*Ai sto dialo!*' the old lady said. May she go to hell. "She told me Hope must have killed him otherwise she wouldn't have run away. Repeated it at least a hundred times. Yeah, the family has washed their hands of her all right. I'm with them. I can't wait to see the back of her. What time is she leaving?"

"She's not. Stathis called and he wants us to keep her here for the time being."

"But we always take suspects to Piraeus. We take them on the hydrofoil, sign some papers and hand them over. It's standard operating procedure. Has been since I joined the force."

"I know," said Costas.

She longed to say more, but stopped, knowing no good would come from criticizing Stathis to an old-timer like Pappas. Like the army, the police department was hierarchal, those on top giving orders to those below. You might not like those orders or the men who gave them to—in her experience, it was always men—but you obeyed them. How you felt had no bearing on the matter.

"Look at what she did to Constantinos," Pappas said. "It's just not right. She should be locked up in Korydallos Prison and locked up good. It's because she's American, isn't it? That's why Stathis is giving her special treatment, to keep them off his back. If she were a migrant, it'd be different."

* * *

What Pappas said about the victim's mother bothered Costas; and she opened the murder book and reviewed her notes after he left. Sure enough, everyone in the family had been implicating Hope since the beginning, nearly every word they'd all said implying she was the killer. Recognizing the police needed a viable suspect, the family had done its best to give them Hope. She was their sacrificial lamb.

Costas had dismissed much of what they'd said, attributing it to grief. But now she saw there was a pattern, almost a conspiracy of sorts; and she wondered how they'd gone about it. If as a group, they'd decided to accuse her beforehand.

Hope had finally quieted down when Costas went to check on her. Her hair and clothes were stiff with blood; and her face was speckled with it.

"There's a bathroom in the back," Costas told her. "Why don't you wash yourself off? You'll feel better."

Hope waved her away, but a few minutes later, Costas heard the water running.

* * *

Hope's friend, Margaret Vouros, turned up later that night. "I heard she got hurt when you arrested her, that one of your men threw her off the boat."

There was an accusatory note in Vouros' voice that Costas didn't like.

"We did nothing to her," she barked. "When we asked her to come with us, she refused and started fighting. Broke the nose of one of my men."

Costas unlocked the door of the cell. "Stay as long as you want. When you're ready to leave, just call me and I'll come and let you out."

Seeing Vouros standing there, Hope jumped up and embraced her. "Oh, Margaret! Margaret! Thank God, you're here."

Taking her by the hand, she pulled her down next to her on the cot. "You won't believe what they did to me! I was getting ready to board the boat and they started shouting and knocked me down. Then that bitch," she nodded in Costas' direction, "handcuffed me and locked me up in here. I tell you, only in Greece. Something like that would never happen in the States."

"Oh, come on, Hope," Vouros said impatiently. "Worse things happen in the states. If you're black, they don't knock you down. They shoot you."

They went back and forth, sparring about the advantages of living in the United States versus those of living in Greece.

"Let's not do this tonight," Hope finally said. "I'm in trouble, Margaret. Bad trouble."

There was an edge of panic in her voice. "The cops think I killed Thanasis, but I didn't. I swear I didn't. I dreamed about leaving him, sure. And killing that damned mother of his, but that's all I did was dream. I'd never hurt him. He was the love of my life."

"Why'd you take off?"

Hope shrugged as if her fleeing had been of no consequence, a momentary whim. "I just wanted to get away."

"You *do* know that's why they came after you."

"I know. I know. It was stupid. And then I hit that cop in the face. I don't know why I did that either. I just wasn't thinking."

How many times had she heard Hope say that over the years? Vouros wondered. As if it excused anything. She never took any responsibility, never owned up to anything she did. Nor was Hope overly fond of reality—the cold, hard facts of life. Unfortunately, reality was fast closing in on her. At best, she'd end up in jail for five years. At worst, she'd would be in there for life.

"Do you have a lawyer?" she asked quietly.

Hope shook her head.

"What about money?"

"Don't have that either. Thanasis' mother controlled the purse strings in the house. The first day of the month, she'd dole out my share and expect me to make it last. Whenever I complained or said I needed more, she'd talk about the war and how there was no food and everyone she knew died of hunger."

"I can loan you some. You don't want a court appointed lawyer, not in a case like this."

"I don't know what to do, Margaret. One minute I'm crying about Thanasis and the next I'm worrying about going to jail. Terrible as he was sometimes, I loved him with all my heart. He never meant anyone any harm. He was just a kid, a big, dumb kid."

For once, Hope had gotten it right, Vouros thought. Thanasis Papadopoulos had been exactly that—a big, dumb kid. One of those men who'd gone from boyhood to middle age without ever achieving manhood.

"No one ever made me feel the way he did," Hope added, her voice softening. "I just couldn't get enough him. It was like I was an addict. I was addicted to him. I remember thinking it was a miracle when he asked me to marry him, that a man like that would want *me*."

You would have thought some of this would have worn off over the years, Vouros told herself, such sexual enthrallment. It was as if her relationship with her husband had sucked something vital out of her and left nothing in its place.

Both of Hope's hands were wrapped in gauze, soggy now and streaked with red where her wounds had bled through. The whine Vouros had long associated with her had intensified; the self-pitying tone Hope inevitably employed when speaking of herself.

"I just can't believe this is happening. The police say he had a massive wound at the back of his head and cuts on his hands and forearms. Defensive wounds, they say, most probably from fighting off someone he knew. Me, they're saying! It was me!" Hope's voice became shrill.

"I don't know who could have done it. Sometimes he'd go into the cave in the afternoon. I found him passed out there a couple of times. His drinking was getting worse. He couldn't really control it anymore." The complaint was in Hope's voice again, that abiding sense of grievance. "I thought after what happened in Athens, he'd stop, but he didn't."

"What happened in Athens?" Vouros asked.

Hope refused to meet her eyes. "It's not important. It was a long time ago."

"Is that where you found him? In the cave?" Vouros wanted to keep her talking, thinking it was therapeutic, would do her some good.

"Yes, I was so happy. I was pregnant and he told me he'd find us a house of our own. Everything would be better."

Five and a half months pregnant, Hope was beginning to show. If something wasn't done, there was a good chance the baby would be born in jail. Pity, at least on Vouros' part, had long been the basis of their relationship, but at least now it seemed justified.

She handed Hope the stack of books she'd brought for her and stood up to go. Hope clung to her, wetting the fabric of her shirt with her tears. "What am I going to do, Margaret? What's going to happen to me?"

Removing Hope's hands, Vouros slowly extracted herself. "I'll do what I can for you, but I don't know what's going to happen, Hope. Maybe you'll get lucky and they'll decide there were extenuating circumstances and you had cause for hitting that policeman. I think that's the best you can hope for at this point."

"Hope never got me anywhere, Margaret. Never did me a bit of good. My sister-in-law's right. My name should have been Hopeless."

* * *

Costas left the station at five a.m. Unexpectedly, Simonidis had appeared out of nowhere and offered to take over for her, saying he couldn't sleep and might as well work.

Still deeply shaken, she drove to her apartment and parked under the trees by the old school. She sat there for a long time, mulling over what had happened at the harbor. Stathis would find out—he always did—and once he did, she would lose her job.

There was a line of red at the horizon and the sky was slowly growing light, Homer's 'rosy-fingered dawn.' Touching the scratches on her face, she bowed her head and wept.

If she wasn't a cop, what was she?

Chapter 12

Patronas' wife, Lydia, eyed the ringing phone like a live grenade. "Oh, for God's sakes, Yannis, answer it!"

The *Flight of the Valkyries* continued to sound. rising to a jarring crescendo.

Reluctantly, Patronas picked up the phone. "Good morning, sir."

Stathis wasted no time. "Costas fouled up and she's off the case. How soon can you get to Spetses?"

"It will take me some time. I'll have to fly from Chios to Athens first and then take a boat from there."

He knew where Stathis was going and he didn't want to go there. He might have solved a number of homicides, albeit in fits and starts, but he had no illusions about his abilities. For every step forward he took, on average he took five back. He knew because he'd counted. Hit or miss about summed it his approach—'miss' being the operative word.

Nor did he have any illusions about Stathis. The only reason his boss was summoning him to Spetses was because there was no one else. Murder was rare in Greece; and, consequently, most police officers there had little or no experience dealing with it. Unfortunately, Patronas did, having solved three homicides in the past two years. They'd damaged him, both physically and emotionally, those cases. What he'd seen would haunt him till the day he died.

The motives for those killings had varied widely, but not one had involved a spouse, so the case on Spetses would be a first for him.

In his experience, wives often made their husbands' lives hell—God knows his first wife, Dimitra certainly had—but as a rule, they didn't kill them. Not outright anyway. They took their time, drained the joy out of their days the way vampires did blood, leaving nothing behind, but empty husks. Their mates damaged, but alive.

"Sounds pretty straight forward, sir," Patronas said, seeking to weasel out of the assignment. "A simple domestic. No reason for me to get involved."

"As I told you before, the chief suspect is a foreign national—an American. From New Jersey of all places." Stathis paused to let this sink in. "New Jersey," he repeated.

No good would come from pointing out Hope Erikson's point of origin was irrelevant, be it New Jersey or someplace else. Reality in Stathis' mind was whatever he said it was.

"I need you to solve the case and solve it fast," his boss went on. "Press is already on it and we can't afford to have what happened in Italy, where they arrested that American and had to release her years later. Big *fassoria*, brouhaha, that caused. Gave Italy a black eye and made everyone involved from the prosecutor on down look like idiots. Your case has to be air-tight and able to withstand the closest scrutiny. And you'll need to work fast, Patronas. Fast, fast, fast. I can't stress that enough."

Patronas tried one last time to escape. "But Spetses is out of my jurisdiction, sir. I don't want to encroach on local law enforcement."

"You can and you will. Melissa Costas is off the job as of this morning. She's totally inadequate and should never have been appointed to run the department."

"I beg to differ with you, sir. Colleagues of mine say she's extremely competent."

"A false impression," Stathis said airily. "The suspect, in addition to being American, is also pregnant which Costas failed to tell me when she briefed me about the case. I only learned about it today from the newspapers. Seems Costas and her men botched the arrest and threw her down the stairs. No doubt it was an accident, but it doesn't look that way on the internet. One of her men has her in a chokehold, for God's sakes; and all of them are covered with blood. Check it out. You won't believe it."

Patronas' heart sank. This was the real reason he was being dispatched to Spetses: To clean up the mess.

"Any chance this Hope woman is innocent?" he asked.

Stathis snorted. "Highly unlikely."

Guilty already. His boss was moving at the speed of light on this one.

But then due process never meant much to Stathis. "The law should never be an impediment to justice," he often said, the two, at least in his mind, being mutually exclusive.

Yes, time had stopped for his boss. Right around 1984.

Napoleonic in both temperament and stature, he had served both the Junta and the current leftist regime with equal fervor; and if by some sad twist of fate, the Nazis returned, Patronas had no doubt Stathis would transform himself yet again. Don a brown shirt and go goose stepping down Stadiou Street.

"Defendant is from a wealthy American family," Stathis continued. "Father was a banker, so you'll need to tread lightly, Patronas. America has been a far better friend to Greece than Europe ever was. We might be overrun by migrants now and governed by socialists, but the old order still stands and one day it will return to power. You don't want to antagonize those people."

Patronas smiled to himself. His vision of his boss in a brown shirt hadn't been that far off.

Stathis was an interesting man. Although a total fascist, he was enthralled with the United States, convinced everyone there was rich, the streets of New York and Los Angelos indeed paved with gold. Too bad there were drug addicts on every corner of those streets, Patronas had reminded him, opioids taking down thousands and thousands of America's young.

"Where is this woman now?" inquired Patronas. "The spouse from New Jersey."

"You know how it is with this government, everyone is equal. She's in jail. A real hellion, she broke the nose of a policeman there in three places. I want you to gather that team of yours and get going. Bring me enough evidence to charge her for murder."

More foolishness of Stathis as the two associates he was referring to— Giorgos Tembelos and Papa Michalis, an elderly Orthodox priest—had no professional training in forensics, nor were they particularly adept at police work. They hardly constituted a team. A pair of magpies would have made better cops.

The priest was fond of detective shows and believed because he watched them, a kind electronic knowledge transfer took place. Also, he talked too much. With Papa Michalis, talking was like a disease.

The other member of the so-called 'team,' Giorgos Tembelos, was

Patronas' best friend. Cretan, he was loyal to the point of madness and Patronas would have trusted him with his life. That said, he was probably the laziest cop in all of Greece. He didn't like taking notes during interviews, so he didn't. He slept during stake-outs and misplaced key pieces of evidence. The list of his sins was long and ever growing.

With a sigh, Patronas told Stathis, he and his team would get there as soon as they could.

"Good, good," Stathis said. "See that you do."

* * *

Getting the suitcase down from a shelf of the closet, Patronas opened it and began to pack. He folded his spare uniform up and stowed it inside, along with a sweater and ten days' worth of clean underwear. Rummaging around, he found his swimming suit and threw it in as well and closed the bag. He could hear Lydia in the kitchen, clearing away the dishes.

She joined him a few minutes later. "Is Father going with you?"

"Yes, he's meeting me at the airport. Tembelos, too."

Lydia touched his sleeve. "I wish you didn't have to go."

She'd been urging him to retire ever since they got married, afraid he'd be injured facing down a suspect. "They call them killers for a reason," she often said. "Killers, Yannis. Killers."

Patronas was undeterred. There was something to be said for getting away from home and eating what he wanted. Pizza, for example, which Lydia heartily disapproved of, and *loucoumades,* fried honey balls, which he dearly loved and hadn't been allowed to eat since they wed.

Lydia would always shake her head when he proposed getting some. 'Sugar," she'd say as if they were speaking of arsenic. "Sugar."

Patronas planned to eat them both on Spetses. Also, French fries with handfuls of salt. Ice cream.

As Stathis was frequently delinquent in paying for the team's services—the boats, hotels and meals involved—Patronas and his men had taken to filling a valise with food before they left on a case. A somewhat problematic solution as the priest always ate more than his share, taking a huge salami and whittling it down like a beaver. A nocturnal beaver, he always did his eating at night while Patronas and Tembelos slept. Tembelos had spotted teeth marks on the last one and threatened to beat up Papa Michalis if he did again.

No, not a team, Patronas thought morosely, eyeing the stained valise. More like the Three Stooges, Larry, Curly and Moe.

* * *

As a general rule, Patronas tended to side with husbands in domestic disputes, the result of his own turbulent marital history. His first wife, Dimitra, had wanted to kill him and probably would have, given half a chance. Run him through with a pitchfork, the weapon of the devil, whose handmaiden she surely was. What men did to women, he'd never much thought about, a lapse, Lydia frequently pointed out to him.

She did that a lot, Lydia, pointed things out to him, one of the few flaws along with the food in their otherwise perfect union.

They'd been married less than a year and for the most part it had been an idyllic chapter in Patronas' life, although there were clouds looming on the horizon. It had started out innocently enough when pizza disappeared and mysterious substances replaced it on his dinner plate. Kale and a strange grainy thing she called 'quinoa' and said the ancient Incans ate.

"And where are those Incas today?" Patronas had asked, poking at it suspiciously with his fork. "Extinct, that's where."

"Nonsense," she replied. "Quinoa is a wonder food."

Other changes were also in the works. Just two weeks ago she'd taken him to a hair salon and instructed the stylist to give him a 'make-over.' Not wanting to make a scene, he'd gone along and now sported a ridiculous, hipster haircut as a result. With shaven sides and a great wad of hair on top, it made him look like *Tintin*, the comic book character, and had caused much derisive laughter when he ventured into work the next day.

And worse just this morning, she'd suggested he might want to shave off his moustache, claiming it 'dated him,' but he'd dug his heels in and refused. It had been with him a long time, that moustache, well over forty-five years, and he couldn't bear to part with it. It would be like putting shaving cream on his soul.

All these efforts were preposterous given that he barely cleared five-foot one and was losing his hair. He wasn't tough. He was puny and weak and more than a little pigeon-toed. An aging Charlie Chaplin if the truth be told; and he wished with all his heart that she would recognize this and leave him alone.

What was it the ancient Greek philosopher, Menander, had said? 'Marriage is an evil most men welcome.'

He picked up a framed photograph of Lydia on the dresser. They'd been on a boat when it was taken and her coppery hair had been loose, like a cloud of sunlight around her. She had a look of pure joy on her face, that infinite reservoir of joy that so defined her.

Not necessarily evil.

Not all the time anyway.

He touched the photo affectionately. No, sometimes marriage could actually be a blessing.

Chapter 13

As Costas had feared, Stathis relieved her of her command as soon as he saw the news about Hope Erikson on the internet. "You are no longer in charge of the department on Spetses," he said. "Nor are you to play any substantive role in the investigation of the murder of Thanasis Papadopoulos."

"What are you saying? Are you firing me? Am I still a cop?"

"Yes, you are a cop. Not a very good cop, but a cop."

His voice hardened. "In fact, you might be the single most incompetent cop I have ever had the misfortune of working with. Knocking down a pregnant suspect. What the hell did you think you were doing, Officer Costas? When I saw what happened—it's all over the internet by the way, foreign and Greek sites alike—I wanted to fire you on the spot, but my superiors held back. Apparently, the American ambassador called last night and got everyone's back up. 'Who is he to tell us what to do?' they said. 'Who we should keep on the force and who we should fire?'

"Your incompetence never even made it to the table." Stathis was shouting now. "Pure unadulterated bullshit if you ask me, but there you have it. Now you listen and you listen good: You are to obey every order Patronas gives you. You are not question his directives. nor undermine his authority in any way. As of this moment, you are on the equivalent of foot patrol. And, I cannot stress this enough, if you make another mistake, no matter how minor it is, you are off the force."

"I won't disappoint you, sir."

"You already have." And with that, he hung up the phone.

Not quite the fate of John the Baptist, but professionally, it was close. Her head wasn't on the platter yet, but if she didn't watch her step, it soon would be.

Constantinos called not long after to warn her reporters were swarming the department and she might want to dress as a civilian when she came into work. "I doubt that they'll recognize you out of uniform, but they might, so be careful. They're everywhere."

Depressed, Costas opened the door of her closet and pawed through her clothes, seeking something appropriate to wear, eventually pulling out the black dress she'd purchased for her mother's funeral. She took a shower and washed her hair, then put it on. A dress, it necessitated the wearing of high heels as well. Her version of sackcloth and ashes.

A television truck was parked haphazardly in front of the police station, a good-looking man standing next to it with a microphone in his hand. An American, Costas judged, seeing the earnest expression on his face.

Wanting to put forth her version of events, Costas held an impromptu press conference later that day. It deteriorated almost immediately, an Italian reporter shouting questions about police brutality on Spetses. After an abrasive exchange, involving much yelling back and forth, Costas ended the press conference and threw him out of the station.

"You stood tall," Pappas said admiringly. "Just like Metaxas with Mussolini. You stood up to him."

In 1940, the Greek Prime Minister, Ioannis Metaxas, had refused the ultimatum from Mussolini that demanded Greece surrender to Italy, an event that precipitated Greece's entry into the war.

Aside from the fact that both she and Metaxas had stood up to Italians, Costas didn't see the connection. What she'd done wouldn't result in war. Only in her unemployment if Stathis got wind of it.

Pappas was bewildered when she burst into tears. Not knowing what to do, he brought her a glass of water and set it down on her desk. "Sorry, boss. I didn't mean to upset you."

"I'm not your boss anymore," she said, wiping her eyes. "I've been replaced by a man from Chios, Yannis Patronas."

"I know him," Pappas said. "He's a pugnacious little guy. Took on Stathis once, the only one in the department who ever did. Got fired as a result, but they hired him back six months later. He's a great cop. Totally dedicated. Lives and breathes policework."

* * *

Unlocking the door of the cell, Costas leaned in and spoke to Hope. "Although it is customary, you will not be going to Piraeus today. We will be escorting you there the day after tomorrow."

"Why do I have to go to Piraeus?"

"To go before the magistrate, who will determine what charges are to be filed against you, whether or not you will be charged for assaulting a police officer."

Hope's eyes were wet. "I need a lawyer. Get me a lawyer."

Returning to her office, Costas called all the lawyers she knew on Spetses, seeking to find one willing to represent the American. It wasn't her job, but she did it anyway as a kind of penance.

There were very few attorneys on the island; and none of them wanted to get involved. "Call the embassy," they all said in one form or another. "You said she's American. She's their problem."

Costas worked the rest of the morning, going through the phone messages her men had left for her. Five of the calls were from Stathis and she crumbled those up and threw them away, two from an American official at the embassy, and any number from reporters, the first clocking in at five a.m.

After she finished responding to the messages—by email or text, she was in no mood to talk to anybody—she set about preparing the office for Patronas. She drafted the final entries for murder book and wrote them all in, making sure everything she knew could be found in its pages. She wanted him to he'd have something to start with when he took over, not have to repeat everything from the beginning.

As an afterthought, she penned a note, stating Hope Erikson should be evaluated by a psychiatrist. Not that she was a danger to others, but she might well be one to herself. But then she thought better of it and threw it away. She was off the case. What happened to Hope Erikson wasn't her responsibility any more.

She straightened the books on the shelves and dusted the furniture with a rag, swept the floor and watered the geraniums on the window sill. They were dying, just like her career.

* * *

Wearing a shapeless black dress, Melissa Costas was waiting for Patronas and his associates when their ferry docked on Spetses.

Odd, the funerary garb, Patronas thought, wondering why she wasn't in uniform. Perhaps someone had died in her family.

Stranger still was the police car she was driving. No windshield, dents everywhere, it looked like it had been attacked by King Kong. Costas didn't volunteer any information about it either and he didn't ask. Already Spetses was proving to be more of an adventure than he'd anticipated.

"Where do you want to start?" she asked him after they'd introduced themselves. She was mystified as to why he'd brought a priest with him, but, remembering Stathis' warning, didn't dare ask.

"The crime scene," Patronas replied. "After that, I want to speak to the victim's family and that American woman you have in custody."

* * *

Pieces of crime scene tape hung in shreds around the entrance to the cave. Buffeted by the wind, they rose and fell like macabre party decorations. The interior smelled faintly of hydrogen peroxide, iodine and alcohol, chemicals Patronas associated with forensic work. In addition, there was another scent, far uglier that he recognized from previous homicide cases. The smell of violent death, of feces and blood. Fear, too, he imagined.

He'd insisted on inspecting the cave alone. Walking around the perimeter, he focused on the rock walls, noting the pattern of the blood splatter. Costas had objected when he told her his plan, saying she wanted to accompany him, but he dug his heels in, saying he needed to form his own impression. He'd meet with her later today after he finished the tasks that he'd assigned himself, go through the murder book with her and discuss her assessment of the victim's family.

Turning on his flashlight, he ran the beam across the limestone walls. Spotting a crack in the rocks in the back, he inched his way towards it. The opening proved to be far larger than it looked. With some effort, any normal sized adult could squeeze themselves through it.

He eased his way through the crack and found himself in an extension of the cave, a dank cavern full of stalactites and stalagmites the color of dirty snow. A kind of rough tunnel led off from it and he headed toward it. The walls of the tunnel were damp and he guessed they had been formed by water seeping into the rock and hollowing it out. The water was still there, a stream running through the tunnel and pooling sluggishly at his feet.

Getting down on his knees, he dipped a finger in and tasted the water. Brackish and salty, it could only have come from the sea, meaning there was a connection between the cave and the distant waters of the channel. He stared at the water for a long time, wondering if a man could have used the stream as a way to get into the cave undetected

However, the stream disappeared a few minutes later, flowing through an opening much too small for a man to pass through. Although Patronas could hear it trickling, he could no longer see it.

Overhead, bats covered the jagged roof of the tunnel, the ground beneath his feet gray with their droppings. He paused, not sure whether to continue on or go back. Costas was waiting for him with Tembelos and Papa Michalis at the taverna. Perhaps he should leave this part of the cave for the forensic specialists.

They would have the final say, but he was convinced he'd discovered the route the killer had taken. According to Costas, Hope Erikson had staggered out of the cave screaming, her clothes soaked in blood. A memorable exit, very theatrical. Costas also reported Hope had been the only person in the vicinity at the time.

Still, Costas wasn't convinced the American was responsible. She and Patronas had discussed it in the car, going back and forth over who else it might have been responsible.

"There's no way someone could have left the cave that day without someone noticing," Patronas had said. "Given the nature of the victim's wounds, they would have been covered in in blood."

The existence of the tunnel changed all that, raised any number of possibilities.

He heard something in the tunnel, a faint sound. It seemed to be coming from the place where he'd started. Unnerved, he tried to brush it off.

"It's just the wind," he muttered. Yet there was no wind in the cave. The air was absolutely still.

He started walking again, faster now. Five minutes later, he stopped and listened hard, but the only sound he heard was his own tortured breathing.

Reluctant to return the way he'd come, he headed deeper into the cave. He had no idea where he was going. All he knew was he had to get away. He'd nearly lost his life wrestling with a suspect in a cave in Chios, and he was mortally afraid of being trapped like that again. He stumbled forward and moment later, the darkness lifted and he was standing outside in a patch of sunlit grass.

Looking around, he sought to get his bearings. High above him, the rocks were pockmarked with shadowy indentations, the limestone porous and deeply eroded. Could be the cave where the family had stored its supplies wasn't the only one in the cliff. There might well be others. Again, he thought the possibilities were endless.

He was in plateau high above the beach. Pine trees covered the surrounding hills; and the air was fresh and full of birdsong.

The victim's house; was very close, less than twenty meters by his estimate. Given the distance, anyone in the family could have entered the cave by the back entrance, confronted the victim and killed him, exited and cleaned themselves off. The busiest time of day at the taverna, there would have been no one around to see them.

He needed to put a team together—Costas and her men, Tembelos and himself—and scour the area, draw a grid and go over the cliff centimeter by centimeter, find the clothing the killer had cast off that day. Patronas had no doubt it was there.

* * *

"I found a tunnel," Patronas told Costas. "It runs under the cliff and ends within a stone's throw of the victim's house."

Costas instantly understood the implications. "Show me," she said.

Stepping over the crime scene tape, Patronas led her into the cave and squeezed through crevice. retracing his steps and walking swiftly through the tunnel and out into the meadow. Playing his light along the ground, he'd searched for signs of an intruder while he was inside, but had seen nothing, only his own footprints in the thick piles of dung. The rancid little stream of water was still there, burbling along beside him; and above him, the bats slept on, undisturbed.

After they exited the cave, Patronas told Costas to wait and he walked to the victim's house, timing the journey with his watch.

Less than five minutes.

"Could have been any one of them," he said, returning to her side.

* * *

"We've got our work cut out for us," Patronas told his colleagues, Giorgos Tembelos and Papa Michalis. "We need to find out who knew about that tunnel. It may well prove the key to the case."

He spent the rest of the afternoon interviewing members of the victim's family, summoning Daphne Papadopoulos and speaking with her first.

"I told that policewoman all this yesterday," she complained. "Where I was and who I saw. We must have gone over it a hundred times."

She also claimed to know nothing about the tunnel. "I hated that cave. I never went in there if I could avoid it."

Her expression changed when Patronas brought up Hope's pregnancy. "If she's convicted, will you and your husband seek guardianship of her child?"

"No, never," she snapped.

They might have been speaking of a leper, so swift was her reaction.

Startled, Patronas entered what she'd said in his notebook, underlined it and starred it.

In Greece, people always professed affection for children. It was required behavior, an involatile rule in the culture. And newborns were held especially sacred. Daphne had told him she had no children; and one would think she would welcome the presence of a baby in her life, not spurn it as she just had.

He himself loved children and would have gathered up all the lost ones in the world and given them a home if it were up to him. Built an ark and rescued them just as Noah had the animals. A baby? Who wouldn't want a baby? What was wrong with this woman?

"Let me understand. You won't help Hope when the time comes?" he asked.

She shook her head.

"You *do* know that Hope will not be able to keep the baby with her indefinitely. At some point she will have to surrender it and it will be placed in an orphanage."

When she didn't respond, Patronas stood up and indicated the interview was over. He knew it was unprofessional, but he didn't want her anywhere near him. He wanted her gone.

Daphne's husband, Vasilis, said basically the same thing when Patronas raised the issue with him. "Listen, you see our situation," he said. "We can barely afford to eat, let alone take care of a child. We'll see that it has a home if that's what you're worrying about. Somewhere safe to go. But beyond that…" He made a hopeless gesture with his hands.

"I'm surprised," Patronas said. "If it were me and my brother died, I'd want his child."

"People are different," Vasilis said.

No doubt the older brother, Stavros, got the lion's share of the profits from the taverna given that he had three children to support; Vasilis, and his wife, Daphne receiving far less. Money often played a role in human relations, Patronas had learned since joining the police force twenty-three years ago. Still, it didn't explain the antipathy Daphne and her husband had expressed toward Hope and her child. Something else was going on.

Patronas found he didn't have much use for Chryssoula either. Given to striking poses, she acted like she was in the middle of a magazine shoot, not a homicide investigation.

Her husband, Stavros, was also irritating. Irreverent and profane, he'd pointed out a tourist in a bikini and made lewd jokes. Neither he or his wife seemed overly upset by the murder.

Still Patronas decided upon reflection he'd give the two brothers the benefit of the doubt. Greek man, they couldn't cry. No, tears would have embarrassed them. Perhaps Stavros' laughter was like Zorba's in Nikos Kazantzakis' famous book who'd danced on the beach for hours after his son died. Danced until he could dance no more. Vasilis was more of a puzzle.

Stoic and dry eyed, the victim's mother was far more familiar, describing her dead son as loving and dutiful in a monotone. *"Chyso mou,"* my golden one, she told Patronas. "The joy of my life."

A true daughter of Sparta, she said after the initial shock, she had not allowed herself to cry. It would have lessened her pain, she said, and she wanted to keep it alive, to keep it fresh. Patronas had no doubt she would build a shrine to him in her heart and light symbolic candles there every morning and every night, speak of her loss until the day she died. After his father died, his mother had done the same. He'd never understood it as a child, her need to cloak herself in sorrow, but now he believed it had given purpose to her life. She was there to remember, to bear witness. But, unfortunately, a witness was all she ended up being. Everything else had leached away.

"He never hurt anyone," the old woman went on. "Why this happened, I do not know."

Patronas had the feeling she was holding back, that there was some crucial fact about the victim she didn't want him to know. Perhaps it was only his alcoholism. As a Greek mother, she would never admit her son was a drunk.

It was interesting the way that played out sometimes. A friend of his had a son, who was a heroin addict. "Trust me, Yannis," he'd told him, "when something like that happens, people just devour you. They just eat you alive. Everyone we know abandoned us when we told them about our son. People, who'd watched him grow up, who'd known him all his life. They treated all of us like vermin. They assumed because he used needles, he had AIDs and would infect them. He came to my brother's house one Easter; and I saw my sister-in-law throw away the glass my son had used, his plate and the silverware. Do you have any idea how that feels?"

Maybe having an alcoholic son was the same. Maybe Thanasis was something to be hidden away, closeted. It could be she thought his problem would reflect badly on her, that if she told people she would be found wanting as a mother.

Chapter 14

Costas relayed what she knew of Spetses society to Patronas and Papa Michalis on the way back to town in the cruiser. "The Papadopoulos family is an anomaly as far as I can see," she said. "Most of the people here have money, wealthy Athenians, who've summered on the island for decades."

"What's their connection with Spetses?" Patronas asked. "What brought them here?"

"Stavros said the family had two souvenir shops in Athens, but lost them during the economic crisis. 'No customers, no money,' were the words he used. Supposedly, the taverna is a way for them to survive."

"You check it out?"

She shook her head. "I was going to, but I didn't get the chance."

Patronas had ordered Tembelos to stay behind in Aghioi Anargyiou and keep watch on the tunnel. "There's a good chance the killer left something behind in there; and he'll come back to retrieve it. Clothes would be my guess. He'll come at night if he comes at all, so you need to be prepared."

Given his friend's inherent laziness, Patronas doubted he would manage to do what he was supposed to do. Far more likely, Tembelos would fall asleep as soon as the sun went down and stay asleep until morning. He might even snore, alerting the killer to his presence. It wouldn't be the first time.

Patronas had already called the forensic team in Athens, stating they needed to return to Spetses as soon as possible and go through the cave again, dust an additional area for prints. He'd also erected a sign with a skull and cross bones on it outside the cave, warning people not to approach.

"But you and Costas went in there," Tembelos complained. "If there was any evidence left to be found, you contaminated it."

"We'll give the forensic people a sample of our DNA when they get here," Patronas said, conceding the mistake. "Hopefully, they can work around it."

Costas had been all about setting up search lights and working all night, but Patronas had dissuaded her. "Tembelos is a good man. He'll call us if he needs help. We'll search the area first thing in the morning. Chances are we'll miss something if we do it in the dark."

* * *

Hotel Ambrosia was old and sparsely furnished, the sole decoration in the lobby, a plethora of dusty potted plants. The toilet didn't always flush, the owner warned Patronas, nor was the air conditioning particularly effective. "Keep the windows open and you should be all right."

In other words, high on flowerpots, low on amenities.

According to the online site Tembelos and Patronas had consulted, Hotel Ambrosia was the cheapest place on Spetses.. As always, Stathis' travel stipend had been meager—ten euros a day per person—and they wanted to be able to eat. To that end, they'd also booked only one room, even though there were three of them, a catastrophic miscall given what the owner had said about the toilet.

The room was on the third floor; and Costas hurried up the stairs ahead of him, a show of youth and athleticism that did nothing for Patronas' ego. He was already having trouble with her. For one thing, she towered over him and he had to look up every time he spoke to her. Such had been his lot since age fourteen when everyone else in his class had shot up, but he'd stayed right where he was, rooted to the earth and waiting for a growth spurt that never came.

Papa Michalis' face fell when he saw the accommodations. Sniffing the air, he complained bitterly. "The owner said the toilet doesn't always flush. This is obviously an untruth. Given the smell, I'd say it never does."

* * *

When Patronas arrived at the police station, Costas led him through the lobby and down a lengthy corridor. The lobby was stuffed with furniture. In addition to a sofa, there were upholstered chairs everywhere and a coffee table with piles of government forms neatly stacked on top. Unlike the station on Chios, there were no Interpol photos of suspected arms smugglers or bearded terrorists on the walls, nary a *desperato* in sight. The air conditioning was on and seemed fully functional. All in all, not a bad place to be.

Opening the last door, Costas pushed it open. "This is my office."

She hesitated in front of the metal desk. "But given my loss of position, I can no longer justify using it, so I'm turning it over to you. I cleaned out the drawers and sorted through all the files. I think you'll find everything is in order."

Picking up a black spiral notebook, she handed it to him. "Here's the murder book. I'm sorry if it's incomplete, but this was the first homicide I ever worked and I didn't really know what I was doing. As for the police station, I have, had, four men serving under me: Petros Simonidis, who's working the front desk, Michalis Constantinos, Alexis Ritsos and Giorgos Pappas. I'll introduce you to them later."

She then went into a lengthy explanation as to why her men hadn't been there to meet him. "As a general rule, Spetses is very quiet. Once in a while people get drunk or there's a domestic situation we have to be deal with, but that's it. That said, everything changed after the murder. Hope Erikson fled; and Stathis ordered me to go after her and detain her. She hit Constantinos in the face and broke his nose in three places. He's still in a lot of pain and I sent him home to get some rest. The other two, Ritsos and Pappas, are in Aghioi Anargyiou, monitoring the family in case one of them tries to leave. I probably should have introduced you when we were there, but you wanted to see the cave and then I forgot about it."

Costas was obviously nervous, vibrating like a tuning fork; and Patronas kept hearing the same defensive note in everything she said. He wasn't her superior. They were equals. She didn't have to justify herself to him.

"Look," he said. "I didn't volunteer to come here. Stathis ordered me to. I am fifty-four years old and my career as a policeman is just about over. I have never been a particularly ambitious man; and I'm certainly not seeking to advance myself now at my age. Homicide cases are tough and I would happily never work another. They are depressing and they scar you for life. Yet here I am in your office, preparing to investigate yet another one. I know Stathis demoted you, but that doesn't mean we can't find a way to work together."

"Stathis won't like it."

"Stathis won't know."

Costas searched his face. "If Stathis finds out I countermanded an order, he'll fire me."

"Then we won't tell him. Listen, Officer Costas, we all make mistakes. I shot up a herd of goats during a stake-out once, killed nearly forty of them. They didn't go quietly either, the wretches. They bawled and whimpered and shat themselves. That was over five years ago and Stathis has never let me forget it."

"He said you were a great detective."

Patronas chuckled. "I'm not. Believe me, I miss a lot of stuff. The truth is I've seen very little action and only fired my gun once in my entire career; and as I said before, that was at goats. Mostly I do what every cop does, I sit and I wait. That's the essence of police work in my opinion— waiting. Waiting for a judge to issue a warrant, waiting for a suspect to show himself or make a mistake, waiting for my shift to be over so I can go home. There is also a fair amount of confusion and boredom, smoking and staring off into space. Frustration and stupidity."

They both laughed.

He proposed they get something to eat and they walked to a carry-out restaurant, named Pita Pan, and ordered *tyropitas*. After they finished eating, she offered to show him the harbor and they walked down to the quay. A ferryboat had just arrived; and there was a long line of horse-drawn carriages waiting for passengers, the animals standing absolutely still in the heat.

They sat down on a bench overlooking the sea. The ferryboat departed a few minutes later. A huge hydrofoil, its massive wake slammed into the quay, shooting spray high in the air.

"You might want to talk to Margaret Vouros," Costas told Patronas. "She's a friend of Hope Erikson. She knows her as well as anybody."

"Do you think Hope did it?"

"She's certainly capable of murder in my opinion, but then I think most people are if you push them hard enough. As I told Stathis on the phone, I'm not convinced she's the one responsible. He wants it to be her, that's for sure. I don't think we have enough evidence at this point, not nearly enough, but Stathis disagrees."

"Victim's relatives are a strange lot. Brother dies and there's not a sad face among them."

"When I spoke with them, I had the distinct impression they were hiding something."

Patronas nodded. "Especially Sophia, the victim's mother. You have any idea what it was?"

"I thought at first they might be hiding drugs in the cave and smuggling them into Athens, but Spetses is so small, sooner or later I would have heard about it and I never did. Not a word about any illicit dealings involving any of them."

Chapter 15

In a hurry, Patronas decided to take a horse-drawn carriage to the old harbor where Hope Erikson's friend, Margaret Vouros, lived. Like the Hotel Ambrosia, this was another a bad idea, the horse, nearly comatose, clip clopping along at a leisurely pace, munching on flowers as the spirit moved it.

Worse, it had bells on its bridle which jingled and jangled, and a crown of pink plastic roses on its head which Patronas eyed with disdain. A cop on a mission, he had better things to do than stop and smell the roses. The plastic roses.

Children were throwing bread to the fish in the harbor, schools of them breaking the surface as they fought for the crumbs, their silvery bodies flickering in the sunlight. A little boy dragged a net across the water and gathered up a few, laughing as he showed them off to his friends before dumping them back in the sea.

Patronas smiled, remembering when he'd done the same as a boy, casting his little net off the pier on Chios and bringing up fish. They hadn't been much the ones he'd caught, minnows mostly, but the sight of them, slippery and glistening with wet, had made him shout with joy.

"*Expiasa psaria! Expiasa psaria!*" I caught some fish. I caught some fish.

Greece had been a paradise for children then; and he wondered if it still was, if Spetses was as sunlit and golden for these children as Chios had once been for him.

* * *

In spite of her age, Margaret Vouros was dressed like a teenager in jeans and t-shirt that read 'God made the first pot and it was man,' a reference to

Adam, Patronas assumed, God having fashioned him out of clay. Or had it just been his feet? Patronas couldn't remember. Feet of clay? Yes, maybe that was it. He'd have to ask Papa Michalis.

Vouros had a wild look about her, bushy hair, bushy eyebrows. The kiln was on and her face was slick with sweat.

She wasted no time. "I have reason to believe Hope is being framed for the killing," she said. "Railroaded by her in-laws and the police here for a crime she didn't commit."

"Framed? Railroaded?" Patronas asked uncertainly, unfamiliar with the English terms. He was afraid some colleague of his had lost their mind and it was a version of water boarding.

Vouros nodded. "It's a convenient solution. One that won't disturb the status quo or frighten away tourists. Wife gets angry, kills husband and everyone goes home happy. Happens all the time. Hope is the perfect candidate. She doesn't know how to defend herself or negotiate the Greek court system on her own. Even though she's been here for years, her Greek is terrible. She can barely order food in a restaurant."

"How long has she been here?"

"Ten years, give or take."

Patronas had an opinion on this which he kept to himself. "You think she's innocent?"

"I didn't say that. I said I think she's being treated unfairly."

"What do you suggest we do? Let her go?"

"Yes. She's all alone and confused. She doesn't belong in jail."

Patronas didn't bother answering. Judging by her appearance, Vouros was in her mid-sixties. If she hadn't learned how the world worked by now, she never would. Justice was never a sure thing, not here, not in America. And certainly not when you broke the nose of a policeman.

"It seems that we are at cross purposes, Mrs. Vouros," he replied. "I can't release her. She assaulted a colleague of mine and I have strong feelings about that. It also makes her a criminal; and my job is to catch criminals and put them in jail. Not release them and put them back out on the streets."

"She's had a hard time. Granted, many of her problems are self-inflicted, but her husband was an alcoholic; and as you undoubtedly know, alcoholics are hard to deal with, especially in Greece where everyone just looks the other way. She sought to stage an intervention at some point, to get him into some sort of treatment program; but his family did everything in their power to undermine her, her mother-in-law especially, who believed Hope was the reason for his troubles. 'He's not happy,' she said. 'That's why he drinks.'

"I've dealt with my share of alcoholics," Vouros added after a moment's hesitation. "My father was one, so I understand what she was up against. Alcohol is like a cobra. You think you can control it, but then one day it rears up and sinks its fangs in you and you discover those fangs are made of steel."

Patronas examined her for a few minutes, wondering what had provoked this outburst, where her husband was on this warm summer's evening.

"Do you think someone in the family could be responsible for the murder?" he asked.

"I don't know them well enough to say. Everything I've told you is second-hand, Hope's version of events, and you know how that is in a marriage."

He nodded, remembering what Dimitra had said about him during their divorce proceedings, how he hadn't recognized himself in her words. The only one he'd agreed with was 'absent,' and that he surely was and had been for years. In heart and soul and body.

"Hope told me her in-laws were trying to pin the crime on her," Vouros said.

Costas had written something similar in the murder book, stating Hope's in-laws had implied she was guilty every time she'd spoken to them.

"Do you think there's any merit in what she said?" Patronas asked.

"Yes. It isn't just that she's American, it goes deeper than that. Her husband could stay out all night and drink up whatever money they had, spend a fortune on *ProPo* tickets, the national soccer lottery, it didn't matter. They forgave him everything. Hope, on the other hand, could do nothing right. Once she and her mother-in-law were planting vegetables and Hope asked which end of the garlic she should stick in the ground.

"'*Pos mporei kapoia na einai toso ilithia,*' the old woman said. How can anyone be so stupid? Every single day that was what Hope heard. 'How can anyone be so stupid?"

Patronas found himself agreeing with the mother-in-law. Garlic was garlic. How could anybody *not* know which end of it was up?

"Why didn't she leave?"

"I asked her that recently and she said she loved her husband and couldn't imagine her life without him. Sometimes love can exact a terrible price, Chief Officer, end up being a kind of slavery, a total subjection of self. I'm sure you've seen your share of prostitutes in bondage to their pimps. I think with Hope it was something similar. Thanasis had some kind of hold over her. Maybe sexual, maybe psychological. I don't know. Also, her parents are both dead, so she no longer has a home to return to, nor the will or confidence in my opinion to go forward and forge a new life. At this point, everything just seems too hard for her."

Although Patronas listened patiently, he had no idea what she was talking about. Obviously love figured into it, love as a kind of emotional bondage, not the kind of love he believed in, the type that involved heavy breathing and damp sheets. Something vaguer and harder to pin down and which, if his first wife was to be believed, he wasn't very good at.

*　*　*

After introducing himself, Patronas pulled up a chair and sat down across from Hope Erikson in the cell at the police station.

Staring off in space, she barely acknowledged him, listlessly, curling and uncurling a strand of hair around her finger. The movement was so mechanical, Patronas thought she might be catatonic. There was something unengaged about her. Dislocated. Perhaps her attitude was deliberate—something she'd cultivated since being arrested—but then again, maybe it had a deeper source, some underlying pathology beyond her control. There were fancy names for such disorders, but he refused to use them, preferring to think of them as defects of character, something deeply wanting in a person.

His wife, Lydia, who prided herself on her enlightenment, had called him backward and nearly boxed his ears when he'd told her he felt this way. "Defects of character? Good God, Yannis, that's like saying 'someone is possessed by the devil!'"

Turned out Hope Erikson *was* possessed by the devil, albeit a different one than his wife had had in mind. Hampered by a world view that began and ended with herself, she was a textbook narcissist, so much so she might have served as a clinical illustration of the disorder.

The two of them spent the next two hours together, Patronas gradually learning the story of her life or rather her truncated version of the story. According to her, no one had ever understood or appreciated her. Her married life had been a struggle always. From start to finish, everything had gone wrong for her.

In his mind, Patronas questioned what kind of mother she'd be once the baby came. She seemed incapable of acknowledging anyone's feelings, save her own.

He kept returning to the cave, whether or not she'd known about the back entrance.

"Yeah, yeah," she answered. "One of the Stavros' kids climbed through that hole in the wall; and we all went in afterwards, looking for him

Mentally, Patronas had prepared a list of suspects. He'd eliminated the victim's mother already. On crutches, she wouldn't have been able negotiate the uneven terrain in the cave. As for the others, accessing it would have been easy for them.

"What about the men," he asked. "Stavros and Vasilis? Did they go with you?"

Hope snorted. "How would I know? It was so dark you couldn't see a thing."

"Your sisters-in-law, Chryssoula and Daphne?"

"I think they were both there. I know Chyrssoula was. As for Daphne, you'll have to ask her."

If Hope was indeed innocent as Vouros alleged that left a dwindling number of suspects. But then again, Vouros might well be wrong; and the killer was sitting right across from him, vacant-eyed and fiddling with her hair.

The idea frightened Patronas. But then, psychopaths always did.

"When you went into the cave the day of the murder, did you feel like there was someone in there with you?"

She looked up sharply. He had her attention now.

"Yes, I kept hearing a kind of rustling sound. Even before I found Thanasis. But then that cave always creeped me out."

The room they were sitting in was nearly identical to the one at the police station on Chios; and, judging by the smell, used for the same purpose—to house drunks both foreign and domestic. The misuse of alcohol was fast

becoming a theme in the case—Hope had said her husband was a drunk—
the cobra, Margaret Vouros spoke of, hissing and baring its fangs.

* * *

Patronas stayed up late that night at the hotel, reading the murder
book in bed and underlining parts of it. With three beds lined up in a row,
space was limited in the room. One misstep and he'd land on Tembelos, or
worse, Papa Michalis. The set-up reminded him of his time in the army,
crowded into the barracks at night. Same sounds, same smells.

The priest had been in a talkative mood all evening, musing aloud
about the case. "You know, the wife may well be guilty, as she's American
and Americans are exceedingly violent people, absolutely in love with
guns. Big ones, little ones…Guns, guns, guns."

Patronas turned a page in the murder book. "Victim wasn't shot."

The old man continued as if he hadn't heard. "I do have one question
though. If she did do it, why in such a public manner? She and the victim
lived together; she would have had ample opportunity to kill him. She
didn't have to slash his throat. It's not a particularly efficient way to kill
someone and worse, it's exceedingly messy. That said, logic *does* dictate
that as the spouse she's the guilty party, but then logic will only take you
so far in human affairs. Man is many things, but in my opinion, but
logical isn't one of them. There's been no logic on display recently, not
since 1940 onwards."

Only Papa Michalis would think 1940 was recent. As for the rest, the
priest had many theories about mankind, all of which Patronas had heard
before and had no desire to hear again. There was the question of evil,
whether it was innate—the result of some Neanderthal ancestor or faulty
DNA—or the result of childhood abuse. There was also a third possibility
that Satan walked the earth and meddled in human affairs.

"There's too much of evil in the world to be the work of man alone,"
Papa Michalis frequently said. "There must be a malevolent force operating
somewhere in the universe."

"Satan?" Patronas always replied.

"I'm serious," the priest would inevitably answer and off they'd go.

As a policeman, Patronas had seen enough evil—it was real, he accepted that—but he was sure it wasn't Satan who was responsible. There was no need for Satan; man did the job all by himself. Evil wore a human face.

Papa Michalis always tended to overstate his case and tonight was no exception. He repeated every word any number of times, influenced no doubt by the liturgy of the church which also repeated itself, everything in sets of three, six, even nine during the Easter service, which is why Patronas never attended. Once was sufficient in his mind, three times repetitious and boring, nine times and you wanted to set fire to the priest with your candle.

The old fool also had much to say about the nature of women, a subject he had no right to discuss, Patronas felt, given that he'd been celibate his entire life.

"Aristotle wrote eloquently on the subject," the priest intoned. "The female is a female by virtue of a certain lack of qualities; we should regard the female nature as afflicted with a natural defectiveness."

"What they are not, in other words?" Patronas said.

"That is correct."

"Which is *men*."

And with that, Patronas returned to his reading.

Costas had made a comprehensive record of every interview she'd conducted since the start of the case. She'd done an excellent job in Patronas' view; and he saw no reason to duplicate her efforts. His interview of Margaret Vouros had been a waste of time. She'd repeated what she'd told Costas almost word for word. She doubted Hope was guilty. Her passivity would have precluded her killing her husband. It was all there in the book.

There *were* a few things Costas hadn't followed up on, the loss of the stores and family's subsequent departure from Athens being the most notable. As she'd told him, Stathis had pulled her off before she'd been able to pursue it. The question of smuggling also needed to be explored further. If Stavros and his brother, Vasilis, were as unsavory as she alleged, they might have been moving any number of things—drugs, women, even children.

Patronas wasn't convinced Hope Erikson was as innocent as Margaret Vouros claimed. Two Americans? They could have cooked up her testimony together. What was it they used to say? "The lady doth protest too much." Or in this case, the ladies. Anything was possible.

The priest had finally nodded off and was sleeping peacefully, his beard laid out neatly on top of the sheet. Not so Tembelos, who was murmuring sweet nothings in his sleep, dreaming of women no doubt, his friend devoted to the chase even with his eyes closed.

Like a toy train, he went around and around attractive females, but never jumped the tracks and approached any of them. A married man, there would be no further stops on his line.

The main reason was Tembelos' wife, a hot-tempered Cretan named Eleni, who employed a scorched earth policy when it came to her husband. "I'll pull your heart out through your mouth!" she'd yell; and Tembelos, for one, believed her. God only knew what she'd do if she caught him in the arms of another woman. The word "eviscerate," came to mind, as did others—dismemberment, disembowelment.

Poor Tembelos. If a man was indeed the sum of his parts, he was a castrato.

Chapter 16

Patronas rented a motorcycle early the next morning, a bright yellow Yamaha. Costas had offered to drive him to Aghioi Anargyiou in the damaged cruiser, but he'd refused, wanting to be able to come and go as he pleased.

Costas was at the harbor now, waiting for the forensic team to arrive from Athens. They would join Patronas later and go over the cliff together, searching for new evidence.

Tembelos had called Patronas earlier and reported he'd seen nothing untoward during the night—only bats, thousands and thousands of bats, which, according to him had all left the cave at the same time.

"A goddamned cloud of bats. They have teeth, you know. Sharp, pointed little teeth, I'm done here, Yannis. You want somebody to keep a look-out at the cave, you do it."

"Stay where you are," Patronas ordered. "I'm on my way. We'll rendezvous at the taverna."

"Rendezvous?" Tembelos repeated.

"It's French. It means to meet up with. To liaise"

"To liaise?' Jesus, Yannis. Do you hear yourself?"

In the past, Patronas had been a staunch defender of the Greek language and never used foreign words in conversation if he could avoid them. He never bought a hamburger, for example. He bought a '*biftecki*,' which was essentially the same thing. 'Rendezvous' was a marked departure for him.

"Lydia called me narrow-minded when I told her about my desire to purify my Greek," he explained to Tembelos. "She said other people had tried that in the past; the Nazis, for one, only with the gene pool. That it had been a bad idea then and it was a bad idea now. She was very emphatic."

"And you listened to her?" his friend screeched.

"I had no choice, Giorgos. Like I said, she was very emphatic."

"With two wives under your belt, you'd think you'd know by now there is no peace to be had in marriage. You have to stand your ground and fight, Yannis. Fight and fight hard. Wives are like Hitler. You can't concede anything. You can't go giving them Poland."

* * *

"We're off," Papa Michalis shouted when Patronas started the motorcycle. "In hot pursuit of the killer!"

Except it wasn't hot pursuit, more like lukewarm, their combined weight slowing the vehicle down to a virtual standstill. Whenever Patronas tried to go faster, the motorcycle would buck like a horse and stall out. A sick horse, a horse with epilepsy.

Uphill was nearly impossible, downhill slightly better as they were able to coast.

Patronas had laid down some ground rules before they started. "You will sit behind me, Father, and hold onto my waist in a calm and relaxed manner. You will not to scream in my ear under any circumstances, even if a cement mixer is heading straight toward us. No clutching me around the neck or behaving in a reckless, hysterical fashion."

All of which the priest ignored. At one point, he pointed to a tourist bus coming their way and let loose a terrible yell. Startled, Patronas hit the brakes; the bike tipped over; and they both fell off. The bike's engine kept going, its wheels spinning around and around on the ground. The priest's robe had somehow gotten entangled in the spokes, little strips of black cloth tearing off with each rotation.

Patronas helped him up. "You all right, Father?"

"I'm fine." The priest jerked the robe free. It came away in pieces, shreds of fabric, some big, some small, not quite covering what needed to be covered.

Patronas didn't know whether to laugh or cry. "Father, your robe..."

"Bah, what I wear is not important. It's what's inside that counts. The Bible is very explicit on that score: 'Lay not up for yourselves treasures upon earth, where moth and rust doth corrupt, and where thieves break through and steal. But lay up for yourselves treasures in heaven, where neither moth nor rust doth corrupt, and where thieves do not break through nor steal."

"Forget about the moths. Your garters are showing. You need a new robe."

After much discussion, Papa Michalis called the merchant in Athens, who supplied the priests in the church, stated his robe had been destroyed in the line of duty and the bill for the new garment should be sent to Stathis Haralambos in care of the police department in Piraeus.

Patronas smiled. He was a wily one, Father. Never paid for anything if he could help it. Nor did Stathis. It would be interesting to see how this played out. If the department ended up paying for the robe or if Papa Michalis got stuck with the bill. The duel of the cheapskates.

The victim's mother, Sophia, was standing over the grill. flipping skewers of meat with an oven mitt, pausing now and then to fan the flames with a folded newspaper. The two brothers, Stavros and Vasilis, were drinking coffee with their wives, Stavros' three children sitting at the table with them.

"This is your chance," Patronas told the priest. "Victim's mother is all alone. She'll see your *rassa*, robe and tell you anything you want to know. Women of her generation were raised to honor the clergy. It is one of the basic tenets of village life. They consider people like you representatives of the body of Jesus and agents of God."

Patronas managed to work a little sarcasm into the last few words.

"Don't be disrespectful," the priest said. "Don't go bandying your atheism about."

"Go talk to her."

"I don't know." The old man looked down at his tattered robe. "I'm a mess. I don't really look the part."

"Did you hear me? I said 'go talk to her.'"

"Yes, Yannis, I heard you. You're speaking very loudly. It's hard not to."

And with that, Papa Michalis headed off without another word. In his haste, he'd left his cane behind and was limping slightly, his robe so tattered it looked like a large animal had eaten off parts of it.

Approaching Sophia, Papa Michalis introduced himself. As Patronas had anticipated, she immediately stopped what she was doing and joined him at a table, calling to the Pakistani to bring them food.

"*Ligo apo ola*," she said. A little of everything.

Stavros and Vasilis had gotten up from the table and taken over for their mother at the grill, their faces partially obscured by smoke.

Papa Michalis stared at them. What he was looking for he didn't know. A furtive glance, a sign of guilt? Stupid, he knew. Mengele, the butcher of Auschwitz, had been a handsome fellow, charming it was said. Monsters did not always present as such.

* * *

"How do you want to proceed?" Costas asked Patronas. The forensic team was already inside the cave, checking the area around the crevice in the back for fingerprints. At the rate they were going, it would take them all day. They hadn't even entered the tunnel.

"We'll divide the area up and fan out," Patronas said. "You can do one part and Tembelos and I will do the other two."

Pushing their way through the thorny underbrush, the three of them spent the rest of the day in the baking sun, working their way forward on their hands and knees across the face of the cliff, searching for blood-stained clothing. The white limestone seemed to magnify the heat; and Patronas kept wiping his face, sweat pouring off of him and stinging his eyes. He'd drawn a grid before they'd started and he marked off each square as they completed it. Traversing the site was as hard physically as anything he'd ever done; and by the time he finished, his body was aching and his head felt like someone had taken an axe to it.

Tembelos was laboring under the distant pines while Costas had taken the area nearer, working almost alongside him. "You said you heard something when you were in the tunnel," she said. "Could it have been footsteps? And if so, were they light or heavy?"

A good question. "I don't know," Patronas said. "They were too far away to say for sure."

He hesitated, debating whether he should tell her about what had happened to him on Chios, how he'd almost died in a cave and suffered panic attacks now every time he went near one, convinced there was yet another killer lurking in the darkness, waiting for him. In the end, he decided against sharing the story. He wanted her to trust him, not see him as a victim of post-traumatic stress, a man whose perceptions were compromised.

Papa Michalis joined him a few minutes later. "Well, I spoke to her."

"She tell you anything?" asked Patronas.

"Something exceedingly odd in my opinion. 'See that no harm comes to her, Father,' she said. 'Hope can't help what she is.' I found it extremely charitable, given the circumstances."

"Sounds to me like Mama doesn't think Hope did it either."

* * *

Patronas was in the police station when the preliminary report from the coroner came in. A detail-oriented individual, the coroner had gone into great detail, carefully outlining the nature of the victim's injuries—measuring the dent in his skull and logging it in—and the order in which the wounds had been inflicted. The angle of the initial strike indicated either the assailant had been exceptionally tall, or far more likely, that the victim had been sitting when he was attacked. He'd also identified the kind of wine in the bottle, a local red, most probably from Messina, and given its age, young, not yet fully mature. He *had* found the victim's blood on Hope Erikson's dress and person, consistent with her story that after finding her husband dead in the cave, she'd embraced him, sobbing and calling his name.

When Patronas called him to go over the findings, the coroner volunteered he was dissatisfied with the test results on the wine bottle and intended to examine it again, using the latest technology, hoping to pull up a better image of the fingerprints. In addition to Hope's, fingerprints from other family members were also in evidence, but none that impacted the crime scene directly. Stavros' were on the rack that held the wine bottles as were Vasilis'. Daphne's and Chryssoula's were also there, indicating they, too, had visited the cave in the days leading up to the murder. DNA was in process, but it would take more time, three additional weeks if not longer.

"The broken bottle was surprisingly clean," he told Patronas. "So much so, it might well have been wiped."

Not an impetuous crime then, a systematic one.

After thanking him, Patronas hung up the phone and sat there thinking.

Summoning everyone, he convened a meeting in the conference room. He'd seen such gatherings on television—detectives talking cynically about 'perps'—and thought it might be worthwhile. The four men, who served under Costas, didn't know what to make of the idea; and it took some arm twisting to get them there. Filing in, they sat down at the far end of the table, well away from Patronas, Tembelos and Papa Michalis.

By and large, Simonidis and Constantinos were uncooperative, sulky like kids in detention, while the two older men, Pappas and Ritsos, were nearly comatose from boredom. As for Tembelos and Papa Michalis, it probably would have been better if he hadn't invited them.

"I propose we let justice run its course," Tembelos announced at the onset. "Hope Erikson was covered in blood. Ergo Hope Erikson is the guilty party. The powers that be are satisfied with that solution. Therefore, we should be, too. I say we pack our bags and go back to Chios.

"What about the coroner's report?" Patronas asked.

"Fuck the coroner's report."

Patronas reminded him that while the blood on the American's dress might be compelling, it was not necessarily evidence of guilt, given that she was the one who found the body. However, the coroner had said there was no evidence suggesting she was innocent either. He'd obviously found this important and had underlined it three times in his report and added a row of exclamation points. It was only that, an absence, he wrote. Patronas shouldn't read anything into it at this point. As an equation, it was flawed. She could have wiped the bottle and or donned gloves before she picked up and killed him.

Unable to sort out the coroner's convoluted language, Patronas had read that portion of the report back to him on the phone. "What does this mean?"

"It means Hope Erikson might have done it, but then again, she might not have. At this point in time, there is insufficient evidence to draw a definitive conclusion either way."

"What about the family?"

"Except for the mother, they were all in the cave at one time or another, so, yes, they're still in the mix. Once the DNA results come back, I should know more."

* * *

"Anyone in the family could have done it," Patronas announced to the group in the conference room. "Even the victim's mother. She says she's going outside to hang up some laundry and heads into the cave, hits him over the head and bang he's dead."

"Bang? Where'd that come from?" asked Ritsos, stirring in his chair. "Weapon was a wine bottle, not a gun. Anyway, a mother would never kill her son."

"He's right," Simonidis agreed. "A wife, sure, no problem, but not a mother."

The discussion subsequently deteriorated, the men going back and forth about the pitfalls of marriage, one of which was death as was the case here. Tembelos was definitely in the "evil most men welcome" school of thought and by and large, so were the others. Patronas hadn't really made up his mind. Women were complicated, no question about it. Dimitra had been nothing to write home about; and Lydia, well, she had her good and bad days.

As was his wont, Papa Michalis took it to a whole new level. "Women are inferior to men," he declared. "God fashioned Eve from Adam's rib which means from the very beginning, they have been incomplete."

"Old Testament claptrap," Patronas said. "No one came from anybody else's rib."

"What? You're one of those? You think we evolved from apes?"

"I do," Patronas said. "Some of us more so than others. You, for one, would look very nice right about now eating a banana."

Undeterred, Papa Michalis continued. "The deceitfulness of women is well documented in the Bible. Look at Eve in the Garden of Eden, consorting with the snake."

Remembering his first marriage, Patronas couldn't really argue with him. There *had* been a snake in that garden, but it hadn't been an external one, it had been her. She'd been the viper. Hell, Dimitra had been a whole nest of vipers.

Just when Patronas thought the conversation couldn't get any worse, down it went, the participants moving on to domestic abuse cases they'd covered, all, judging by their reaction, they found hilarious. The husband who'd thrown his wife out of the house because she served him leftovers, tossing the offending items out after her.

"*Keftedakia*," Ritsos squealed. "It was raining meatballs."

"Willful," the priest intoned. "Women are willful. They are not like men."

"Different," Patronas insisted. "If you ask a man about the significant women in his life, he'll enumerate the ones he slept with, starting with the first and going forward, maybe give a few details about their physical attributes, the quality of the encounter. Women, on the other hand, it is all about feelings with them."

Lydia was trying to educate him on this score and had a whole closet full of words to describe his behavior, most of which he didn't understand. Disengaged? How could he be disengaged if he was sitting right there? She might as well have been speaking Norwegian.

Melissa Costas hadn't said a word. She just sat there in her chair with her head down, doing her best to remain invisible.

Seeing the strained look on her face, Patronas was ashamed of his colleagues' casual misogyny.

By and large the police force in Greece was a man's world; and not 'man' in the poetic sense of the word, man, the hero or the saint. No, man in all his crassness and testosterone-driven glory, man who pissed on the toilet seat or forgot to flush, who spoke lewdly to women or pawed them without their consent, men who made a mass and expected others to clean it up.

Feeling guilty, Patronas asked Costas to stay on after the meeting, "You were right. The coroner's report raises doubts about Hope's culpability."

"No proof of guilt or proof of innocence.' That's hardly conclusive. Anyway, it's out of our hands now. Stathis ordered me to take her to Piraeus tomorrow and hand her over to the authorities there."

She walked over to the window and stood with her back to him. "If you want to know the truth, I feel sorry for her. No matter what happens, she's got a long hard road ahead of her."

"She assaulted a police officer. She broke his nose."

"That was in the heat of the moment. He pushed her too hard. She didn't mean to do it."

"I'll go with you tomorrow and see what I can find out about the family. Chase down any leads I come up with. If what you say is true and Hope Erikson didn't do it, then someone else did and we need to discover who that was."

Patronas was relieved about the direction the case was taking, the complexities slowly revealing themselves. From the beginning, it hadn't felt like a simple domestic to him. Costas had had the same sense. Something hidden had come to into play that day, be it smuggling or some unknown family dynamic. And now the coroner's report was reinforcing that feeling.

* * *

It was close to ten o'clock when Patronas finally left the police station. He'd sent Tembelos and Papa Michalis back to the hotel ahead of him, desperate for a few minutes of solitude.

Spetses was unique in his experience, a warren of perfectly preserved neoclassical buildings; and he wandered around on foot, examining them in the light of the streetlamps and marveling at their beauty. The looming bulk of the Poseidonion Hotel dominated the landscape, an expansive paved square in front of it. The area was packed with people, locals mostly out for the evening; and the atmosphere was festive, vendors selling *malli tis grias,* cotton candy; and toys that lit up the sky when they tossed them in the air, whistling and glowing like meteors as they descended.

An impressive statue of Laskarina Bouboulina, a heroine of the Greek War of Independence occupied pride of place at the center of the square. Facing the harbor, she was depicted with a fearless expression, a pistol tucked in her belt.

Poor, poor Bouboulina, Patronas thought, who'd fought in the war against the Turks, only to lose the one at home and be killed in a family feud.

Perhaps there was a lesson here. One he should take with him when he went to Athens.

Chapter 17

Taking care not to wake Tembelos and Papa Michalis, Patronas removed the sheets and blanket from his bed and left the room. He strapped them to the back of his rented motorcycle and drove to the outskirts of Aghioi Anargyiou and lumbered up the hill to the back entrance of the cave, crouching down and using the pine trees as cover, not wanting to alert the family of his presence.

He laid his blanket down about two meters away from the opening, unwilling to venture any closer to the cave at night.

He scooped up some pine needles and tucked them beneath the blanket to soften the rough ground beneath him, savoring their scent and the dry, dusty smell of the earth. Overhead, the tops of the trees formed a circle around him, a patch of starlit sky showing through the dense foliage.

The sounds of the birds awoke him and he sat up, stiff and covered with pine needles. Brushing himself off, he hurried back down through the woods to the place where he'd parked the motorcycle.

Before driving off, he surveyed the cliff one last time, not knowing what he should do about it. Whether he should to ask Costas to continue the surveillance or let it go. Whoever the killer was, they must have removed whatever evidence there was already. They wouldn't have waited until now to do it. Two full days had passed since Thanasis Papadopoulos had been murdered, three since he and his men had arrived on Spetses. More than enough time enough to clear out anything that could incriminate them.

He felt there *was* something sinister about the cave, had sensed it the first time he'd been inside. Violence always left its mark even on the earth; and Thanasis Papadopoulos' death had been violent. But what if that violence wasn't finished and instead had only just begun, what if the killer had developed a taste for it as sometimes happened.

He'd asked Papa Michalis to visit the taverna while he was in Athens and insinuate himself into the Papadopoulos family. To work his charm on the old woman, Sophia, the victim's mother. He needed to warn him to be careful. To never be alone with any one of them. To decline a ride if they offered and take a taxi.

* * *

Seeking to buy time, Patronas hemmed and hawed, telling Stathis there'd been "developments" in the case and "it was all coming together." His boss didn't ask what exactly was coming together which was fortunate as nothing was. Instead, he complained about the press which had been highly critical of the way the Greek authorities were handling the case, specifically the mayhem that had accompanied the arrest of Hope Erikson.

Fortunately, the reporters hadn't figured out yet who Patronas was; and he'd been able to come and go in peace, unlike Melissa Costas, who was fast becoming a prisoner in the police station, unable to move without a crowd of them, engulfing her and shouting questions. Patronas had watched the news on television the previous night; and the murder had been the main feature, the clip of Hope Erikson on her hands and knees being played over and over. "Blood on the beach," the CNN reporter had intoned. "Murder in Paradise. Love triangle leads to death." Another newscaster had alleged a Somali immigrant was responsible. A British tourist had seen him with a bloody bottle in his hand.

Patronas was convinced nothing good would come of such speculation. It would only bring more pressure to bear on Stathis and his colleagues and goad them into acting prematurely. In his experience, homicide investigations took time and as a detective, he was more like the tortoise in Aesop's fable than the hare. Slow and steady, slow and steady won the race.

* * *

Patronas' wife, Lydia, also alluded to the press on the phone, saying she'd seen him on television. "Don't slouch. Stand up straight, Yannis. Cameras add pounds. And for God's sakes, tuck in your shirt."

Patronas listened with growing impatience. If he was to make the boat to Athens that morning, he needed to get to the harbor. He had no time for this.

If Tembelos was right and marriage was indeed war, now was a good time to seize the day and tell her off. To announce in no uncertain terms that he was fine just the way he was, short and rumpled and eminently suitable as a man. He, of course, didn't say this to Lydia. He just hung up on her.

She called right back, complaining about the poor connection and how the phone kept cutting off. "Are you all right, Yannis? Do you want me to come there?"

"God, no."

In keeping with Tembelos' World War II analogies, the ensuing fight was like the Battle of Stalingrad. Nothing, but burned-out buildings and dead bodies stacked up like cordwood as far as the eye could see, Patronas' among them, frozen solid in the permafrost. Even long distance, Lydia was a formidable opponent. His own private panzer. She ran him over, then for good measure, backed up and ran him over again.

He ended up groveling and begging for forgiveness. "I'm sorry. I don't know what got into me. I'm under a lot of pressure. Stathis has been riding me hard."

This seemed to mollify her; and they'd ended up avowing their love for one another and exchanging endearments. Unfortunately, Tembelos had been standing next to Patronas during the entire conversation and heard every word.

"Poland," he mouthed silently, shaking his head. "Poland."

* * *

"Would you look at this crowd," Tembelos said. "It's a human anthill."

Dodging a diminutive woman with a suitcase, Patronas nodded. He had once welcomed the annual invasion of foreigners—more than twenty-four million strong—who came pouring into Greece every summer. Now he felt like his country was in danger of being destroyed by them, that if things didn't change, Greece would become a place that people visited, but where no one would want to live.

In front of them, a Swedish woman was boarding the boat; and Tembelos was caressing her with his eyes. Not all of her, just the protruding parts.

Patronas was in no mood for his friend's shenanigans. He'd slept badly and was so tired he was having trouble forming sentences. Subject, verb, he told himself. Subject, verb.

"*Stamata*," he hissed. "Stop it! You are on duty."

Reluctantly, Tsembelis shifted his focus to the day ahead. They'd arranged to meet Costas at the dock and take the first ferry to Piraeus together, then go their separate ways. Costas to court with Hope Erikson, he and Patronas to Moschato, where the Papadopoulos family had lived prior to moving to Spetses.

Costas appeared a few minutes later with Hope Erikson in tow. The American's hair was soaking wet and she was wearing a frilly pink dress with a white collar. Not a felon or a murderer, Patronas thought, taking her in. No, when she appeared before the judge in Piraeus, the look she was going for was schoolgirl.

"Sorry I'm late," Costas said. "I know it's not in keeping with police protocol, but I took her to my apartment first so she could take a proper shower. Who knows when she'll get another chance?"

The hydrofoil appeared right on schedule. Bright yellow with a strip of dark blue at the bottom, it was part of a fleet that had once heralded a new era of sea travel in Greece. However, that had been a long time ago; and the so-called Flying Dolphin was showing its age, patches of rust darkening the hull.

The narrow hold was configured like an airplane, two rows of seats with an aisle down the middle. The windows were caked with salt and the air stank of diesel fuel.

Before they got underway, Costas removed Hope's handcuffs—a necessary precaution in case the boat went down—and cautioned her to stay where she was during the voyage, not get up and move about.

Hope laughed good naturedly. "What if I have to pee?"

"I'll take you," Costas said.

Tembelos nudged Patronas. "You know, Costas wouldn't be half bad if she relaxed a little," he said in an undertone. "Way she moves, it's like she's wearing Kevlar underwear or something, stiff, stiff and more stiff. Even her hair."

"I agree, the hair is unfortunate," Patronas said. "Far more suitable for a geisha than a cop."

Costas was sitting two seats ahead of them and Tembelos studied the back of her head. "You're right. That bun of hers…all that's missing are the chop sticks."

"I never really got Japanese culture," Patronas said.

"Me, either. It's a mystery in my mind. Sushi? Who wants to eat raw fish? Not to mention *hari kari,* killing yourself when someone wrongs you. On Crete you'd go after them, you wouldn't rip open your *own* guts with a knife. You'd rip out somebody else's."

Clutching a little cosmetic bag, Hope Erikson was sitting directly across the aisle; and Patronas watched her for a moment. The bag was covered with polka dots and about the size of a wallet; and he wondered why Costas had let her bring it. The guards would just take it away from her when she arrived at the prison. Given the situation, the American seemed surprisingly relaxed, looking out the salt-splattered window with a placid expression on her face. She was scheduled to go before the magistrate at noon. After that, where she ended up was anyone's guess.

"What do you think is going to happen to her?" Tembelos asked, following his gaze.

"They'll probably lock her up in Korydallos Prison. She's obviously a flight risk. She tried to escape once and is sure to do it again."

"She could have gone quietly. She didn't have to break Constantinos' nose."

"Should have, would have, could have," Patronas declared. "Such are the choices we make."

"Watch yourself, Yannis. That preachy note, you're beginning to sound like Papa Michalis."

* * *

The Flying Dolphin arrived in Piraeus on schedule; and the four of them disembarked, climbing up the steep staircase inside and out across the top of the ship. Stathis had sent a prison van to pick up Costas and Hope Erikson and they left immediately for the courthouse.

Grabbing their suitcases, Patronas and Tembelos joined the long line of people waiting for taxis on the curb.

Tembelos yawned. "You clear this little jaunt with Stathis?"

"Yes. He authorized two nights in a hotel plus meals. His usual, ten euros per day. Any more than that and we'll have to pay ourselves. I have to admit he wasn't happy when I proposed coming to Athens; and it took me some time to convince him. 'You've got a viable suspect in custody,' he said, 'Why not leave well enough alone?'"

"He has a point, Yannis. You're like a pit bull. Once you get hold of something, you can't let go."

Patronas raised his eyebrows. "A pit bull?"

"Yup. Once they bite down, that's it. They'll die before they release you. That's you in a nutshell. Chomp, chomp, chomp."

"You're saying I'm tenacious."

"I'm saying you're an asshole."

"One person's asshole is another person's tenacious."

"Listen, Yannis. You got me up at the crack of dawn and brought me here without so much as a crust of bread or cup of coffee. Way I'm feeling, I'm going with 'asshole.'"

* * *

Before meeting with Stathis at the police station, Tembelos and Patronas stopped at local fastfood chain and ate breakfast. Patronas thought it prudent to drink coffee before speaking to his boss, a lot of coffee. Best to be alert around Stathis, vigilant. If he didn't like what you said, like Zeus, he'd let fly with a verbal thunder bolt and fry you right down to the ground. His tongue lashings were legendary.

Stathis was bent over his desk, laboring over a spread sheet, when Patronas and Tembelos arrived at his office. He didn't look up when they came in, just kept working. His boss had always been a big one for figures, Patronas remembered, firing off reports full of cost saving suggestions based on obscure and random equations. A bureaucratic warrior, Stathis, one whose weapon of choice was the bottom line.

Still got that moustache, I see," Stathis told Patronas, when he finally got around to acknowledging them. "Would have done Stalin proud, that moustache or Kaiser Wilhelm. You should get rid of it."

Tembelos, he completely ignored.

Knowing his time was limited, Patronas hurriedly summarized his findings. "The investigation is going well. We should close the case by the end of the week."

"If so, why are you here?"

"Loose ends, sir. There are a lot of loose ends."

Patronas outlined his plan as fast as he could. "First, we'll visit the apartment building in Moschato where the family lived and speak to the neighbors, then to the owners of the stores they rented, try to establish why they pulled up stakes and moved to Spetses." Although it was risky, he threw in a few good words about Melissa Costas.

"I wanted to tell you how impressed I've been by her," Patronas said. "She has a keen mind and has demonstrated great investigative skill, spotted things at the crime scene no one else saw. She's been a great resource, unique in my experience. It's been one of the highlights of my professional life working with her."

Stathis smirked. "What are you? Her mother? If I were you, Patronas, I'd worry more about my own professional standing than hers. As you might have gathered, I'm not happy about your trip here. The only reason I allowed it was because you insisted. 'We must exercise due diligence,' were the words you used if I remember correctly. 'Leave no stone unturned.'"

He pointed to the door. "So you and your sidekick there, whatshisname, go find some stones and start turning them over."

* * *

"Twenty years, I've worked for that man and he still doesn't know my name," Tembelos complained. "'Whatshisname!' Can you believe it?"

Opening his palm, he thrust it back in the direction of Stathis' office. The *moutza*, it was a universal gesture in Greece, an expression of defiance and contempt, the equivalent of shoving shit up someone's nose, in this case the boss.

"Melissa said Stathis is like the hydra," Patronas said. "Cut off his head and someone worse will take his place."

"Who could be worse than Stathis, I ask you? King Herod? Himmler?"

Chapter 18

Named for the variety of grapes that once had grown there, Moschato, a suburb of Athens, was home to approximately 25,000 people. Graffiti covered the walls of many of the buildings, even two elderly vehicles parked out in the street. A few of the images were compelling, but most were little more than scrawled initials, phrases in Arabic.

Patronas and Tembelos were on Koumantea Street, one of the major thoroughfares in Moschato, looking for the number Stavros Papadopoulos had given them. In addition to apartment buildings, there were stores along the road, signs in Russian in some of their windows, other languages—Urdu maybe—Patronas didn't recognize.

"It's hard to believe we're in Greece," Tembelos said. "Where did all those people come from and who invited them here?"

"I don't know," Patronas said.

The migrant situation was even worse on Chios where there was no work, no jobs to be had. But given the current economic situation in Greece, he doubted the newcomers in Moschato were faring much better.

With very little open space, a number of residents had transformed their balconies into play spaces for their children. One unit, Patronas saw, even had a swing and a slide. He had spent his formative years out in the open, roaming the hills of Chios with a group of friends, and he couldn't imagine growing up here.

The taxi driver, who'd driven them here from Piraeus, was from Epirus; and had spent his childhood herding goats in the mountains outside his village. The sound of car horns reminded him of the tinkling of their bells, the driver had said, the most poignant expression of homesickness Patronas had ever heard.

Four story apartment buildings lined both sides of the street the family had lived on, featureless cement structures with few identifying characteristics. There was no roster of names or doorbells to push when they found the number Stavros had given them—such accoutrements were far too dangerous now in Athens—forcing them to wait until someone appeared, a woman with a shopping cart full of vegetables. Viewing them with suspicion, she demanded to see their IDs before letting them in. A recent arrival, she said she knew nothing of the Papadopoulos family and quickly vanished into her ground floor apartment.

Many apartment buildings in Greece had once employed people to take packages and screen visitors in the lobby. Patronas mother had hated the one in her building on Chios. *Koutsompolides,* she'd called her. Busybody.

Patronas had hoped there would be such a person in this building as they were often excellent sources of information. But there was no one. Paved in black marble, the lobby was just a big, empty space.

With such a large transient population, Patronas doubted the residents would know much about their neighbors; and that would make their job much harder. You could easily remain anonymous in Moschato, live here for a time and then one day be gone; and no one would be the wiser.

The family had lived on the top floor, occupying three of the ten units. Splitting up, he and Tembelos worked their way down either side of the hall, knocking on doors and asking people if they remembered them.

A sharp-eyed old lady reported she'd lived next door to Thanasis and his wife, Hope, for over a year. "That man you're asking about, he never came home until late; and he and his wife fought about it, shouting at each other in English. I don't know English and couldn't understand what she was saying. All I knew was she was very angry."

"Do you think he had a girlfriend?"

"Probably." Her face soured. "They all do."

She didn't remember any event that would have triggered their departure. "They kept to themselves, especially her. She never greeted me, even when the two of us were alone on the elevator."

"What about the rest of them?"

"The same. Only the mother was good. She'd bring me food sometimes and sit with me in the evenings."

A young woman answered the door of the next apartment. "Why are you asking about them?" she demanded. "What right do you have? What have they done?"

Around nineteen, she had a tattoo of a spider web on her neck and seemed strangely agitated, bouncing back and forth on the balls of her feet. In spite of the heat, she was wearing a long-sleeved shirt, tugging the sleeves down over her arms as she came to the door. But she wasn't fast enough and Patronas spotted the tracks on her arms. A heroin addict.

Even if he could convince her to talk, whatever she said would be worthless, far too risky to introduce in court. Patronas had been in this situation before. Junkies were called that for a reason. Human flotsam and jetsam, they were totally unreliable. In recent years, the drug had grown in popularity throughout Greece, junkies lying on the sidewalks near Victoria Station in Athens, used syringes washing up on local beaches.

"Tell me why you're here?" the girl insisted.

"It's a police matter. Part of a homicide investigation."

"Homicide?"

"That's right."

"Do you have a warrant? Don't you have to have a warrant to talk to me?"

"Not to talk. Only if I come into your apartment and I don't."

She seemed to relax at that point; and, eyes downcast, she admitted she had known Stavros Papadopoulos. In fact, they'd hung out together.

"Hung out?" Patronas frowned.

"Yeah, like that," she said and slammed the door in his face.

The couple in the next apartment said while they might recognize the various family members on sight, they had never spoken to them and knew nothing about them or their history.

An elderly woman, who lived by herself, welcomed him into her flat, saying she understood how difficult his job was; her husband had been a policeman. "During the Civil War, if you can imagine."

She nodded when he asked her about Hope Erikson. "Yes, yes, she was an American woman, married to one of the brothers. I remember she was pregnant at some point, but then she wasn't and I assumed she'd had a miscarriage. She was well along, too—at least six months—and losing a baby at that point must have been terrible for her. I thought about reaching out to her, but in the end decided not to. We had no language in common. There would have been no way to communicate."

Beyond that, she contributed little else of substance. The family had been very upset at one point, she said. "I saw them in the elevator and they were all wearing black and it was obvious they'd been crying. I knew they weren't weeping for her. They were tough, those women, not the kind of people who'd go to pieces over a miscarriage. I do remember the American and her husband had a fight once, a terrible one out in the hall. His mother finally came out and put an end to it. "*Tha se koutsompolevsoune.*" People will gossip about you. "She also said something about little Achilles, her grandson, but I couldn't hear exactly what it was. I was on the way into my apartment; and I didn't want them to think I was eavesdropping."

"When was this?"

"2015."

She went on to say it hadn't just been one baby, but several Hope had lost. "She was pregnant two or three times, always with the same result. Given what happened with the other child, I thought it was very sad."

"You think her husband had anything to do with the miscarriages?" he asked. "Did he hit her when they fought? Did she have any bruises?"

"No, never. It was all her. She was the one who couldn't carry a child."

The final person Patronas spoke to was a government pensioner named Christos Antonopoulos. Well into his eighties, it had taken him a long time to come to the door when Patronas knocked, laboriously pushing his walker ahead of him one step at a time.

The old man volunteered he'd seen a little boy with one of the couples. Not the American and her husband, one of the others, the Greeks.

"There were four children if I remember correctly," he said. "Three in one family, one in the other."

One of the children had been in an accident, he went on to say, and after a lengthy stay in hospitals, both here and abroad, had subsequently died.

And there it was.

Getting out his mp3 player, Patronas turned it on and asked him to repeat what he'd just said.

Closing his rheumy eyes, the man slowly complied. "It happened in the street in front of the building. The child was playing, I think, and there was some kind of accident. He was a real cute little fellow. No more than four or five years old. And I remember the family was distraught when it happened. They took him to the hospital in an ambulance, not in a car. I know because I heard the siren and went down to see. That's when I knew it was serious."

"Was there a follow-up investigation? Did the police interview you?"

"If there was, they never spoke to me. Family would have been better off calling the Golden Dawn than the cops. They would have found the culprit and taken care of him."

The Golden Dawn was a group of right-wing thugs, posing as a political party. Its members had been responsible for number of attacks on migrants, at least two of which were fatal. Patronas loathed them, loathed the ideology they espoused and those who believed in them; and he fought to be patient with the old man.

"Was there a funeral?"

"Not here. I would have seen the sign and gone to it. Maybe they took him back to their village." Tired now, he was trembling a little, clutching the walker so tightly, his knuckles were white.

"Thank you," Patronas said. "You've been very helpful."

The woman Patronas had spoken to, the one who said her husband had been a cop, had also mentioned a dead child, but he hadn't followed up on it, hadn't established whose child it was. He'd just assumed she'd been talking about Hope and her miscarriages, a potentially grievous error.

Returning to her apartment, he banged on the door. "I know one of the families had three children. Do you remember if the other family had a child?"

"Oh, my, yes. A little boy four or five. He was killed in a car accident, right out in front. They took him abroad if I remember correctly, but even the doctors there couldn't save him. I thought his grandmother would die, too, she was so heartbroken."

"Why didn't you say anything before?" Patronas asked.

"I did. I told you the women were all in mourning and I saw them crying in the elevator. Who did you think they were crying for? They were crying for him."

"Do you remember the child's name?"

"Yes. They called him Achilles. Little Achilles. His grandmother didn't call him that though. She called him, 'to paidiaki mou," my little child. Panagia mou, how she loved him. After he died, it's a wonder she didn't die too."

* * *

Patronas and Tembelos ate lunch at *Ermis Psitopoleio*, a taverna in Moschato listed on Trip Adviser. Suspicious of modern technology, Patronas had objected when Tembelos had consulted his phone.

"We're Greek and this is our city," he'd said. "We don't need some app on our phone to find out where to go. We can ask the locals."

"You see any locals here?"

It was true. Moschato was like the United Nations, every nationality, but theirs, well represented. Patronas shook his head. In their own country, Greeks were an endangered species.

The food proved to be tasty and cheap; and even better, the bill came to less than twelve euros for the two of them, well within their daily stipend. Impressed, Patronas congratulated his friend on his selection.

"Modern life, Yannis." Tembelos waved his phone at him. "You should try it."

They lingered at the table for a few minutes, going over what they'd discovered that morning.

"The child's death was certainly the catalyst," Patronas said, "the event that triggered the murder. One of the women I spoke to mentioned it, but I misunderstood and nearly missed the reference. I must be getting old, losing my edge."

"We know now, Yannis, and that's the main thing," said Tembelos. "As you know, policework is an imperfect science, practiced by imperfect people, you, me, Costas, just to name a few. We do the best we can, but we don't always get it right the first time or sit up and pay attention when we're supposed to. We're not mind readers. We can't see inside people, what makes somebody want to kill."

A taciturn man, it was an unusually long speech for Tembelos.

Patronas nodded. As his friend had pointed out, they had what he needed now and could go forward. That was the main thing. In his mind, he reviewed the implications of what they'd learned about the accident. In his opinion, it would significantly alter the outcome of the case.

Sophia, the victim's mother had said her family had known much sorrow; and Patronas now knew the source of that sorrow. The loss of the child would have affected everyone in the family. Grief was a powerful force. Like a riptide in the ocean, it could easily pull someone under, lead them to commit unspeakable acts.

After leaving the taverna, he phoned the police station on Spetses and spoke with Simonidis. "I want you to access the police logs in Moschato in 2015. Start with the death notices that year and work your way forward—anything you can find on Achilles Papadopoulos."

According to the neighbor, 2015 was the year the women in the Papadopoulos family had been in mourning. They hadn't been crying over Hope and her lost baby. No, it had been little Achilles, they'd been grieving for.

"Do you want us to question the family about it?" Simonidis asked.

"Hold off for now. Let's get the facts first, then confront them. At this point, we don't know what actually happened. There has to be a reason they didn't tell us about the accident. Thanasis's mother alluded to it, but she was the only one; and she didn't go into detail."

"I don't get it. It doesn't make any sense."

"It was a car accident, and my theory is Thanasis ran over the child and the boy's father killed him for that reason. For whatever reason, members of the family know this and are covering up for him."

"If as you say, the accident was in 2015, that was three years ago. Why wait until now to go after him?"

"Hope's pregnant. Could be that was too much for him."

There was a lengthy silence. "How come if Thanasis Papadopoulos was responsible, the police didn't arrest him?"

"Again, we don't know that. Could be for want of evidence, they declared it a hit and run and filed it away. There might have been no witnesses willing to come forward at the time or maybe the boy's parents didn't know who'd done it at that point. Maybe they only learned after the fact. Or maybe they suspected, but weren't sure. Who can say? Without evidence—at least a good description of the car and the driver—there would have been no point in pursuing it anyway. Given the circumstances, I probably would have done the same thing those cops did—written it up and forgotten about it. Someone loses a child; you don't push them for details. You do your best to console them and leave them alone."

He paused, thinking it through. "Find out for sure who the boy's parents were. It must have been Vasilis and his wife, but I'm going to need proof. Once we have it, the rest will follow."

He then called Costas in Piraeus and filled her in. "Is Hope still with you?"

"Yes. She's still waiting to go before the magistrate."

"Ask her what she knows about the car accident, specifically if Thanasis was the driver of the car."

Chapter 19

"Millions of tourists and they're all in front of us," Tembelos complained to Patronas. They were in the tourist district of Monastiraki, searching for the store the family had rented there.

After exiting the subway, they headed up an alley lined with souvenir shops. A vast assortment of merchandise was on display on the pavement on either side of them, everything from museum replicas of ancient vases to obscene statues of satyrs with erect penises in clay, marble and bronze. Evil eye paraphernalia was everywhere as were a plethora of olive oil soaps piled up in straw baskets. You could spend five euros on a t-shirt—Patronas liked the one with a quote from Solon—*Midena pro tou telous makarizeis*. Call no one happy until they're dead—or thousands on a piece of gold jewelry, so gaudy Elizabeth Taylor might have worn it in *Cleopatra*. The choice was yours.

"Jesus, will you look at those." Tembelos pointed to a pair of leather sandals that laced all the way up to the knee. "Tourists buy that crap because they think it's Greek. Don't they realize the last person to wear stuff like that was Spartacus?"

"Maybe that's the look they're going for. Not sartorial splendor, but gladiatorial."

"What the hell is that supposed to mean?"

"They want to look like gladiators?"

"But why?"

"What can I say? They're tourists; it's what tourists do."

Led by guide waving a flag, a group of Chinese tourists was in front of them, all wearing hats against the sun, a few of the women with open umbrellas. There were so many of them, they proved impossible to get around; and Patronas flashed his badge and signaled for the guide to get them out of his way.

He'd called ahead and the owner of the building the family had rented was standing in the doorway waiting for them. He repeated what he'd told Patronas over the phone. As far as he knew, there'd been no reason for the brothers to leave Athens. They'd been doing well financially. But one day they asked to be let out of their lease, packed up and left.

"It wasn't easy for them. They had a lot of merchandise to get rid of."

"What did they do with it?"

"Sold it. These people all know each other. They buy and sell all the time."

"You ever hear about one of them losing a child?"

He shook his head. "No, never. There was a time when they all seemed pretty upset. I remember thinking something bad must have happened. But they never told me what it was."

"When was this?"

"Three years ago, 2015."

* * *

The second store was located in Gaza and the landlord there remembered the family well.

"They had a hard time of it," he said. "I remember when they gave up the store and were preparing to leave Athens, jewelers came from all over the city to buy what they had, seeking to pay them less than it was worth, grab their gold jewelry at a cut-rate price. Stavros fought them. You could hear him shouting, calling them *kleftes,* thieves. Had to, I suppose. They needed the money."

Patronas and Tembelos exchanged glances. "Why did they need the money?" Patronas asked carefully.

"They had a lot of hospital bills. One of them had a little boy—I don't remember which one of them it was—and he'd been hit by a car and was in terrible shape. Pretty much had to be taken apart and put back together again. In the end, they took him to Germany. They had no choice, I guess; it was either that or let him die here in Greece. It was sad. In the end, they lost him anyway."

"Do you know if anyone else in the family was in the accident?"

"Sure, his uncle."

"Do you remember the name of the uncle?"

"I'm not sure, but if I had to make a guess, I'd say it was Thanasis. He disappeared for a couple weeks around the same time."

"Was he the driver of the car?"

"Again, I'm not sure. All I know is it was a terrible time for the family. Going back and forth to the hospital and trying to manage two stores, it was impossible. One night, they forgot to close the door of the store, can you imagine? All that gold. Fortunately, no one broke in and took it. They were spared that at least."

"Do you know when the child was hurt? What year the accident was?"

"Sure, the summer of 2015. He died about four or five weeks after it happened; and by then they'd lost everything. They tried to make a go of it, but eventually they gave up and let the store go. I felt sorry for them and let them stay on a little longer for free."

* * *

Patronas and Tembelos spent the night in a hotel in Theseion, a popular tourist area in the center of Athens. Not wanting to exceed Stathis' stipend, Tembelos had again searched the internet and it was the least expensive place he could find.

The neon sign in front of it was missing two letters, the 'e' and the 'l,' spelling 'hot' instead of 'hotel,' which the place definitely was, sweltering, in fact.

Only one room was available, the clerk informed them, a double located on the top floor. He demanded payment in advance before giving them the key which should have alerted them all was not well in Hotel "Hot." He neglected to inform him that 'double' referred only to the mattress. There was only a single bed in the room rather than two twins as was customary in Greece. Nor did he mention the bathroom was communal and located at the far end of the hall.

There was also no elevator which meant by the time Patronas climbed up the four flights of stairs with his suitcase, he was stuck as Tembelos was unwilling to make the long trek back down. A group of beefy Eastern European men in undershirts were standing in the hall, milling around and smoking. They were as big as the Russian weight lifting team

Patronas had seen in Athens during the Olympics. Tough men the size of mountains.

"I feel like a rabbit surrounded by wolves," Tembelos said, nodding to the group.

"Bears," Patronas whispered. "Russian bears."

Aside from the bed, there was nothing, not even so much as a waste basket, in the room. The duvet on the bed was an inauspicious brown color as were the curtains; and the furry rug on the floor might well have started out life as a dog.

Seeking fresh air, Patronas opened the door of the balcony and stepped outside.

The view took his breathe away, nearly all of Athens spread out at his feet. The citadel of the Acropolis towered over all of Theseion; and he could see the Roman theater of Herod Atticus directly below it. Nearly every era in Greek history was represented from the agora, the marketplace where Socrates had once held court, to the old mosque where the Ottoman Turks had worshipped. The ancient cemetery, Keramikos, lay to the west as did the outcropping of rock, the Areaopagos, where St Paul had preached the gospel.

A little white train was ferrying tourists back and forth. Patronas and Tembelos had seen it earlier in the day, circling the Tower of the Winds, a Roman water clock at the center of Athens. The guide onboard had been reciting information about the Tower, saying the Romans had built it, believing the direction of the wind could predict the future.

Dubbed the 'Happy Train,' it was well named, Patronas remembered, full of tourists snapping pictures, the conductor ringing a bell at every stop it made. Now looking down on it, he was struck by the contrast between it and the Acropolis, the juxtaposition of Greece's monumental past with its tourist-plagued present.

As a young student, he had been moved to tears when he'd learned of the incredible advances his ancestors had made in nearly every field of human endeavor, from charting the heavens to building a primitive computer to navigate the sea. How proud he'd been as a boy to claim that heritage.

His mother had been a different kind of patriot. In her opinion, the greatest gift their ancestors had bestowed on civilization wasn't the statues of Praxiteles or the words of Aristotle, but Greek Orthodoxy. The kingdom of piety and priests. She and Patronas had argued about it, something he now regretted.

Patronas looked up at the Acropolis. The color of old bones, the marble seemed to glow from within. To illuminate the sky itself.

Fifty years later, he could still cry for Greece. Only tonight his tears would be in mourning. Grief for the world of his youth, for the paradise that once was and was gone forever.

With a sigh, he went back inside and got ready for bed. It was going to be a long night. He'd shared a bed with Tembelos on a previous occasion and it hadn't gone well. Lost in a dream, Tembelos had embraced him and given him a watery kiss, basically licked him. And not just once, multiple times.

At least Patronas hoped it had been a kiss. Judging by the sounds Tembelos had been making, he could have been dreaming he was a cannibal and gnawing off his face.

* * *

The hotel advertised continental breakfast, but it was only continental in the sense that Australia was a continent, the taste and texture similar to what Patronas believed he'd find in the outback. Dry bread, dry cake and coffee that tasted like poison.

He and Tembelos had left the sliding door open the previous night and a pair of drunken tourists—a boy and a girl—had stationed themselves directly beneath their balcony. After a bout of furious kissing, they'd started singing, the discordant sounds filling the night air.

Irritated, Patronas leaned over the railing of the balcony and bellowed, "I'm a police officer and I'm trying to sleep. Be quiet!"

In response, the pair defiantly switched to rap, belting out lyrics which expressed much four-letter disdain for the police and advocated their destruction. "I ain't the one chugga, chugga…Fuck the motherfucker with a gun…" After which, the boy urinated on the side of the building.

This was followed by another bout of kissing and God knows what else, the girl squealing, the boy grunting in a rising crescendo. Their coupling complete—it hardly qualified as love making in Patronas' mind—they resumed their serenade.

Tembelos rolled over in bed. "Put them out of their misery, Yannis. You've got a gun. Shoot them."

Chapter 20

A large number of migrants were on the subway to Piraeus, single men from Pakistan and Africa standing next to Patronas and Tembelos in the car.

"Where are all these people going?" Tembelos gestured to the bags the men were carrying. "To sell purses in Piraeus or packs of tissues to motorists on the national highway? How do they survive? How do they live?"

Patronas had long wondered the same thing. Did someone pay these men? The ones peddling the leather goods always seemed to be African; and they were everywhere, squatting down on the pavement all over Athens, their wares laid out on blankets in front of them; and yet he'd never seem a single one of them make a sale. The goods they were selling. dubbed 'maimou,' monkey, by the Greeks, as in 'monkey see, monkey do,' were all imitations and had no intrinsic value; and he doubted anyone local would subsidize them. It was impossible, given Greece's current situation. No one had the money. Perhaps Turkey was shipping them in to destabilize the country. In the past, they'd burned down the forests, so why not this?

The thought depressed him. Although the train was full, he and Tembelos appeared to be the only Greeks; and for a moment, he felt as if he'd left his homeland behind and passed into another dimension. As if he were the famed Spartan warrior, Leonidas, facing the Persian army with his army of three hundred men. How would Greece ever survive this onslaught, he asked himself, this inrush of people who had no ties to the country, no knowledge of its culture or ancient tongue?

Piraeus had once been the most Greek of destinations. The movie, *Never on Sunday*, had been filmed there, its star, Melina Mercouri, playing the free-spirited prostitute who lived in the port. Explaining why she never worked on Sundays, she had belted out the famous song by Hatzidakis, 'Ta paidia tou Piraeia.' Patronas doubted Mercouri would recognize Piraeus now.

Before boarding the boat back to Spetses, he and Tembelos stopped to buy koulourakia—bracelet-sized rings of bread covered by sesame seeds—and ate them as they made their way up the ramp. Although it was early, it was already hot and they sat outside on the deck.

"Soon we will be on our back to Chios," Patronas announced. "We're done, Giorgos. We've got means, motive and opportunity."

"You're sure it was one of his brothers who killed him?" asked Tembelos.

"Yes," Patronas said. "We just have to determine which one it was."

"You ruled out the boy's mother?"

Patronas nodded. "Killing required physical strength. I doubt a woman could have done it."

Chewing thoughtfully, Tembelos mulled this over. "Vengeance then. The part of Crete I'm from, Sfakia, it would certainly have played out that way. Someone kills a member of your family; you go after them with everything you've got. It's mandatory, demanded by the culture. As a man, you must do unto him what was done unto yours."

Normally, Patronas felt a sense of relief at the end of a case, but not this time. Now all he felt was an abiding sense of loss. If his theory was correct, grief had been the motivating force behind the murder, overwhelming grief. He wouldn't be jailing a psychopath this time or serial killer, only a heartbroken father.

As a homicide detective, Patronas had strong feelings about murder. It was a despicable act, judged a mortal sin by every society in the world; and from what he'd seen, it set off shock waves that lasted for generations. He wasn't sure it was unnatural—this killing of others—the result of some errant chromosome in the human heart—or if it was an inevitable part of life on earth. Given its growing frequency, he was beginning to believe it was the latter. Predators walked every square inch of earth and one of the worst was man.

Achieving justice for the victim had long been his goal as a police man, the one that kept him going. He didn't see himself as an avenging angel like the Cretans Tembelos, had spoken of. He was more of a custodian in his view, the person who sweeps up after a killing and restores the world to rights.

Yet there would be no restoring anything this time. All there'd be was sadness.

Of all of the people involved, Patronas felt sorriest for the victim's mother, Sophia. Her family had known much sorrow, she'd said; and now she would know even more when the police came for her son, be it Vasilis or Stavros, and arrested him for the murder.

* * *

The ferry made a number of stops on the way to Spetses. Standing on the deck, Patronas watched the island of Hydra pass by to the west of him. The port was full of nineteenth century mansions, mute testimony to the prosperity the island had once enjoyed, when it had been a famous maritime center and home to 10,000 sailors. Boats of every description filled the harbor, the rigging on the sailboats clanging furiously in the wind.

Like Spetses, Hydra had played a significant role in the Greek War of Independence; and cannons, dating from that time, still dotted the shoreline. Modern tourism had also begun there, the result of *A Boy on a Dolphin*, a popular movie with Sophia Loren that had been filmed on Hydra in 1957.

Patronas didn't know whether to laugh or cry when he read that in his guidebook. Such misfortunes continued to happen. *Mamma Mia* had also brought tourists flocking to Greece, brides from all over the world seeking to re-enact the film's wedding scene on the island of Skopelos, turning what had once been a peaceful corner of the Aegean into a circus.

The ferry continued on, passing a number of smaller islands, one with a small lighthouse at its base. Patronas saw a fissure in the cliff below it. Red, it looked as if the rock had been split by a massive axe and lay wounded.

* * *

"Simonidis found the information you requested," Costas told Patronas as soon as he got to the station. "Papa Michalis also wants to speak to you. He said to tell you that he'd spent the last two days with the victim's family and thinks he might hold the key to your understanding of the crime."

Simonidis reported he'd found a brief entry about an accident in the precinct of Moschato. Flipping through the pages of his notebook, he recited: 'a four-year old boy, Achilles Papadopoulos, the son of Vasilis and Daphne Papadopoulos of Moschato, Athens, was injured on Koumantea Street in an accident on July 2, 2014 at 3 p.m. He was subsequently transported to KAT, the Athenian trauma center, in an ambulance.'

"Daphne and Vasilis," Patronas said. "Well, well…"

But Simonidis wasn't finished. "However, there was no mention of Thanasis Papadopoulos on that date," he droned on, "not as the driver of the vehicle, nor as a passenger in it. I did find an entry for him, but it was three weeks later, July 25, 2014. A policeman found him on the sidewalk in front of his apartment building with multiple injuries, apparently the victim of a mugging."

Patronas frowned. Without proof, there went his theory. He could almost see it, galloping over the hill like a horse.

They'd ordered pizza for lunch; and the table in the conference room was littered with the remnants of their meal. Frustrated, Patronas shoved the boxes away.

"You're saying you found no evidence that Thanasis Papadopoulos was driving the car that injured the child?" he asked, his voice rising.

"That right. None whatsoever. Although a Ford Fiesta *was* registered to him, there was nothing in the records to indicate that Thanasis Papadopoulos or his car were involved in the crash. From what I read in the police report, the child might have just stumbled and banged his head on the curb. It was all very unclear."

"Did the police check Thanasis Papadopoulos' blood alcohol level when they found him unconscious on the sidewalk? Was he drunk?"

"Again, there's no mention of it in the report."

"It doesn't add up. A neighbor in Athens said Thanasis had been hurt, too. And the owner of the store the family rented swore he'd gone missing around the same time."

"Missing and hurt aren't necessarily the same thing," Costas interjected. "He might have gone on a bender. It's also possible your witnesses got their dates mixed up. They saw him with bandages and assumed his injuries were the result of the same accident, not realizing there was a three-week discrepancy between the two events."

Nodding, Patronas conceded the point. "What do we do now?"

"We bring in Daphne and Vasilis and play them one against the other,"

Tembelos suggested, "And if that doesn't work, we go after Chryssoula and Stavros and do the same thing. Sooner or later, one of them will talk."

"It could be Thanasis was responsible for the child's death and the boy's father beat him up," Costas said, thinking aloud. "That would fit."

"Then killed him years later?" Simonidis said. "Why wait so long?"

"Perhaps over time, his grief turned murderous," offered Papa Michalis. "It does that sometimes. Witness those vendettas on Crete."

"What about Hope Erikson?" Patronas asked, turning back to Costas. "What's her status?"

"She's now housed in a cell with six other women. The attorney the American embassy found for her is demanding she be moved, but I don't think the transfer will take place anytime soon."

Papa Michalis reached for a napkin. "From the start, I was never convinced she was the guilty party," he said, dabbing his mouth primly. "Granted, she's a difficult person, but not without merit. For one thing, according to everyone I spoke to, she loved her husband with all her heart. 'Beyond reason,' one of her sisters-in-law said. By all accounts, her affection for him was genuine and deeply felt. Unfortunately, these feelings did not extend to his family, which she despised, nor his country, which she hated. As for the accident, I believe she didn't tell us about it because she knew or believed her husband, Thanasis, was culpable, that he and he alone was responsible for his nephew's death. She couldn't admit it, not to the police, not to herself. To do so would have disturbed her fantasy life, her childish, but much cherished belief that she and Thanasis had a perfect marriage."

"Two nights ago, you told me just the opposite. You said that 'you believed *she* was the killer," Patronas said. "'She's American,' you said, 'and Americans are extremely violent people."

"I have since changed my mind." Papa Michalis said. "This was a crime of vengeance, pure and simple. A grief-stricken father lashing out and taking down the killer of his son."

"You keep saying 'father.'" Costas complained. "Why couldn't it have been the child's mother?"

But she was a voice crying in the wilderness.

"It's highly unlikely the perpetrator was a female," Papa Michalis said dismissively. "As a general rule, women don't kill."

Costas fell silent, unable to think of a single case she'd studied at the police academy that contradicted what the priest had said. Historically, there'd been a few women murderers—the Roman empress, Livia, came to mind, who'd poisoned everyone who came between her son, Tiberius, and the throne. Lucretia Borgia was another. Certainly, not many and none that she knew of in Greece.

The group went back and forth, discussing how best to proceed. "I think we are all in agreement," Patronas said. "In all likelihood, Vasilis Papadopoulos was the perpetrator."

Stroking his beard, Papa Michalis nodded. "He's by far the most likely candidate. Seeking revenge is pure folly, of course, but there you have it. It might have eased his grief initially—taking action always does—but in the end, it led to an act of utter depravity, the slaughtering of his brother like a Paschal lamb. 'Vengeance is mine, sayeth the lord.' Not yours, not mine, and certainly not Vasilis Papadopoulos."

"He sayeth?" Patronas repeated. Even for Papa Michalis, it was extreme.

The priest then went into a long, rambling discussion about the nature of vengeance. "When you seek after it, dig two graves."

Patronas cut him off. "You've had your sayeth, Father. Now let someone else speak."

"I propose we interview Daphne and Vasilis Papadopoulos separately first thing tomorrow," Tembelos proposed. "Ritsos and Pappas have spent the most time with them, so they're the ones who should bring them in. And afterwards, if that doesn't work, we bring in other two, Stavros and his wife."

Chapter 21

Isolating himself in the office, Patronas lingered at the station, reading the murder book and taking notes. He wanted to be well prepared when he confronted Vasilis Papadopoulos the following day. With any luck, he'd take him by surprise, hit him hard and elicit a confession. Uneasy, Patronas wasn't looking forward to the interview. He hated every aspect of this case and desperately wanted to be done with it.

His mind kept drifting back to a conversation he'd had with Lydia earlier that day. "Your ex keeps calling the house," she'd told him. "I asked her what she wanted, but she wouldn't tell me. All she said was she needed to talk to you. I told her you were in Spetses, working on a case; and I gave her your cell phone number."

"I wish you hadn't done that."

"She sounded upset. I didn't know what else to do."

They chatted a few more minutes. "I solved the case," Patronas said with a touch of pride. "Turns out it was the victim's brother who did it. A revenge killing."

If he was expecting a word of praise, some form of congratulations, it was not been forthcoming. A lengthy silence ensued.

"You're a strange one," Lydia finally said. "Other men give their women flowers and chocolates. You give me killers and ex-wives."

And with that, she ended the call.

* * *

Costas was on duty at the front desk; and Patronas could hear her answering the phone and moving around. The reporters had all disappeared, leaving Spetses in search of fresh game elsewhere; and once again, the island was quiet.

Switching on the lamp, Patronas returned to his reading.

A few minutes later, Costas knocked on the door and stuck her head in. "You want to go

get something to eat? There's a nice fish restaurant nearby, Patrali's. It's within walking distance."

Patronas hesitated. Besides his two wives and, of course, his mother, he'd had little experience dining out and making small talk with women. And eating in a restaurant with Costas would be tough. She'd just sit there with a sour expression on her face. It would be like spending the evening with Stathis.

"Aren't you on duty?" he asked. "Who's going to work the front desk?"

"Ritsos is here."

"Just give me a minute," he said.

Not wanting to hurt her feelings, he sat there for few minutes, wondering who he could call. Tembelos had already left the station and gone back to the hotel to sleep; and Patronas never dined with Papa Michalis if he could help it. A prodigious eater, the priest would order half the things on the menu and dribble a goodly portion of them on his beard, then pick out whatever was salvageable and eat it. No, definitely not Father.

Patronas eventually settled on Margaret Vouros, thinking she'd be a good buffer between himself and Costas' and it would be a nice way to thank her for her help with the investigation. Vouros sounded pleased when he called her and said she'd meet him at the station within the hour and they could go from there.

The stars were out by the time she arrived. Costas had gone home during the interval and changed her clothes, trading in her uniform for a flowery dress with flounces. It didn't really suit her, that dress, Patronas thought. With her personality, she was far more winter than spring.

Given the choice, he would have drawn her in monochromatic tones, shades of gray or perhaps khaki, yet there she stood, all decked out like a rose garden. She'd also been drinking. He could smell it on her breathe and was far more relaxed than he'd ever seen her, looser.

He hoped the looseness would stop there and was glad he'd had the foresight to bring Vouros along, worried he might well need a chaperone before the night was over.

This was a first for him and he didn't really know what to do. Far shorter than average, he was not a particularly handsome man; and women rarely, if ever, made passes at him. So what was that dress about? He could almost hear his wife's voice saying, 'it's not all about you, Yannis.' But he thought just this once it might be.

The absence of cars was a relief after the cacophony of Athens, the only sound the soft lapping of the waves. They left the police station and strolled through the center of town, passing Boboulina's house before turning onto Anargiou Street. Vouros knew the area well and pointed out various landmarks along the way, various museums and the city hall. Patronas breathed deeply, savoring the scent of jasmine and *nychtolouloudo*, floating on the air, the latter a flower that only bloomed at night.

As soon as they got to the taverna, Patronas set about ordering the fish, selecting three kilos from the ice-filled display out front, as well as a vast assortment of appetizers. He then moved on to the land of forbidden foods, items Lydia had told him would kill him if ate them—fried crawfish, fried squid and fried cheese, finishing up the list with an ungodly amount of grilled octopus.

Patrali's was built out over the water; and the three of them watched the water pooling and eddying around the illuminated rocks below while they waited for their dinner.

In spite of the lateness of the hour, taxi boats were still making their way to Peloponnese, their lights flickering like fireflies in the darkness.

Patronas proposed they get a bottle of wine. "You have any preference?" he asked Costas.

"No," she said. "I drink everything."

As Patronas had anticipated, Costas proved to be a difficult dinner companion and fussed about everything from the wine—too warm, bring ice—to the tomatoes in the salad—not fresh, chop some more. Nothing satisfied her.

Psira, Patronas thought, nitpicker. The same quality that made her a good cop made her a pain in the ass at the table.

Conversation soon lagged, none of them being particularly adept at small talk; and in an effort to get things going, Patronas poured more wine into their glasses, emptying the bottle before the food arrived. Holding the bottle up, he signaled for the waiter to bring him another.

Costas pushed her plate away. "I'm sorry. I'm just not very hungry.

Ever since Stathis demoted me, I've been a mess. I can't eat. I can't sleep. All I want to do is cry."

And cry she did, blowing her nose on the napkin. "I gave up my life to be Chief Officer here. It's all I had and now it's gone."

"*Ola kala.*" Patronas said, seeking to calm her down. Everything's all right.

"You know what 'all right' is for me? It's being a cop. That's it. That's where I begin and end. My alpha and omega. I don't have anything else."

* * *

Patronas and Vouros ended up eating all the food while Melissa Costas got drunk. The fish proved to be delicious, the fried crayfish even better; and he rooted around, scarfing up the last bits like a truffle pig, wiping his plate with a chunk of bread and popping it in his mouth. Even though he was full, he kept eating, bread, French fries, whatever was left on the table. Anything to block Costas out. That fountain of misery, sitting across from him at the table. Fountain, hell. She was fucking Niagara Falls.

He'd given up trying to comfort her.

Vouros didn't know what to do either and kept offering her advice. Terrible advice in Patronas' opinion, beauty tips that had no bearing on the situation.

"Have you ever thought of cutting your hair?" she asked at one point. "You're a little…" Vouros hesitated, searching for the right word, before settling on "severe."

Costas patted her hair self-consciously. As usual, she'd gone overboard with the hairspray and it bounced back as if on springs. "Really? You think so?"

"Yes. Also put on a little make-up. Pretty yourself up. You're a cop, not a nun."

But within minutes. it was back to the job or in Costas' case, the lack thereof.

"I was like you once," Patronas said. "For a long time, I thought being a cop was all that I was. I'd gotten divorced, so I wasn't anyone's husband any more. I had no children, so I wasn't anyone's father. And I'd long since ceased being anyone's son. Without the job, I was nothing."

More than a little drunk himself, he went onto to describe Dimitra and what she'd done to him, the consequences of their divorce. How he'd been left without a roof over his head and been forced to sleep in the office. "Without Papa Michalis and Giorgos Tembelos, I would have lost my mind."

Costas refused to be consoled. "I don't have anyone. Everyone I know hates me, even my men. Do you know what Pappas call me? 'Alecto,' In case you don't know, *Alecto* was one of the furies of Greek mythology. You know the ones. They had heads like dogs and were the scourge of humanity. *Alecto* was the worst of them. Her name means unceasing anger."

"*Alecto*," she repeated, her eyes wet

"You have a friend," Vouros said. "You have me."

Surprised, Costas smiled.

"You should do that more often," Vouros said.

"What?"

"Smile."

* * *

After paying the bill, Patronas and Vouros put Melissa Costas in a carriage and sent her home. She was so drunk; she could barely stand.

She thanked them more than was necessary, muttering garbled words about how much their support meant to her.

"You're a good cop," Patronas said. "Never forget that, Melissa. One of the best I've ever worked with. It's been an honor serving with you."

The two of them had to hoist her up—the dress, it was so tight, it was a struggle—and set her down inside the carriage. She couldn't manage it herself.

Patronas was very careful not to touch anything he shouldn't. No accidental pat on the derriere, no hand going where it didn't belong. When Costas' dress rode up, he stepped back and let Vouros handle it, kept his eyes resolutely averted.

He paid the driver in advance and gave him Costas' address. "See that she gets home all right. We were celebrating and I'm afraid she's had a little too much to drink."

"No problem," the man said. "I've spent my life ferrying tourists around. Drunks are my specialty."

Costas endeavored to wave, but couldn't quite pull it off. *"Yia sou,"* she called. Bye.

She continued to call, her voice growing fainter and fainter as the carriage vanished over the hill.

* * *

After returning to Hotel Ambrosia, Patronas had just gotten into bed when his cell phone rang. Fumbling around, he hastened to answer it.

"Hello," he said, keeping his voice low, not wanting to wake up Tembelos and Papa Michalis, fast asleep in their beds on either side of him. "Hello, who is this?"

"It's me, Yannis," his ex-wife said. "Dimitra."

They spoke awkwardly about her time in Italy. Strained, but amicable. Eventually she got down to it. "I'm coming home, Yannis. I'm sick. I've got cancer."

As always, she was very matter-of-fact. "They want to start chemo and I know it makes you sick. My mother is too old to drive me to the hospital and I was hoping you would. I know things didn't end well with us, but you are the only family I have. I don't have anybody else."

Family? Him? Patronas supposed after twenty years it was true.

There was a long pause and it sounded like she was crying. "I'm sorry, Yannis. I know you don't like me. I'm sorry to be asking this of you. But I don't have anybody else. I'm all alone."

"Of course, I'll help you, Dimitra," he said, not knowing what else to do. "I'll drive you and do whatever else you need."

After he hung up, Patronas walked out on the balcony and stood there for a long time, staring out at the night. He didn't bother searching for the stars. There was no point, not tonight. A wave of despair washed over him.

Dimitra had always had that effect on him, their time together like a continual solar eclipse, nothing but darkness closing in all sides, the air growing colder, then colder still as the light disappeared from the sky.

The call had awoken Tembelos and he joined him out on the balcony a few minutes later. "What were you thinking, Yannis?" he asked. "You just got married. You can't go driving Dimitra around Chios."

"She can't drive, not in her condition. She said her cancer is well advanced."

"Bah! Dimitra's like Rasputin. She'll never die."

"It might work, my helping her," Patronas said with a sinking heart. "All things are possible."

Chapter 22

Patronas offered to get Daphne Papadopoulos a cup of coffee when she first arrived at the station, asking her how she liked it and supervising Simonidis while he made it in the kitchenette, making sure he prepared it the way she wanted it—*metrio*—medium sweet.

Whatever truths he uncovered today would be painful ones; and he wanted to make the process as easy as he could for her. Costas had volunteered to sit in during the interrogation, but he'd demurred, not wanting to crowd Daphne or upset her further. He would bring in Papa Michalis when he went after her husband, Vasilis, but until then it would just be the two of them, he and Daphne, sitting across the table from one another in the conference room.

In preparation, he'd readied the space beforehand. discarding the debris on the top of the table and wiping it down. As afterthought, he'd opened all the windows; and he could hear birds now, calling in the bushes below. He wished they'd be quiet. The singing of birds had no place, in here, not this morning, not today.

Daphne had dressed up for the interview—her two-piece suit more suitable for church than for speaking with a homicide detective—and unlike the previous times Patronas had seen her, she wore no make-up today. Her face was scrubbed clean; and her glossy hair was loose, curling softly around her shoulders. She looked younger than he remembered and far more vulnerable.

Before getting underway, he started the mp3 player, not wanting to distract her once they got started. He glanced down at it now to make sure it was working, then picked up a pen and opened his notebook, intending to bolster the recording with his own observations.

He quizzed her first about the cave, who in the family might have known about the back entrance.

"We all did," she answered. "Chryssoula's son had gone exploring and found that opening in the rock and went through it. He's a curious one and I guess he wanted to see what was on the other side. It took us hours to find him. We must have searched every square inch of that cave."

An overly long explanation. Perhaps too long.

"Did your husband, Vasilis, participate in the search?" he asked.

"Of course. Like I said before, we all did."

"Did you leave the cave immediately after you found the boy or were you curious, too, and follow the tunnel to see where it went?"

"I came right back out. But it was very dark in there and I can't speak for the others."

"What about your husband? Was he with you?"

"He came out a few minutes after I did."

"How long? Five minutes? Ten?"

"Ten maybe."

Long enough.

What Daphne said was consistent with what Hope Erikson had told him about the discovery of the tunnel. Anyway, it didn't matter. He'd verified Vasilis knew about it; and that was the main thing.

Taking a deep breath, he moved in for the kill. "I don't know if you know this. But I went to Moschato and spoke with the people in the apartment building where you used to live. I know about the accident, Daphne. I know what happened to your son, Achilles. I realize this is difficult for you, but you need to tell me what you remember about that day."

In his mind, they'd come to the end of the road, the two of them. All that was missing was the beginning of the story, how it had all come about.

"I've figured most of it out," Patronas said gently. "I just need you to verify it. It must have been terrible. Losing a child like that. The hardest thing in the world."

"It was," she said. "My life ended that day."

"*Sillipitiria*," 'I'm sorry with you.' The standard expression of sympathy in Greece, Patronas knew it was inadequate, but he recited it anyway, wanting to acknowledge her loss.

He let the silence drag on, a technique he often employed during interrogations. As a general rule, it disturbed people and they rushed to

152 • LETA SERAFIM

fill the void, prattled away like children. But Daphne didn't say a word.

Hating himself, he hammered away at her. "I've got all the time in the world. I can sit here all day and all night if I have to. You're not going anywhere until you tell me what happened that day."

She began to cry then, tears welling up and spilling down her face. Worse were the sounds she was making, the whimpering and cries of pain.

"I'm sorry," she said, choking back a sob. "It's still so vivid in my mind. I was upstairs, folding laundry when it happened. My mother-in-law was supposed to be watching him, but he got away from her. He did that. He liked to hide from us and make us come looking for him. Sometimes, he'd run out in the hall and get in the elevator, push the button and ride it up and down. That's what we think he did that day. Only he didn't stop there. He ran outside, something he'd never done before.

"Thanasis drove up in his car and started to park in the street in front of the building, but he was drunk and ran up on the sidewalk instead. He hit Achilles head on and sent him flying, crushing both of his legs and his pelvis. Terrible fractures, where the bones break through the flesh. I didn't even know it had happened. They had to come and get me."

Fighting to control herself, she buried a fist in her mouth. "He was in KAT for what felt like an eternity. It wasn't very long, I realized later, only two weeks, but for me, it was forever. There is no night or day in a hospital. Time has no meaning.

"The wound in one of his legs got infected and the doctor wanted to amputate. But Vasilis refused and we took him to Germany instead, to a specialist a person we knew recommended. It was horrible. He slept most of the way there on the plane; he was very sick by then. His skin was gray and he was feverish. I was sure I was going to lose him, but he woke up after we landed in Munich and was himself for a little while. He was very excited in the ambulance on the way to the hospital and he must have asked me a thousand questions. 'Why are they talking like that, Mama? Why aren't they speaking Greek? Where are we?'

"We spent ten days in the hospital there. Everybody around us was jabbering in German and we didn't understand half of what they said. The doctor seemed to know what he was doing, but in the end, it didn't make any difference. Achilles just kept getting worse and worse. He was feverish and drifting in and out of consciousness, the infection ravaging his body.

He was so little and they stuck tubes in him everywhere. Even in his neck. I told them not to, but they said they had to. They didn't have a choice."

Unable to continue, she stopped for a few minutes.

"When did he die?" asked Patronas quietly.

"August fifteenth. The same day as the Holy Mother. I never left his side the whole time we were there, except to go to church that day. It was hard to find an Orthodox church, but I managed. Vasilis didn't want to come, so I went there by myself and prayed to *Panagia*, the Holy Mother, to save my son, to save Achilles. 'You know, I told her. 'You know what it is to lose a child. Spare me this loss.' There were a lot of people there, Greeks like me, and I remember I felt a little better being among them. I came back to the hospital and sat down in my usual place, in a chair next to Achilles' bed, and I reached for his hand. He was in a coma by then and I don't think he even knew I was there. Later that night, he made a funny sound, a kind of rasping; and his eyes flew open, but only for a few seconds. All the machines started ringing and the staff came running, but it was too late by then. He was gone."

"You said Thanasis was drunk when he hit him with the car."

She nodded. "You could smell it on him and he was slurring his words. Even after he sobered up, he had no idea what he'd done. I don't think he ever realized. What happened to other people never really mattered to Thanasis."

"Did you speak to the police after the accident?"

"Yes. Two officers came to the hospital and questioned us. Seeing how upset I was, they left me alone and Vasilis did most of the talking. My mother-in-law had made him promise not to tell the police Thanasis was involved and he didn't."

"Why?"

"I don't know. All I know is Vasilis did as she'd asked and kept his brother out of it. "It must have been a hit and run accident,' I heard him say. 'It's a very dangerous intersection.'

"Which meant Thanasis got away with it."

"That's right," she said, rage flaring up and spreading like a fiery brand across her face.

A piece of the puzzle dropped into place. "Someone beat Thanasis up after the accident. That was your husband wasn't it?"

She nodded. "After Achilles died, Vasilis just went crazy; and, as soon as we got back from Munich, he cornered him and beat him half to death. He would have killed him, too, if his mother hadn't gotten between them. 'Enough,' she kept shouting. 'Haven't I suffered enough?'

"Where was Hope when all this was going on?" Patronas asked.

"Around. She was afraid the police would come and take Thanasis away. That's all she cared about. My son didn't matter to her. They were the same in that, the two of them.

"We buried him in the village. By then all the money was gone—not just our money, everybody's. We couldn't pay the rent in Athens and Stavros arranged for us to move to Spetses. It never got better, at least not for me. I don't think it ever will. Even now years later, I'm still suffering. Vasilis and me, we sit in silence at night without turning the lights on and go to bed without speaking. Losing a child…. It's like being burned alive, only the scars are invisible. No one can see the scars."

She took a long shuddery breath. "Before we left Athens, I packed up all of Achilles' things and put them away. But it didn't help. Nothing helped. His death is still with me. It will be with me until the day I die."

"Given what happened, how could you live in the same house as Thanasis?"

"I was too numb to protest when Stavros arranged it; and I ended up having a lot of medical problems after we got to Spetses. The doctor said it was because of stress, but it wasn't, it was because of him. Having to be around him all the time, to be around that worthless, worthless man, who took my child's life. I wanted to silence him. To shut him up forever.

"I know what you're thinking, Chief Officer." Raising her head, she looked Patronas straight in the eye. "You think I killed him. But I didn't. I wasn't sorry he got killed. No, not at all. In fact, I rejoiced in it. My only regret was that it took so long, took all those years for someone to do it."

"That's why you didn't want Hope's baby," Patronas said.

"That's right. I couldn't raise his child. It would have been impossible for me."

Daphne Papadopoulos went on to say she had a witness, a woman could attest to her whereabouts at the time of the murder, a local resident, who'd been at the taverna that day, and whose table she'd waited on. She rattled off the woman's name and address; and Patronas wrote the information down.

He stood up and opened the door of the conference room. "This is still an active homicide investigation," he said. "You are not to leave Spetses under any circumstances."

"Where would I go, Chief Officer? The only place I want to be is with my son and that will never happen."

* * *

When Patronas questioned Daphne's husband, Vasilis, he grew enraged, yelling he wasn't the one who killed Thanasis. "I swear on all that is holy, I had nothing to do with it. On the memory of my dead son. Do what you want to me. Give me a lie detector test if you want or swab me for DNA. It won't make any difference. I'm innocent."

"You beat him up," Patronas said. "You nearly killed him."

"My mother made me promise I wouldn't touch him again and I haven't. It wasn't me, Chief Inspector. You need to look elsewhere for your murderer."

"Your mother orchestrated your silence?"

He nodded. "She's been pulling our strings ever since it happened. Even at the hospital, she dictated what Daphne and I were to say. There was my poor son, lying there with tubes in his neck, tubes everywhere; and there she is, standing by his hospital bed, telling me I mustn't say anything to the police about Thanasis, not tell them he was the one behind the wheel of the car that hit Achilles. Begging me with tears in her eyes to let it be. To protect my useless brother and keep our family intact."

"And you went along with her."

"Sure, I admit it. And you know why? Because I didn't know what I was doing that day. My kid, dying right there in front of me, I was out of mind."

His willingness to take a lie detector test troubled Patronas. Even though the results would be inadmissible in court in Greece, it seemed unlikely he would volunteer to take such a test if he'd done it. It would invite destruction if he were guilty, be an act of self-immolation.

* * *

Stavros Papadopoulos readily admitted his brother, Thanasis, had been responsible for the accident and talked at length about the consequences of it, specifically how much the child's injuries and death had cost them.

It took Patronas a few minutes to realize Stavros was speaking literally—about money—not about the emotional toll on the family.

"Thanasis bankrupted all of us without blinking an eye," he said. "We were hanging by a thread as it was and then that trip to Germany...You won't believe how expensive it was. Thousands and thousands of euros. We got some money from the government, but it didn't come close to covering the cost. The hotel rooms and the meals, the private ambulances and airplane tickets. It all added up. We were willing to pay it, of course. Don't get me wrong. We all loved Achilles and would have done anything to save him. But in the end, it ruined us. We had to let the stores go, had to let everything go.

"After the accident, I thought Thanasis would change, but he didn't. He was still drunk half the time and full of himself. Knowing what he'd done, it was very hard to be around him. But he was my brother and I did what I could for him."

"When we first questioned you about the murder, why didn't tell us about the car accident?"

"My mother made me promise I'd keep quiet about it. She's funny that way about the family. To the outside world, everything has to be perfect, even a wreck like my brother. I realize now I should have said something to that woman cop, but then hindsight is always 20/20, isn't it? My mother changed after Achilles died. All she talks about now is dying. How her life is over and there is no reason to live any more. I'm her son and I love her. That's the reason, I did what I did. Withheld evidence or whatever the hell you people call it. Things were bad enough for her, I didn't want to make them worse."

Like the others, Stavros insisted he'd had nothing to do with his brother's murder. "Why kill him? The damage was done. Killing him wouldn't restore Achilles to life or give us back the stores. There was no point."

* * *

Dressed appropriately for once, Chryssoula Papadopoulos was wearing a pristine white dress and a hand-made cardigan with little pink flowers embroidered on it. Gone were the gold lame shoes and glittery eye shadow, and sadly, the spectacular décolletage.

She volunteered that after the accident she'd kept her children as far away from Thanasis as she could, afraid they'd meet a similar fate, die as Achilles had, at their uncle's hand. "He was so irresponsible; you couldn't trust him with anything. And he didn't care. You'd yell at him and he'd just laugh. That's why we got a separate house. I insisted on it before we moved to Spetses. I told Stavros I wouldn't go otherwise."

Chryssoula then gave a little speech about how much she'd loved Achilles, weeping and dabbing her eyes with an embroidered handkerchief she'd brought with her. As with everything she did, there was a theatrical element in this display of grief, something that didn't ring true.

Patronas cut her off. "I heard you son got lost in the cave."

Caught off-guard, Chryssoula didn't know what to answer and she flailed around, looking for Stavros.

"I sent your husband home," Patronas said, enjoying her discomfort. "You're on your own here, Chryssoula. What I actually want to know about is the tunnel, the one leading off from the cave. Whether or not you knew it was there."

She shifted uncomfortably in her seat. "Yes, I knew. We discovered it the day my son went missing."

"How about where the tunnel led? Did you discover that, too?

"I don't know what you're talking about."

It was a little sad, Patronas thought, how obvious she was, her decision to stonewall him showing itself triumphantly on her face. She wasn't very subtle, Chryssoula. If you played poker with her, you'd win every hand.

Leaning closer, he fired off question after question. "Did you know that it leads directly to your house? Almost to the front door? That it's less than a five-minute walk away? We believe the killer used it afterwards, that he changed out of his bloodstained clothes in the cave and left them there."

"It's not possible. It's too dark in there."

"Ever hear of a flashlight?"

Patronas watched her for a moment. "What's the matter, Chryssoula? Stavros say something incriminating to you? Did you find bloodstains on his trousers when you went to do the laundry?"

Calling her continually by her first name was a breach of protocol, but Patronas didn't care. He wanted to keep her off-balance. "Let's go back to the flashlight. Did your husband keep one in the cave in case of emergencies?"

"No, no. Maybe one of the others did. I don't remember."

"There are only two others. If you had to choose, which one would you pick?"

After stalling for a good twenty minutes, she allowed that her brother-in-law, Vasilis, might have, adding as an afterthought that he had hated Thanasis.

"It seems everyone did, you, Stavros, Daphne…"

That stopped her. "I didn't kill him," she said abruptly. "I can prove it. I have witnesses."

Wearily, Patronas took down their names. then dismissed her with the same admonishment, he'd given Daphne. "Do not to leave the island."

He showed her out of the conference room and shut the door behind her, then sank back down in his chair and lit a cigarette. For more than an hour, he sat there, brooding and smoking.

Without a confession, he didn't have enough evidence to go forward with the case; and a confession had not been forthcoming. Everyone he'd interviewed had sworn they were innocent. And worse, he believed them.

Chapter 23

"Well, what do you think?" Patronas switched the mp3 player off.

Stymied, he'd played the recording of the interviews back for Costas and Tembelos, hoping they might pick up something he'd missed. A long, drawn out process, it had taken over two hours to go through the tape from start to finish. Patronas had left the conference room. when his interview with Daphne Papadopoulos played, unable to listen to it a second time.

Tembelos leaned back in his chair. "Everyone hedged. Four people, one after another, saying virtually the same thing. I'd say they rehearsed their answers beforehand and agreed on how much to say. Sounds like they were working off the same script."

Patronas nodded. He had come to the same conclusion. The question was why. "We need to track down the witnesses Daphne and Chyrssoula mentioned, verify they were at the taverna at the time in question."

"I'll get right on it," Costas said.

Costas had kept a low profile since their abortive outing with Margaret Vouros. She was still drinking, that much was clear. Her eyes had been red when she'd started her shift that morning, her hands a little shaky. Still she seemed to have it under control. You'd never be able to tell she had a problem just by looking at her. Her uniform was always freshly ironed, her hair as tightly contained as ever, shellacked into place at the nape of her neck. Patronas had known his share of drunks; and he doubted she'd be able to keep it up much longer, this little charade of hers. She needed to rein it in and do it yesterday.

He made a mental note to speak to her. Stage one of those American things Lydia was always talking about. What were they called? 'Interventions.' Do whatever was necessary to save her.

It would be on him. He'd never tell Stathis, not in a million years, not even if Costas shot a suspect in a drunken rage or crashed that miserable cruiser into the police station.

* * *

His boss called Patronas on his cell phone later that day and demanded he charge Hope Erikson with first degree murder. "You're wasting time," Stathis said. "Book that American woman and be done with it."

"I'm not sure that's the appropriate course of action," Patronas said, pushing back. "I am not convinced she killed him, not convinced beyond a reasonable doubt."

Stathis exploded. "Fuck you and your reasonable doubt, Patronas. You're a cop, not a juror. You have until the end of the week to wrap this up or I'm pulling you off the case."

Three days.

Patronas walked over to the window, opened it and lifted up the screen. The birds were still there, hopping from branch to branch in the bushes below. barn swallows from the glossy look of them. He'd bought a pepperoni pizza for lunch, and he gathered up the remains and threw it down to them.

"One swallow does not a summer make," he said aloud, recalling Aristotle's words, "Nor one day of joy, a happy life."

He wished Aristotle had seen fit to discuss homicide in his writings, wished the philosopher could point him in the right direction. Wished someone could.

Did the ancient Greeks kill each other? he wondered. Surely, they must have. Murder had always been a part of human life. That poor soul in Switzerland, the one the hikers found frozen solid in a glacier, had been murdered, according to forensic anthropologists, shot dead by an arrow four thousand years ago. It had gone on during the Ice Age and would continue to do so as long as men walked the earth.

But who the hell was the killer this time?

With a sigh, he returned to work. The surface of his desk was covered with paper — computer print-outs, photographs of the crime scene and the medical report from the coroner, In addition, there was a stack of manila folders, carefully labeled with each suspect's name. If only generating paper would generate a solution, his problems would be solved.

Costas called in to report she had contacted one of the witnesses from the taverna and taken their statement, but had been unable to locate the other. "According to her relatives, she's in Athens and should be back tomorrow."

"Keep at it," Patronas said. "I am at a loss as to what else we can do. Initially, I was convinced Vasilis was the killer, that he'd confess and we'd close the case today, but now I'm not so sure. I keep thinking I'm missing something."

"Something someone said?" Costas asked.

"Or didn't say."

* * *

Patronas drove to Aghioi Anargyiou with Papa Michalis later that afternoon in Costas' wrecked cruiser, intending to speak to the victim's mother, who if her two sons were to be believed, had conspired to cover-up the car accident in Moschato and forced them lie to the police about their brother's involvement. Her behavior didn't make sense to Patronas; and he wanted to hear her side of the story.

Dimitra had called before he left, and he was in an ugly mood. To the priest's dismay, this manifested itself in his driving which had always been interactive—lots of verbal abuse and hand gestures directed at other drivers—but today was terrifying.

Papa Michalis gave a nervous squeak and grabbed the dashboard. "You seem a little agitated today, Yannis. What's the matter?"

Patronas and Papa Michalis went back a long way, even roomed together for a time after Patronas' marriage fell apart; and he understood instantly when Patronas told him about the phone call from Dimitra, knew better than anyone else how Patronas felt about his ex-wife. Hate didn't begin to describe it.

"Dimitra." The priest shook his head. "I thought after the divorce, you'd finally gotten rid of her."

"Careful what you say, Father. She's sick. She's got cancer."

"Is that why she called?"

"Yes. She's coming back to Chios and she wants me to drive her to her back and forth to the hospital. I said I would. She's sick and alone. I had to, Father. What else could I do?"

"There aren't many people, who would do as you've done, Yannis, agree to help a person like Dimitra. I wouldn't and I'm a priest, a sort of professional Christian. It would be like befriending a rattlesnake."

"I know, Father. You'll get no argument from me."

After his divorce, Patronas had been cast adrift, his life in total disarray. Dimitra had gotten the house in the legal settlement and kicked him out, then tossed everything he owned out in the street after him. His father's cufflinks and baptismal cross, a framed photo of his dead mother—the only one he had of her smiling—it didn't matter, out it went.

Thoroughly humiliated, Patronas had gotten down on his hands and knees and gathered it all up again, picked up the bits and pieces of his life, put them in the backseat of his car and driven away.

As a result, he had been left homeless for over a year, all his earthly possessions stowed in a cardboard box beneath the desk in his office. Broke, he couldn't afford to rent an apartment, not if he wanted to eat; and he'd still be homeless, camping out at the police station, if fate hadn't intervened and he'd met Lydia Pappas, a Greek-American potter, and married her.

Turned out Lydia had money and, after returning from their honeymoon, she had bought a house for them, a little cottage on the beach in Nagos on the north coast of Chios. Living with her had been a revelation. For the first time in his life, there'd been flowers on the table and scented candles in the bath. In the morning, she wake him with kisses and at night drag him outside to see the moon, singing off-key *Pame na volta, sto feggari!*' Let's go for a walk to the moon. He'd never known anyone like her, never believed such joy was possible. He still couldn't believe his good fortune; and would lay awake at night and watch her sleep, her red hair spread out across on the pillow, so overcome with tenderness he could barely breathe.

"Hard as it might be, I *do* think you're doing the right thing," the priest went on. "Hard as it might be."

He recited a portion of the Bible he especially was fond of: "But let us who are of the day be sober, putting on the breastplate of faith and love, and as a helmet, the hope of salvation."

Patronas nodded, recognizing the truth in what the old man was saying. No question about it, he would need a breastplate and helmet going forward in the future. Dimitra had always been Goliath in their relationship while he had been David. David, armed only with a slingshot, David, small in stature and very much afraid.

Chapter 24

The victim's mother, Sophia, was sitting out in the sun, tracking Patronas' progress across the yard with half-closed eyes.

"You again?" she said.

Patronas nodded. "You've already met my colleague, Papa Michalis. We have some additional questions to ask you."

Pulling up a chair, he sat down next to her and signaled Papa Michalis to sit on the other side, wanting to box her in.

"We know all about the accident," he said without preamble. "The one that killed your grandson, Achilles, in Moschato. What we don't know is why you withheld this information from us. Not once, but three times, first with Officer Costas and twice with Papa Michalis and me. Surely, you knew it was important."

"Ach, Achilles. You're here about Achilles."

Her eyes filled with tears. "I miss him. Every day I miss him, every single day. The pain never goes away. 'Yiayia,' he always said. 'Yiayia, don't leave. Stay here with me.' If only I could, if only I could."

She continued to weep. "Once he said he wanted to marry me. 'We can live together,' he said. "You and me. I'll build a house for us, Yiayia. A house like a castle."

"I'm sorry," Papa Michalis said.

She nodded, acknowledging his sympathy. "He was all that I had. All that I had in the world. My other grandchildren, Chryssoula, she keeps them away from me. I never see them and when I do, they don't want to come near me."

"Why didn't you tell us?" Patronas asked again.

"Why? What good would it do? He's dead, Achilles. Dead and gone."

"It has bearing on the case."

"Achilles died a long time ago. His death has nothing to do with what happened here."

"I beg to differ. I believe it has *everything* to do with what happened here. The car accident was the reason your son, Thanasis, was murdered and you know it. Vasilis said you ordered him to lie to the police about it in the hospital and then again here. Subordination of perjury is illegal and yet you went ahead. We can charge you with obstruction of justice."

"Bah. Throw me in jail. I did what I had to."

"I don't understand why you felt like you needed to protect Thanasis. He was an irresponsible drunk. He killed your grandson." Patronas' tone was harsh.

"He was mine. That's all that matters. It's what you do. He couldn't help the drinking. It was like a hunger he had."

"And now you're protecting Vasilis. How far does your loyalty go? Does it extend to killers?"

Raising a wrinkled hand, she moved to silence him. "Stop talking like that! Leave me alone."

"Vasilis killed him and you know it."

"No, no! That's not our way."

"What isn't? Murder?"

"He promised he wouldn't touch him. He gave his word he would leave him alone."

"But he didn't, did he? You know what I think? I think you suspected Vasilis from the beginning. You thought he'd finally killed his brother."

The fight seemed to go out of her. "I'd already lost so much. First, Achilles and then Thanasis. I couldn't afford to lose any more. I never had much. Only that, only my family. I had to protect him."

"You're saying it was Vasilis?"

"I don't know," she said, breaking down completely. "Maybe he did. Maybe he didn't. I don't know."

She was still crying when Patronas and the priest left, bent nearly double in her plastic law chair. The sound of her weeping followed them to the car.

* * *

"Next time, you go alone," the priest said. "I can't do this anymore. This case, I feel like I'm watching people eat each other. The way you attacked her…I know you're upset, but you shouldn't take it out on other people."

"She was obstructing justice. I had to be tough."

The priest crossed his arms in front of his chest, a mulish expression on his face. "Is that what that was? Is that what you call it? Tough! What's next, Yannis? Thumb screws? The rack?"

Petronas had no regrets about the way he'd handled Sophia Papadopoulos. She had covered up Thanasis' involvement in the accident, forced family members to perjure themselves and implicated Hope Erikson, stated repeatedly her daughter-in-law was the killer. What had Margaret Vouros said? "Railroaded?" That just about covered it.

Chapter 25

"I was sure it was a vengeance killing," Patronas told the head of the forensic laboratory, Dimitris Leandros, over the phone. "But now I'm not so sure. I confronted the victim's brother, Vasilis Papadopoulos, but he swore up and down he didn't do it. You should have heard him. He even volunteered to take a lie detector test."

Patronas had called Leandros in an effort to solve the case, but so far nothing worthwhile had come from speaking with him. Leandros was methodical in the extreme and would not speculate, no matter how hard Patronas pushed. 'Maybe' was not in his vocabulary, nor was 'possibly' or 'might.' It was as if he didn't know there was a subjunctive case. All he cared about was physical evidence, preferable items he could actually touch, a bullet-ridden liver, for example, the bullets perfectly preserved and suitable for analysis. Evidence Patronas didn't have.

"As you know, polygraph tests are inadmissible in Greece," Leandros said. "A situation I am sure your alleged suspect, Vasilis Papadopoulos, is well aware of. Still, it seems unlikely he would volunteer to take one if he was indeed the killer. He would have nothing to gain by it and everything to lose. If the results indicated that he was lying, the police would then have him in their sights."

As always, his logic was impeccable.

"Fuck," Patronas said.

Leandros made a prissy little cough. A dry specimen with a mechanical, almost robotic manner, he disapproved of many of the things his colleagues did, swearing near the top of his list, which was what the cough had been about. He was also violently opposed to smoking; and Patronas had never dared light up in his presence, afraid Leandros would pick up the saw he used on corpses and lop off the top of his head.

Why would anyone pursue such a career? Patronas asked himself as he listened to Leandros go on and on. Seek to educate oneself in dissection techniques, how to weigh brains and preserve internal organs in formaldehyde? Patronas had no idea what Leandros had been like at the beginning, what kind of kid he'd been, but he was a brittle twig of a man now.

Tembelos maintained this was because Leandros spent so much time with corpses and, as a result, had taken on many of their attributes. "He's the original dead man walking."

As always, the coroner refused to be rushed and went over his findings in mind-numbing detail. Forty-five minutes they'd spent on the phone so far.

"I've examined the evidence repeatedly, and it does not support your theory that either of the brothers, Vasilis or Stavros Papadopoulos, was involved," Leandros concluded. "There is only one clear set of fingerprints; and they belong to the victim's spouse, Hope Erikson. There are absolutely no fingerprints belonging to anyone else on that bottle; and even hers are not very clear, more than a little smeared. As I told you before, I believe the bottle was wiped. There are partials elsewhere, yes, but nothing that would have resulted from gripping the murder weapon tightly enough to raise it up and smash it down over the victim's head. This is very significant finding in my opinion. Conclusive."

"You're saying she did it?"

"Let me finish. For the most part, unlike the bottle itself, the shards of glass embedded in the victim's throat were heavily encrusted with blood. The blood was undisturbed which means it is highly unlikely the killer attempted to wipe them or sought in any way to remove them as evidence. Also, given the breakage, the extensive shattering of the glass, I am convinced that even if the killer had endeavored to do so, it would have proven impossible. You simply cannot clean broken slivers of glass. Something would have remained and I would have found it. That said, I did not. I found nothing, nothing to indicate anyone other than the spouse had touched that bottle. The proof in my opinion is definitive and I am willing to testify to it in court. She was definitely in the cave and she touched both the victim and the bottle that killed him with her hands."

He concluded with a flourish. *"Quod erat demonstrandum."* Thus, has it been demonstrated.

"Hope Erikson?" Patronas repeated.

"The very same."

Before hanging up, Patronas inquired about DNA sequencing, when the results of the tests would be available.

"As I told you before, DNA testing takes time," Leandros said testily. "But at this point I doubt it will contradict what I just told you. If I were you, Patronas, I'd zero in on the American."

* * *

Pocketing his phone, Patronas looked over at Tembelos.   "Leandros claims we got it wrong. It wasn't Vasilis Papadopoulos, who killed him, it was Hope Erikson. According to him, the evidence is irrefutable. Which means it wasn't the car accident that led to the murder, but something else as yet unknown."

"After Moschato, I was sure it was the boy's father," Tembelos said. "I would have staked my life on it."

"Same here.   Seems we've come full circle, Giorgos, and we're back where we started. The victim's spouse, Hope Erikson, was the last person to see him alive; her fingerprints are on the murder weapon and his blood was on her clothes. Therefore, she is the guilty party."

"What are you going to do?"

"Go back to Athens and talk to her again, see what she has to say. One thing's for sure, if Leandros is right and she *is* the guilty party, Stathis will give us a medal. He'll be delighted a foreigner is responsible. Anyone, but a Greek. It's a form of patriotism for him."

They talked for a few more minutes before Patronas left the station, walking down the stairs and heading out into the night. Tembelos had elected to stay behind and field any calls that came in.

"You've been working nonstop," he'd said. "Take the rest of the night off for God's sakes."

Costas and the others had departed when their shift ended, exactly at five; and Papa Michalis had returned to the hotel hours before.

Pausing to light a cigarette, Patronas looked back at the building. Lights were on in the second floor where the station was, but the rest of the offices were dark. Freshly painted, it was a handsome edifice, far better maintained than the aging facility where he labored on Chios. The arches over the windows softened the effect of the metal bars on the windows; and there was a well-tended garden in front, full of oleander bushes and date palms, the fonds shifting listlessly in the wind.

Even at this hour, the heat was unbearable; and it sapped his strength. Seeking relief, he walked along the coastal road by the sea. The area was very quiet, the expensive gifts shops and art galleries all shuttered and closed for the night. Only a small carry-out called 'Souvalucky,' was still open.

He'd wanted to buy a dress for Lydia and had priced one in a shop called Katerina's. It had been nothing special, a lightweight cotton shift with embroidery down the front.

"It's on sale," the owner had told him. "Only two hundred thirty euros" Close to a fourth of what his pension would be when he retired. Disgusted, he'd bought a half-kilo of almond cookies instead, *amigdalota*, a local delicacy. Sugar by the cupful, but then what could he do?

A scrawny black cat darted out in front of him. Seeing it, Patronas laughed to himself. As if he needed any more bad luck. Dimitra alone would suffice. A witch on a broomstick would be a blessing compared to her.

After Athens, the darkened streets felt empty, his footsteps echoing in the stillness. Not that Spetses wasn't beautiful, it was, especially now, the cobbled pavement, silver beneath the streetlamps. Close to two a.m., no taxi boats were going back and forth; and very few lights were on. Only a handful on the distant shore, like sequins strewn across the water.

Overhead, the stars were glorious, the darkness so all-encompassing he could see the Milky Way.

He stood there a few more minutes, staring up at the night sky. He wished Lydia was there beside him, wished they'd have years together, studying the stars, picking out Orion and Pleiades and wishing on the ones that had fallen.

To do this a ten thousand times more before Dimitra returned to Chios and a different kind of darkness descended.

Chapter 26

Hope's prison garb was stretched so tightly across her protruding belly, one of the seams had given way. Her hair was greasy, her nails rimmed with filth. Worse, was her color, that grayish pallor Patronas had long associated with those in prison.

The entry point of the Greek penal system, Korydallos Prison had expanded since the first time he'd been there years ago, the complex now housing well over twelve thousand people. According to the newspapers, international pressure was being brought to bear on the government to do something to alleviate the overcrowding, but given Greece's ongoing financial crisis, Patronas doubted anything would be done to improve the lives of those inside, especially since most of them—well over seventy percent — were migrants, people no one cared about, people who had no voice.

Hope Erikson was due to be transferred out of Korydallos within the next ten days and sent to the all-women's prison, Elaiona, in Thebes. The transfer had been arranged in part because she was American and the embassy was pressuring the authorities, but mainly because she was pregnant. Many new mothers served out their time in Elaiona; some of them keeping their babies with them for a full three years.

Patronas had phoned the prison administrator beforehand; and his processing into Korydallos was swift. A guard checked his identification card at the entrance and waved him through a metal gate that clanged shut behind him.

Papa Michalis was right behind him, dressed in a stiff, new robe. Patronas had suggested he accompany him to Karydallos, thinking he might prove useful during the interrogation. The priest had a gift for talking to people; and God knows they'd need it when they confronted Hope Erikson with the coroner's findings.

The interior of the prison reeked of bleach, but, strong as the disinfectant was, it didn't begin to mask the underlying stench of the place, the all-pervasive odor of human urine and waste. The hallways were poorly lit, what windows there so heavily barred, there was no day or night in the facility, only a kind of perpetual twilight.

A second guard led them through the women's wing to the cell where Hope Erikson was housed, unlocked the door and called for her to come forward. "Hope Erikson, *ela amesos.*"

Curious, Papa Michalis peered into the cell. There were six bunks, a woman in a state of undress lying on each of them. The majority of the inmates appeared to be from Eastern Europe, blondes with high cheekbones and pale eyes. Catching sight of him, one of them licked her lips and blew him a kiss.

"Come," she called in English. "Come to me. My name is Magda. I give you good time."

Standing up, she then did a little bump and grind, taking off her bra and twirling it around her head with her hand.

The priest jumped back like he'd been stung by wasps.

"Now you know why they're in here, Father," Patronas said. "They're hookers. Same as Mary Magdalene was before Jesus got a hold of her."

"Ladies of the night?"

"The day, too, most probably."

Getting up from her bunk, Hope grabbed the same small cosmetic bag Patronas had seen her with before, but the guard signaled for her to put it back and she did before exiting the cell, shoving it deep under her pillow.

Patronas was convinced she had something valuable secreted in inside and was afraid her cellmates would steal it while she was away. Some form of contraband probably.

In a hurry, he kept his suspicions to himself, not wanting to get caught up in jurisdictional red tape. If it was indeed contraband, it was up to the guards at Korydallos to find it and deal with it, not him. The clock was ticking and he couldn't afford to waste any time.

After handcuffing Hope Erikson, the guard walked her to another part of the prison, Patronas and Papa Michalis following close on his heels. They were now deep in the heart of Korydallos, numbered metal doors on either side of the corridor. Patronas heard a woman yelling in one of the cells, another voice jeering at her.

They ended up in a small, windowless room with a cement floor, the only furniture, a table with obscenities carved across the top and down the sides and three metal chairs. A steel ring was welded to the floor to secure inmates; and the guard snapped a metal chain to Hope's handcuffs and attached it to the ring.

"I'll wait outside," the guard told Patronas. "Knock on the door when you're finished and I'll take her back to her cell."

* * *

"I'm sorry you ended up here," Patronas told Hope. "Korydallos is a rough place."

"What difference does it make?" she said. "One prison or another, it's all the same."

Before starting the interrogation, Patronas turned on the mp3 player and read Hope her rights. He'd brought the murder book with him as well, planning to supplement the recording with his own impressions. "You said you knew about the tunnel. Did you know where it went? That it led directly to your house?"

"No. I never walked to the end of it. I always got out as soon as I could."

She paused for a moment. "I know it sounds strange, but on the day of the murder, I had the feeling someone was in the cave with me, that the killer was still there."

"You're saying you weren't alone in the cave at the time of the murder?" Papa Michalis said.

"That's what it felt like, like I was being watched, like we were being watched." She'd tacked the 'we' on as an afterthought.

"You and Thanasis?" the priest asked.

"Yes."

Patronas then took over, coldly listing the evidence against her. "The head of the forensic lab says the tests are conclusive: the only person who touched the murder weapon was you. Your fingerprints are all over it. You were the only one in the cave that day, Hope. You and you alone."

The priest and he had agreed beforehand on the roles they would play during the interrogation, settling on a primitive version of good cop/bad cop.

"And which role will you play?" Patronas had asked him.

"The good one, of course," Papa Michalis replied. "Afterall, I'm a priest."

Patronas had wanted to contradict him, to cite the child abuse scandal that had rocked the Catholic Church, the fact that there were many practicing pedophiles in the priesthood, but in the end, he had decided to let it go. Let the old fool think he was a holy man, an angel of God, bedecked in wings and a halo, floating around with his brethren up in the sky.

"That coroner man, he's wrong," Hope said. "Tell him to check again."

"No, he's not. We know you killed him, Hope. What we don't know is why."

"I told you I didn't do it. I didn't touch him."

"Yes, you did. The physical evidence is irrefutable."

Interrupting, the priest recited the famous passage from Corinthians:

'If I have a faith that can move mountains, but do not have love, I am nothing… Love is patient, love is kind…It is not easily angered and does not delight in evil but rejoices with the truth."

"Love does not delight in evil," he intoned. "It rejoices in truth. Truth, Hope. It rejoices in truth. Tell us the truth. I'm sure there were mitigating circumstances. I know you, Hope, I know you wouldn't have hurt him without cause."

She pushed her chair back and stood up. "This is stupid. You need to go. I'm pregnant and I need to rest."

She tried to leave, but the chain held her back. She looked down at it with a puzzled expression on her face, as if surprised to find herself handcuffed and shackled to the floor.

"Did he hit you that day?" Papa Michalis asked softly. "Is that why you killed him? If so, we can plead mitigating circumstances. Maybe get your sentence reduced. We've been to your house and met your in-laws. We saw how you lived there, Hope, what you were up against."

Wearily, she sank back down on the chair. Bowing her head, she sat there for a long time, silently crying.

"You know most of it already," she said, choking back tears.

"Why don't you start at the beginning?" Papa Michalis said. "When you and Thanasis first met? I know it was a long time ago, but I'd like to hear what drew you to him."

She nodded. "I was sunbathing on the beach in Vouliagmeni and he got out of the water and came and sat next to me. I remember I couldn't stop looking at him. He just took my breath away."

Patronas remembered what Vouros had said about the victim, how Hope's husband was the handsomest man she'd ever seen. "He was like a Hollywood screen star in the old days," she'd said. "Absolutely perfect. He had this way of looking at you and drawing you in. He could charm the birds right out of the sky."

Hope hesitated for a moment before continuing. "I never thought someone like that would be interested in me, but he was. We took a trip to Hydra later that summer; and I got sick. Thanasis stayed with me the whole time, sat by my bed and fed me tea with a spoon.

"With a spoon," she repeated, her voice full of wonder. "No one had ever done that before. My parents never paid much attention to me. 'You're a guest in our house,' my father told me once. 'See that you don't overstay your welcome.'

Hope's smile was bleak. "When Thanasis asked me to marry him, it was like all that went away, the feeling that I wasn't worth anything. It was like all my dreams had come true."

Love figured prominently in her tale. Love scrubbed clean, love that could move mountains and turn back time, fantasy love. It was like listening to the soundtrack of a Disney movie, Patronas thought with disgust, one of the early ones with the singing rabbits.

And then it had all gone sour.

"I don't know what happened," she said. "It was like he got bored or something. He didn't come home anymore and if he did, he was drunk. Once I caught him looking at me—it was terrible, that look—like he didn't want me there. Like I repelled him. I wanted things to be the way they were before; and I tried to make it that way. I'd put on make-up and sit on his lap, kiss him and try to get him to make love to me. But he'd just laugh and push me away. 'Too tired tonight, sweetheart' he'd say. 'Maybe tomorrow.'

"Do you think he married you for your money?" Patronas asked.

Hope seemed to crumble. "Maybe." She started to cry again. "I don't know. I never hid the fact that I had more money than he did. Maybe I should have, but I didn't. The first time he saw me, I was staying on a yacht. It wasn't mine—it belonged to a client of my father's—but I didn't tell him that. I let him think it was mine. He was convinced he was dating a rich American. Like Paris Hilton, only not as pretty.

"I got away with it until we were married and he found out the truth. I didn't have a yacht. I didn't have much of anything. My father *worked* in a bank. He didn't *own* one. I *did* inherit some money, but that came later. Thanasis insisted I give the money to him—he said I'd misled him at the beginning and that I owed it to him—and I did. I thought it would help us. He wouldn't have to work with his brothers anymore. He could start something on his own, maybe open another store. I don't know. But he didn't. He blew through most of it and then there was a family crisis and he gave Vasilis the rest. There'd been a car accident and there were a lot of hospital bills."

She said this last in a dismissive way, as if Achilles was of no importance, had no bearing on the story. "Anyway, after that, I was stuck. I didn't have a dollar to my name and no place to go. I had to live off of what my mother-in-law saw fit to give me."

She continued to complain about her financial situation for some time, repeating the same words over and over, always with the same air of grievance. She didn't mention Achilles once by name or express the slightest grief about his death.

Finding her level of self-involvement difficult to listen to, Patronas concentrated on his writing, laboriously entering every word she uttered in the murder book. He desperately wanted a cigarette, wanted to grind it out in her face.

Papa Michalis folded his hands in his lap. "Now, Hope, I want you to describe the day you found your husband's body, what happened in the cave."

As if hypnotized, Hope immediately switched gears and did as he'd requested. "It started in the morning. Thanasis was taking a shower and he'd left his phone out on the dresser. I don't know why, but for some reason, I picked it up and scrolled down through it. I know I shouldn't have, but he didn't always tell me things and I guess I was curious. Most of his emails were in Greek, but there was one in English from a woman named Carol. It had a photograph attached and I clicked on it. It was a picture of a little boy. I'd seen photographs of Thanasis at that age and that child looked exactly like him. I remember thinking they might have been twins.

"Thanasis came out at that point and he saw what I was doing. 'You miserable, little bitch,' he said. 'I can't turn around without you getting into my business.' After that, he got dressed and stormed off, slamming the door behind.

"I couldn't stop thinking about that picture, what it meant. I tried to talk to Thanasis in the parking lot later that day, but he just brushed me off. He said he had work to do and he walked away, heading toward the cave."

"Daphne said she'd seen you and you were very upset," Patronas said

Hope nodded. "I didn't tell her why. I just said we'd had a fight. She told me to go talk to him; maybe it would help."

"And you did?"

"Not right then. Later. I went in through the tunnel—I lied before about not knowing about it—and walked to the place he was sitting. I hated going that way, but I didn't want his mother to see me and tell me to get back to work. Thanasis had already started drinking—I could smell it on his breath—and he was in a foul mood.

'Who's that woman and why did she send you that picture?' I asked him. 'Who is he?' I was pretty sure I knew, but I wanted to hear him say it. 'He's my son,' Thanasis said. 'How old is he?' I asked. 'Six. His name is Petros and he's six years old.'

"I did the calculation in my head. I'd lost four babies by then, one of them the same year his so-called son was born. I'd started bleeding on the street and had to be rushed to the hospital. I was seven months pregnant at the time and I almost bled to death. And where was my loving husband? Where was Thanasis? He was playing around with some slut.

"I asked him who else knew. And he told me they all did. His brothers and their wives. Even his fucking mother. 'Now you know,' he told me his mother said. 'It's not you, Thanasis. It's her. Hope's the reason you don't have children.'

"He was mad by then and trying to hurt me. I asked him where he met the boy's mother and he said in a bar in Glyfada. They'd been together for six months and they'd stayed in touch after she went back to England. 'Not much,' he said as if that made it better. 'A birthday card, something at Christmas. That was it.'

"After he said that, I don't know what happened. Maybe I blacked out. All I could think about was my dead babies. The clothes I'd bought for them and had to throw away, the wooden crib I kept 'just in case.' All those years of trying and hemorrhages and pain.

"You should have seen him. He had such a smug look on his face as if having a girlfriend was something to be proud of. I remember wanting to hurt him."

"Where did you get the bottle?" Papa Michalis asked quietly.

"It was on the ground next to him. He reached for it, but I grabbed it away. I don't know how the glass got in his throat. I must have done it, but if I did, I don't remember. All I remember is picking up the bottle and swinging it at him. I must have kept hitting him. I don't know.

"After that, I left the same way and walked back down to the house. I wasn't feeling anything. I was just dead inside. Everyone was at the taverna by then, even the kids, so the house was empty. I didn't have time to take a shower, so I used a hose to wash myself off outside and put on a green shift, the same one I was wearing when that woman cop interviewed me after it was all over. When I got to the taverna, it was very busy and no one asked where I'd been or what I'd been doing. Stavros and the rest of them could barely keep up with the orders."

Papa Michalis was watching her closely. "Was he alive when you left the cave? Try to remember, Hope, and be careful how you answer. It's the crux of the case. It's important."

"I'm pretty sure he was moaning. It's all a blur."

"Did you get blood on your clothes when you hit him?" Patronas asked.

"Yes. I knew I needed to get rid of them and I put them in a plastic bag and threw them away at the taverna."

Patronas copied this down and starred it. Given that head wounds always bled copiously, the presence of blood on her person didn't necessarily mean she'd killed him. Still, it would be compelling evidence when the case went to trial.

"And later you went back to the cave?" He was trying to establish a timeline.

"Yes. My mother-in-law sent me there to get some oregano. I was glad. I didn't want to leave Thanasis in the cave. I wanted them to find him and for it to be over."

"And you saw your chance and you took it?"

She nodded.

Tearing a piece of paper out of the notebook, Patronas handed it to her and instructed her to write down everything she'd said, date it and sign it.

"What's going to happen to me?" she asked. "Will I be able to keep the baby?"

"Maybe. I know there are women and children in the prison in Thebes. I heard that they're planning to send you there, so you might be able to keep the baby with you for a time. But nothing is certain at this point. Don't get your hopes up."

Hope seized on this. "Hear that Hope? Don't get your hopes up!"

She then began to chant in a sing song voice. "Hope Erikson, she took an axe and gave her husband forty whacks. When she saw what she had done, she gave his mother fifty- forty-one." There was a hysterical edge to her voice.

Not knowing what to do, Patronas banged on the door and told the guard to take her away. He could still hear her as the man led her back to her cell, her crazed, dismembered voice.

"Took an axe, took an axe. Gave Thanasis forty whacks, forty whacks."

* * *

"Do you think there was any truth in what she said?" Papa Michalis asked Patronas.

Patronas looked over at him. "You mean about there being another person in the cave? I doubt it."

"Means, motive and opportunity. It would appear that you have all three."

"Yes. He betrayed her. Still she had a choice, Father. She could have left the wine bottle where it was and walked away. She didn't have to kill him."

"She said he was still alive…"

"That was her conscience talking. I'll wager he was dead before she left the cave."

Pulling out his crumpled pack of cigarettes, Patronas lit one and inhaled deeply. "It's a sad story. All she ever wanted was a baby and there she was almost six months pregnant, sure it would all work out and she would carry the baby to term. And then she finds out he'd fathered a child with another woman and it all comes crashing down on her."

Patronas was no stranger to marital angst. In that, he and Hope Erikson were similar. He'd lived in the same bleak space the American woman had inhabited, spent more time there than he cared to remember.

Like her, he, too, had longed for a child; and his ex-wife, Dimitra, had destroyed that dream, telling him in a fit of rage that she'd been tested and she was fine. He was the one who was sterile. True, he hadn't killed Dimitra, but he'd wanted to, wanted to smash her head in just as Hope had done. He knew firsthand the blinding rage that had consumed her and led her to do what she did, that act of complete and wanton savagery.

He was still badly shaken. "Jesus, Father, what people do to each other."

"Jesus played no part in this."

Chapter 27

Checking his watch, Patronas was surprised to see that he and Papa Michalis had only been inside Korydallos for three hours. On their way out, they'd passed a long line of people, waiting to enter, the metal gates clanging ominously as they opened and shut after each new arrival.

The complex was enormous; and it took them more than fifteen minutes to circumvent it. Razor-wire was everywhere, encasing the exterior walls like massive spider webs, great swaths of it hanging above the courtyard where the inmates exercised like malevolent trapeze wires. Worse were the handwritten signs Patronas saw hanging from some of the cell windows, mute appeals for dignity, solidarity and justice.

They had some time before returning to Spetses and ordered an early dinner at a place called 'Simply Burgers,' and ate it on the steps of a nearby church, Ekklisia Analipsi. The land surrounding the church was weedy and uncared for, the only evidence of human life an abandoned building site in the distance, steel rods protruding from the dusty soil.

Patronas' phone rang, stopped abruptly, then started up again. Worried, he checked the number. It was the administrator at the prison.

"Hope Erikson's gone berserk," the man told him. "You need to get here as fast as you can."

Patronas and the priest had just passed through the gates of the prison when a red helicopter passed directly above them and landed in the courtyard. The sound was deafening, the prison's high cement walls acting like an echo chamber.

It had a white cross on its side which meant it was a medical helicopter, here to airlift someone to the hospital.

Although the blades of the helicopter were still whirling, the medics wasted no time and rushed into the prison with a gurney, heading toward the area where Hope Erikson was housed. A few minutes later, they re-emerged with one of her cellmates, the Eastern European woman, who'd blown a kiss to Papa Michalis.

Soaked with blood, she had lost consciousness, her head lolling from side to side. She had an IV attached to her right arm, a plastic envelope hanging from a metal pole attached to the gurney. The liquid inside was clear, most probably some kind of saline solution. The crew of the helicopter swiftly loaded the woman inside, the engine whining as it picked up speed. Within seconds, she was airborne.

The prison administrator approached Patronas and quickly summarized what had happened. "Hope Erikson sliced one of her cellmates up with a razor. Apparently, she was threatening to kill herself and the woman tried to stop her."

Patronas' eyes were on the helicopter. It was bound for KAT, the trauma center in the north of Athens.

Greatly agitated, the administrator continued to talk. His phone kept ringing, his staff seeking advice on how to proceed.

"Get her out of there," he bellowed at one point. "Put her in solitary."

Eventually, the phone stopped ringing. "The embassy's been informed along with the media," he told Patronas. "We need to prepare a statement."

Patronas and Papa Michalis followed the prison administrator into his office. On the way the administrator went into detail about what he learned from the guards about the incident. He was brief and to the point.

"I have established to my satisfaction that the razor did not come from inside the prison. Hope Erikson had to have brought it in with her, either secreted on her person or in that little bag she always carried. My staff is not at fault. As far as I have been able to determine, they did a thorough job. They said they frisked her before they locked her up and ran her and her stuff through a metal detector; and I believe them. But accidents happen and somehow the razor got passed them."

Patronas nodded. The administrator was working hard to justify himself and his staff.

"Fortunately, another cellmate saw the blood," the man added. "At first, she thought it was Hope Erikson's, that she was having a miscarriage and losing the baby, but then she saw the wound on the other woman's arm. 'I saw blood pouring out of her,' she said, 'and I tore off a rag and wrapped it around her.'"

"Where's Hope Erikson now?"

"Locked up in the *psychiatrio*, psych ward. The guards dragged her there and tied her to a bed. A psychiatrist has been into see her and he shot her full of as many tranquilizers as he could, given that she's pregnant. He'll evaluate her after she's calmed down. Right now, there's no speaking with her. From what he said, she's completely hysterical. *Treli einai.* Crazy.

* * *

Patronas and Papa Michalis spent another hour in the office of the administrator, preparing their own statement about Hope's demeanor during the interrogation. She had not seemed overly distraught, Patronas was careful to write, nor had she spoken of suicide while they were together, nor indicated in any way what she intended to do.

"How can you write this?" the priest whispered, reading over his shoulder. "She *was* distraught. These are *lies*."

"Take that up with God. In the meantime, keep your voice down."

Patronas handed in the statement and stood up to go. "If I were you, I'd say it was an accident," he advised the administrator. "That way no one will be blamed if there's an inquiry. Not my colleague on Spetses, Melissa Costas, who was in charge of Hope Erikson until she left the island, or the guards at Korydallos Prison, who were supposed to be monitoring her. Better for everyone involved."

Unfortunately, unlike Diogenes, Patronas had found the one honest man.

"The facts stand and I cannot change them to protect a colleague," the administrator said. "No question, a mistake was made, but it was made on Spetses, not within the walls of this prison. Now good day, gentlemen."

* * *

Stathis was livid. "Heads are going to roll on this one, Patronas. You had Hope Erikson in custody on Spetses. How the hell did she get that razor?"

Patronas hemmed and hawed, rambling on at length about how carefully the staff had handled Hope Erikson, how diligent everyone in the station had been. "Everything we did was done in accordance with standard police operating procedure. Handcuffs at all times, etc. etc. Everything, sir. If anyone's responsible, it's those guards at Korydallos."

"One more time," Stathis said. "Where did Hope Erikson get that razor?"

"I have no idea, sir. None whatsoever."

* * *

Unfortunately, Stathis found out. Patronas had no idea how he learned about Hope Erikson's ill-fated trip to Melissa Costas' apartment, but he did. The information could have come from anyone. Stathis' sources were many, scattered far and wide throughout Greece, but Patronas suspected someone in the station must have told him, one of the younger men seeking to ingratiate himself with the boss in Athens.

Wasting no time, Stathis fired Melissa Costas immediately.

In a brutal email, he informed her she was being terminated for 'dereliction of duty' and should turn in her badge immediately. She was no longer a police officer. He went on to describe in no uncertain terms what had transpired while Hope Erikson had been in Costas' custody, the exact sequence of events, according to multiple sources.

"In violation of standard operating procedure, you took Hope Erikson, a suspected murderer, to your apartment to take a shower, and, subsequently, left her alone in your bathroom where she stole a packet of razor blades. Razor blades she, subsequently, used while in Korydallos Prison to assault another inmate. The prison authorities found the packet of razor blades on her bunk; and, when they questioned her, she freely admitted she'd stolen them from you, 'when you weren't looking.'" This last Stathis had written in bold face and underlined three times.

Desperate, Costas called Stathis at the station in Piraeus and begged to be reinstated. He was curt and to the point. "You're done as a cop, Costas. Pack your things and get out."

* * *

Stathis ordered Patronas to stay on as head of the police department in Spetses until he could find a replacement for Melissa Costas, Tembelos to serve as his second-in-command.

"For the time being, you're in charge," he told Patronas.

He didn't mention the priest. Evidently, he'd forgotten Papa Michalis existed.

Eyeing the priest with impatience, Patronas only wished he could. Papa Michalis now accompanied him everywhere he went, talking endlessly when he wasn't eating; and sometimes even then, spewing bread crumbs or whatever else he'd ingested all over everyone. Croissants were especially bad, so much so, Patronas had given up eating breakfast with him.

Worse, the priest remained fixated on the case, convinced Hope Erikson was innocent and should be released from jail.

"First of all, she's not in jail," countered Patronas. "She's in the *trelokomio,* the booby hatch. Second, all the evidence points to her; and third and most importantly, the case is closed. We're done, Father. As soon as Stathis finds someone to take over the department, we're on our way back to Chios."

Following the debacle at Korydallos, the media had been relentless; the story being bandied about by reporters was that Hope Erikson's attack on the Eastern European prostitute had taken place because of the unspeakable conditions inside the prison. Earlier that year, an inmate had gone on a hunger strike and nearly died, suggesting a systematic pattern of abuse and neglect. The firestorm continued over the next few days; TV crews parked in front of the prison.

Still recovering, Hope was exploiting the situation for all it was worth, complaining to anyone who would listen about how badly she'd been treated, virtually tortured by police to secure a confession. "I didn't kill my husband," she repeated in both Greek and English. "Someone else did. I'm innocent. I swear it."

One of these statements made it onto the evening news, a CNN reporter talking to Hope as she was being escorted into the courthouse for a preliminary hearing. Patronas and the priest were in the lobby of the hotel when the interview was broadcast and they paused to watch it.

Ever the victim, she kept talking about how exhausted she was, clearly using her pregnancy to appeal to English-speaking viewers. She'd been well briefed by her attorney and knew exactly what she was doing—putting pressure on the Greek authorities in an effort to leverage herself out of prison.

Patronas turned to the priest. "You still think she's innocent?"

"Yes, yes. No question about it. She might be self-absorbed and manipulative, a narcissist to the very core of her being, but no matter. Such character flaws are irrelevant. They have no bearing on the case. A person might be a psychopath—a real, living breathing psychopath—but that doesn't automatically mean that person is guilty. What a person *is* does not preclude innocence."

"Yes, it does Father," Patronas said. "Especially with psychopaths. As a group, they are not known for their benevolence."

Hope's mother-in-law, Sophia, had rushed to her side after the incident with the razor, spending money she didn't have to buy a boat ticket and renting a hotel room near the psychiatric clinic where Hope was now housed. She visited her every day and spoke often with the doctor supervising her care.

Patronas was convinced the old woman was positioning herself to be on hand when Hope gave birth, wanting to have unlimited access to the baby when the time came. She, too, had a master plan: to gain custody of the child if and when the psychiatrist deemed Hope Erikson unfit to be a mother.

"Someone has to look after him," she'd told Patronas. "A child cannot grow up in jail."

"Hope can keep the baby with her until it's three years old. There are more than thirty women like her in the prison in Thebes, Elaiona."

"And after he's three?" The triumph in the old woman's voice was unmistakable. She might have to wait, but one day victory would be hers. "He can't stay with her after that. He'll have to come to me."

There'd been more than a little of rejoicing when she'd said this, a gleefulness that put Patronas off; and he could well imagine the effect it must have on Hope. The old woman continued to dress in black—he'd seen her outside the hospital—reinforcing her vulture-like presence. A *gypas*, carrion eater, if ever there was one.

Patronas had informed Hope's brother about what had happened, but doubted he'd put in an appearance at the trial. He hadn't visited Hope once at Korydallos, nor in the hospital where she'd been taken, nor had he asked how she was when Patronas spoke to him on the phone.

Patronas brooded off and on about his own conduct in the case. He'd known Hope Erikson was in trouble when he'd interviewed her that day in the prison, but hadn't bothered to alert the authorities or get her the help she needed, nor had he shared his suspicions about the contents of the cosmetics bag. He'd just assumed it was cigarettes or pills. It had never occurred to him that she might be hiding razor blades.

The prison administrator had said no risk assessment had been done on Hope Erikson when she'd first arrived at the complex. There simply wasn't enough staff to screen for mental illness. Crazy as she was, she'd been on her own there. And Patronas had known it and done nothing.

At the very least, he might have saved the Eastern European woman if he'd interceded, who in addition to having the artery in her arm severed, had been slashed across the face and nearly lost an eye.

Normally, he felt a sense of closure at the end of a case, but not this time. He remained unsettled by what he'd learned about Hope Erikson, her abiding loneliness and obsessive love for her husband. As her sister-in-law had said, she was indeed 'hopeless' and in all likelihood would spend years in prison—if not for the murder of her husband, then for the assault on Michalis Constantinos and her cellmate at Korydallos. And, worse, her child would be taken for her.

He worried about her baby, too, as yet unborn, and its melancholic future. What joy would it know growing up in Sophia's house?

In the end, he felt as if all the hours he'd put in on the case had been misspent, that he'd wasted his time, seeking to discover the killer of Thanasis Papadopoulos. The victim had been a worthless man, someone who'd left nothing but a trail of misery in his wake. Whoever had cut his throat had done the world a favor.

* * *

Late September, the tourist season was drawing to a close; and Spetses was very quiet. In spite of the lack of activity, Patronas suited up and went into the police station every morning, where inevitably, around eleven o'clock, Papa Michalis and Giorgos Tembelos would turn up and spend the next five hours doing nothing.

Patronas strove to maintain a semblance of order and insisted they write lengthy reports at least twice a week, outlining their activities in detail, which he then attached to an email and sent onto Stathis.

"Make things up if you have to. Pretend you're busy. Turn a lost dog into a lost child. A missing purse into a bank robbery. Whatever you have to do. Money is tight and the government's laying off public employees all over Greece. You don't want to lose your jobs."

Melissa Costas had cleaned out her office three weeks before and vanished without a trace. Although Patronas called her numerous times, she never answered the phone, nor she responded to any of his texts or emails.

Concerned, he drove by her apartment building one evening. A neighbor heard him knocking and opened the door of the adjoining apartment. "I often see her out by the old school," she told him. "She goes there first thing in the morning and walks around the grounds for hours. Always alone, *Kakomira*. Poor thing."

Patronas had mixed feelings about what had befallen his colleague. It had been stupid what she'd done, no question about it, but then Costas was a rookie and rookies make mistakes.

Worried, he called Vouros and asked her to reach out to her.

"I'll tell her I need her help," Vouros said. "That there's a crisis of some kind. What Melissa wants most is to be of service to others. It runs deep in her."

"Most cops feel like that."

Vouros made a strangled noise.

"Maybe," she said in a certain tone. "I suppose you could say that."

* * *

The priest occasionally read the Bible aloud, sharing what he considered to be the more relevant passages with Patronas and Tembelos, who both did their best to ignore him. A strange juxtaposition, such behavior in a police station which by anyone's standards was hardly a holy place, but then that was Papa Michalis. He was full of contradictions, railing against gluttony while happily eating his own food and everyone else's at the table.

In marked contrast, Tembelos dwelt exclusively in the world of the flesh, female flesh to be exact, great expanses of it contained in the girly magazine he brought into work. "Will you look at that!" he'd bellow and hold up a photo. And there for all the world to see would be a naked woman, so physically endowed Patronas doubted she could stand upright.

Papa Michalis would start reading louder at this point, seeking to drown Tembelos out, and end up screeching like a parrot.

Then one morning, the priest went off in another direction. Picking up the murder book, he waved it in the air. "I was reading this last night and I found something you might be interested in," he said. "It seems Daphne Papadopoulos did not offer to take a lie detector test."

He set the notebook down in front of Patronas. "Here. Take a look."

Putting on his reading glasses, Patronas dutifully read the portion the priest was referring to.

"We need to listen to those audio files again," said Papa Michalis. "Daphne and her husband rehearsed every word they said, I'd stake my life on it. If she didn't volunteer to take the test, there was a reason for it."

Opening the drawer of his desk, Patronas handed him the mp3 player. "Help yourself."

After fumbling around, the priest managed to start the mp3 player and Daphne Papadopoulos' voice filled the room.

Forced to listen, Patronas caught something he hadn't noticed before, an evasive note in much of what she said, a hesitation in key places.

He leaned back in his chair, mentally reviewing what she and her husband had told him. He'd missed something, he remembered thinking. Not what one of them *had* said, what they *hadn't*.

And there it was. The priest had found it.

He'd never told anyone—least of all Papa Michalis—that the case still troubled him. Wife gets angry. Wife bludgeons husband to death. Game, set and match. It all seemed a little too pat.

What if Hope Erikson had been telling the truth and someone else *had* been in the cave with her that day. Someone who hated the victim? She had said she felt like she was being watched. What if she actually had been?

She had admitted she hit her husband with the bottle, but claimed he was alive when she left, had sworn up and down she had no memory of ramming the broken glass into his throat.

Taking off his glasses, Patronas rubbed his eyes. "If you had to choose between Daphne and Hope which one would you choose?"

Papa Michalis didn't hesitate. "Why, Daphne of course. It stands to reason. It wasn't Hope Erikson, who sustained the greatest loss at the hands of the victim, Thanasis Papadopoulos. It was the boy's mother. It was Daphne Papadopoulos."

He had Patronas' full attention now. "Go on."

"I know you have little use for the Bible, Yannis. But it does provide some useful insights into human behavior. For example, when David's son,

Absalom, was killed, David begged God to be taken instead. 'Absalom, Absalom, my son, my son, would God that I had died for thee!' And I'm sure Daphne Papadopoulos felt the same way. Her grief must have been terrible, also her rage. If you listen carefully to the audio file, you can hear it in her voice."

Pushing a button, the priest replayed that portion of the interview.

It was exactly as the priest described, Patronas realized as he listened. The first time he'd only heard Daphne's sorrow, her paralyzing grief; but now he heard the rage. She'd loathed Thanasis with every cell of her being.

The priest shut off the machine and handed it back to Patronas. "I never heard anything close to that in what Hope told us. Not here in the police station or later when we spoke to her in Korydallos Prison. There were a number of other emotions, but not that one, not hate. The overriding emotion when she talked about her husband was love. Thwarted love, disappointed love, betrayed love, but always it was love."

"Not hate, love?"

"Correct. Do you remember her description of their trip to Hydra? How she got sick and Thanasis fed her soup with a spoon? It sounded to me like she wanted to go back there and relive that moment in time. You could hear the longing for him in her voice. We've spoken to a number of killers over the years, but she is not one of them. "

"But she admitted it. She said hit him with the bottle."

"Things are not always as they seem. Surely after all these years, you know that. Trust me, you need to talk to Daphne Papadopoulos again. She bears a second look."

The priest tucked his hands in the sleeves of his robe. "May God forgive me, but I always questioned the conduct of the Holy Mother at the crucifixion, the way she wept and carried on at the foot of the cross. It seemed unnatural to me. Even when I was a student at the seminary and awash with religious fervor, it seemed unnatural to me. Why didn't she rise up and defend her son? Fight the soldiers and grab the nails out of their hands? At the very least, bring him some water. Real water, not the vinegar the Romans gave him, vinegar mixed with gall. I know my mother would have. She was a tigress when it came to me. She never would have stood by if I was being nailed to a cross. She would have gone after whoever was doing it with everything she had, fought and raged and screamed and kept coming at them and coming at them until they ran a spear through her and killed her. She would have risked everything to save me and willingly died in my place."

His voice rose. "Absalom, Absalom! My son, my son, would God that I had died for thee.' Mothers are like that, Yannis, and Daphne Papadopoulos was a mother."

They sat there in silence a few minutes, thinking it through.

"This is a heavy burden," Papa Michalis said. "She might welcome the opportunity to confess and be rid of it. Neither one of us has ever had a son. We cannot possibly know what it's like to lose one. How it feels to live alongside the man, who took him from you."

"She said it was as if the ground had opened up and she was cast straight into hell."

"According to Revelations, hell is a fiery lake full of burning sulfur. But maybe it's not, Yannis. Maybe it's only this."

He shook his head. "Ugly all of it."

* * *

Patronas approached Daphne Papadopoulos at the taverna that evening. "Let's go for a walk." he said. "I need to talk to you. Some new evidence has come to light."

She was wiping down a table and she looked up at him, cloth in hand. "Will it take long?" There was a sense of resignation in her voice, defeat.

"Maybe," he said. "I don't know."

Skirting around the two houses, he led her up into the hills. Overhead, the clouds were threaded with gold, alive with the colors of the setting sun; and the scent of the pine trees hung heavy on the air. Chryssoula's children were playing a game of hide and seek in the wooded area behind their house; and Patronas could hear them in the distance as he and Daphne climbed.

Swallows were everywhere, soaring and careening in the tall grass.

Daphne stopped and watched them for a few minutes. "Achilles loved birds," she told Patronas, nodding to the swallows. "If he'd grown up, he might have gone the way of Icarus. Made wings for himself out of wax and feathers and taken flight."

They continued to walk, eventually reaching the back entrance to the cave.

"You were in there that day, weren't you?" Patronas said. "You were in the cave. You followed Hope in there. I checked with the people you said you were serving and they said you disappeared around the time of the murder. They assumed you were in the kitchen, but you weren't, were you, Daphne? You were in the cave."

Patronas hadn't spoken to the witnesses. It was a fabrication, this last, but such was police work.

She shook her head. "Those people are wrong. I was working. I was waiting on their tables just like I said."

"You don't have to worry. This is just you and me talking. I am not going to record what you say. I have no wire secreted on my person. I just want to know."

The strain shadowed her face. "No," she said, backing away. "No."

"It was you, who killed him, wasn't it, Daphne? You picked up the bottle and finished what Hope had started. You cut his throat with it."

Tears filled her eyes; and she tried to get away, but Patronas grabbed her arm and held it.

"I don't blame you, Daphne. Given what he did to Achilles, I probably would have done the same thing."

He could hear Chryssoula's children, calling to one another in the gathering darkness, their game of hide and seek continuing. They were in a different universe than the one he and Daphne Papadopoulos now inhabited.

"I'm sorry," Patronas said, abruptly letting go of her arm. "I wish I didn't have to do this."

She began to cry in earnest, ugly, unchecked sobs that wracked her body and made her gasp for air.

"It was simple actually," she whispered, wiping her eyes. "I saw Hope walking toward the back entrance of the cave; and I knew if I went in the front entrance, the one by the beach, I would get there long before she did and that's what I did. Thanasis had his back to me and I was careful to be very quiet. I hid behind one of the shelves and I waited. They had a big fight and she grabbed the wine bottle out of his hands and hit him with it. There was a lot of blood and she panicked when she saw it and ran out. Thanasis was laying on the ground, holding his head, and I picked up the bottle, slammed it against the wall and broke it, then I jammed it into his neck. 'There,' I told him. "That's for Achilles."

"I'd been wearing a scarf and I took it off before I did it and wrapped it around the bottle. I was very careful. I didn't want to leave my fingerprints behind on the glass. I've seen those forensic shows on television and I knew you'd dust it for prints. I wasn't going to jail for killing him."

"What about your clothes?"

"They were already dirty, so they weren't a problem. I just picked up a can of olive oil and walked back to the taverna, put on a clean apron and went back to work. I figured if anyone stopped me, I'd tell them we needed the oil, that's why I'd gone there."

"What happened to the apron, the one with the blood on it?"

"I threw it into the fire and burned it. I didn't plan to kill him." There was a plea in her voice. "I didn't get up in the morning and say to myself, 'today's the day.' I just saw my chance and I took it."

"In other words, the killing was spontaneous, not premeditated. We are still waiting on the DNA, but once we get it, I'm sure yours will be all over the victim. It's like truth, DNA. It's impossible to hide. We would have caught up with you sooner or later."

Patronas hated what he was doing, hounding someone so damaged; and he felt sick about it. *Maybe everyone is right and we are pigs.*

"I'm sorry," he said again.

She asked to be allowed to spend the night at home and Patronas agreed. The last boat had left Spetses hours ago. There was no way she could get off the island. He saw no harm in it.

"I'll come for you first thing in the morning. You need to prepare yourself. To be ready."

"I will be. I just need a little more time and then you can lock me up forever."

She touched his sleeve. "I know you feel bad about this, Chief Inspector, but I'm glad you came. I'm glad it's finally over."

Chapter 28

"This is for Achilles…." the priest repeated. "Oh, that poor woman."

He and Patronas were sitting in the lobby of the hotel. Tembelos had already gone upstairs to bed; and the night clerk had left hours ago.

"Where is she now?" the old man asked. "Did you take her into custody?"

Patronas shook his head. "I'm thinking of letting her go."

"You can't be serious. You're an officer of the law, Yannis. Your job is to bring suspects in and book them. It's up to the jury to decide who goes to jail and who goes free. And later, upon death, it's up to God to rule on them."

"Damnit, Father," snapped Patronas. "it's always God with you. God has nothing to do with this."

"Of course, He does. You're talking about judgement here, Yannis. What is right and what is wrong. This woman is a murderer. She broke one of the cardinal rules, not just of Greece, but of civilized life. She killed a man."

"She's no threat to anyone."

"Be that as it may, you do not define justice. You only serve it. Arrest this woman and turn her over to the magistrate in Athens. That's what you should do and that's all you should do. Letting her get away with murder will not save her. She's lost, Yannis. Lost since that day in Moschato. You can't fix what's wrong with her. I know you want to, but you can't."

"I don't see what difference it will make. It won't get Hope Erikson out of jail. She assaulted two people. They'll lock her up for that if for nothing else. I don't see the point."

"I'm telling you it must be done," Papa Michalis countered. "You're the one who taught me that. 'Human nature demands it,' you once said. 'We're animals. One of the fiercest predators that ever walked the earth and without the law, we would devour each other.'

Tired of arguing, Patronas started up the stairs.

"Did you hear what I said?" the priest called after him.

"It's hard not to," Patronas said. "You're shouting."

* * *

Daphne Papadopoulos drove off a cliff at some point that night. She was killed instantly and the ensuing fireball ignited the hillside.

The police had returned the KIA to the family after Hope Erikson's abortive ride; and surveying the blackened wreckage, Patronas was sure that was the car Daphne had been driving. She'd chosen the location well, a deserted stretch of road with no guardrails.

Judging by the damage, the car had rolled over a number of times before coming to rest at the bottom of the cliff and bursting into flames. Given the isolated nature of the site, the police had not been summoned immediately. It was only after the fire had spread that a local resident had called the accident in.

So far there'd been no effort made to extract the body, only to douse the flames and prevent them from consuming the surrounding area. Clouds of black smoke continued to billow up from the burning car and there was an acrid, oily feel to the air.

The flames were bright in the darkness and seeing them, Patronas hung his head. This time her hell had been real.

* * *

"She was having trouble sleeping and she would take the car and drive around," Vasilis Papadopoulos said of his wife. "She said it calmed her and I thought that's what she'd done. That's why I didn't notify anybody."

Tears welled up in his eyes. "I don't understand it. She must have driven that road a thousand times." He looked exhausted, the strain of the previous week showing on his face.

"Maybe she dozed off," Patronas said. "It happens sometimes."

Papadopoulos handed him an envelope. "I found this yesterday. She left it for you."

After Vasilis Papadopoulos left the station, Patronas barricaded himself in his office and sat there for a long time, staring at the envelope. He could hear the phone ringing in the front of the station, voices calling. It all seemed very far away, the only reality the paper he held in his hand.

Ripping open the envelope, he unfolded the letter and read it. In it, Daphne Papadopoulos absolved him of all responsibility and stated he had played absolutely no role in what she'd done. It had been her decision and hers alone. "I do not regret killing Thanasis. He brought nothing to this life, he only took away. I did what I did and I am at peace with it. I've been wanting to kill myself since the day I lost Achilles; and now I finally found the courage to do it. I welcome death. I don't know if you know this, but I grew up in Crete, in Heraklion. Katzanzakis' grave is there and his tomb has these words engraved on it: 'I want nothing. I fear nothing. I am free.' And so, I will be when you read this."

As he'd suspected, she had deliberately taken her own life.

A car accident. There were parallels with the death of her son. A certain symmetry. No one had seen the accident, but, judging by the damage to the KIA, she'd sped up before she'd driven off the cliff, thereby eliminating any chance of survive. In the note, she wrote that she had been on this course ever since that day in Moschato, when she'd gathered up her son's broken body and ridden in the ambulance with him to the hospital.

Weeping softly, Patronas read and re-read the note. 'I want nothing. I fear nothing. I am free.'

And he prayed she would be. Prayed she and her son be reunited and don wings like Icarus, only this time survive their long journey across the sky.

Chapter 29

The owner of the rooming house had been endeavoring to turn the front yard of his establishment into a bar with limited success, setting out tables and chairs and stringing lights up in the trees. He'd even installed an exceeding ugly ceramic fountain, water trickling into a basin held by two naked little boys.

"Sounds like a kid pissing," Tembelos observed the first time he heard it.

Perhaps influenced by his age, Patronas had thought it sounded more like a man with prostrate trouble, but he hadn't shared this with his friend. Far younger, Tembelos would find out soon enough. It was Patronas' fervently held belief that time and tide and prostrate trouble wait for no man.

Still, the garden wasn't a bad place in the evening; and he often stopped off there after work and had a beer before heading upstairs to bed.

Aside from the priest, he hadn't told anyone else about the role Daphne Papadopoulos had played in the murder, nor had he shared what she'd written in the letter, that she'd deliberately set out to take her own life. Her husband, Vasilis, was grief-stricken enough. Knowing his wife had committed suicide would only increase his suffering.

He was surprised to see Melissa Costas waiting for him one night, half-hidden in the shadows. The garden was deserted; she was the only customer.

Never easy to talk to, she proved to be even worse than he remembered. Still the two of them soldiered on, talking about Spetses and the weather. A little conversation followed by long bouts of silence.

Signaling the waiter, Patronas ordered a bottle of wine and some appetizers. Costas downed the wine too fast, throwing back one glass after another. Worried, Patronas filled her plate with food and urged her to eat, but she just shook her head. She'd lost weight since the last time he'd seen her, was even more bony, judgmental and grim.

They'd finished one bottle of wine and were starting in on their second when all at once she began to talk, the words just tumbling out of her. She was well on her way to being drunk by then; and Patronas had trouble following what she said.

"I fucked up," she said. "Not just with the razor, with every fucking thing."

"Join the club," Patronas said. "We all did. Don't fault yourself."

"It was Daphne Papadopoulos, wasn't it? She's the one who killed him. I heard after you talked to her, she drove off a cliff."

"Leave it," he said. "I can't bear to think about it."

"It's not your fault, you know. You're a homicide detective. You were just doing your job."

"What I should have done was leave well enough alone, but I didn't. It's like a sickness with me. I have to ferret out the truth, no matter what the cost. Papa Michalis raised the issue of Daphne Papadopoulos' possible involvement and off I went to confront her. There were mitigating circumstances and I should have recognized them, but instead I kept after her. I harassed an already fragile woman and pushed her to the breaking point."

"That's what cops do," Costas' voice was shrill, her self-righteousness reasserting itself. "They get to the bottom of things."

To illustrate the pitfalls of compassion, she went on to describe how a single act of kindness, "that miserable shower," had ruined her life. "All those years I served and I have nothing to show for it. No salary, no pension. How am I going to live?"

Alecto, Patronas remembered her men had called her. Always angry. She'd been well named.

He gazed out at the darkness, his mind returning to the conversation he'd had with Daphne Papadopoulos. To the words he hadn't said, the sorrow he hadn't expressed about the death of her son. Wishing with all his heart he'd left her alone. Her grief was punishment enough. Whatever punishment the court meted out would have been minor in comparison.

"How do you do it?" Costas asked, stumbling over the words. "How do you leave it behind? The work, I mean. When it all goes to hell. No matter how hard I try, I can't get away from it. I keep going over what I did wrong in my head. Over and over again. I just can't turn it off."

"Sometimes I go swimming and that helps a little," he said, eager to change the subject. "I dive in and I swim until I'm exhausted. There's a cove in front of my house and I go back and forth, back and forth until I feel better."

She peered at him. "You do that here?"

"Yes. Ever since Daphne Papadopoulos died. I keep hoping it will make me feel better. Wash my sins away." He sighed. "So far it hasn't."

But Costas wasn't listening. "You know what I do?" She looked down at her empty glass. "I drink."

"I wouldn't do that, if I were you, Melissa. Alcohol might take the edge off at first, but then one day it comes to own you and all you can think about where your next shot is coming from."

Her voice was unsteady. "I think that day is already here."

A few minutes later, she vomited into the bushes. Patronas did what he could for her, holding her hair back and wiping her mouth with a napkin after she'd finished.

A dress rehearsal for Dimitra.

He summoned the waiter, ordered a pot of coffee and two ham and cheese sandwiches and coaxed them down her.

"I've been thinking," he said when she started to sober up. "I might have a solution to your problems."

"Which one?" she said. "As you might have noticed, I have many."

"Your unemployment. I don't know if you know this, but in addition to commanding the police force, I also run a security detail for Harvard University on Chios. Its archeology department has a big excavation going in the northern part of the island; and Giorgos Tembelos and I oversee it for them. We really need someone on-site twenty-four hours a day; and between the two jobs, we're stretched pretty thin. We could use another person."

"Are you serious? You want *me* to come work for *you*?" There was a fair amount of self-derision in her voice, but also a measure of hope.

"Yes, I do. I'll be truthful, Melissa, the job isn't much, but at least you'll get a salary. All you have to walk the perimeter of the site and keep an eye out. Make a note of what the workers uncover in the trenches and make sure none of it goes home with them when they leave for the day."

She thought about it. "I have nothing holding me here," she said, working it out. "And there isn't much to move. The apartment came furnished and things were never that important to me. When would you want me to start?"

"The first of November. That should give you plenty of time."

Patronas had no illusions about her prospects. All he'd done was hold out the promise of a job; it was up to her to do the rest. He didn't know how far gone she was, if she could stop drinking.

* * *

Dimitra called Patronas later that night; and he was unable to sleep after speaking with her, plagued by dark visions of the two of them motoring to the hospital together. He'd heard chemotherapy makes people nauseous; and he feared she'd vomit all over him the way Costas had.

"Compassion," he told himself. "You need to show compassion. She's not the woman you remember. She's sick now."

But he still felt a churning in his gut every time he thought of spending time with her. It was as if he'd been poisoned and his body was trying to expel the toxin.

He still hadn't told Lydia about Dimitra, thinking he'd do it in person when he returned to Chios, gauge Lydia's reaction as he went along and pull back if necessary.

"Abort, abort," Tembelos had urged when the two of them discussed the situation. "It's not too late. Your plane's on fire. Strap on your parachute and jump. Jump, Yannis, while you still can."

The next morning Patronas ate breakfast outside in the garden, enjoying the feel of the sun on his face and the early morning warmth. Somewhere in the distance, a canary was singing, another answering in turn, the two of them trilling back and forth as they welcomed the day.

Tembelos and Papa Michalis joined him a few minutes later and he told them about his conversation with Melissa Costas. "We had a long talk and I offered her a job."

Tembelos slammed his coffee mug down. "You *what*?"

"I told her she could start in November. Not in the police department—Stathis would never allow that—working with us at the dig site."

"You can't be serious."

"Stathis fired her. Way things are, she'll never get another job."

"We're running a charity now?" Working himself up, Tembelos was getting madder and madder. "A rehabilitation service for wayward cops? This might be the craziest thing you've ever done and believe me, Yannis, you've done plenty. You can barely manage one woman and now you're going to have three of them in your life—Lydia, Melissa and Dimitra. What the hell are you thinking?"

Patronas was eating a piece of bread and he dusted the crumbs off his shirt. "I saw a chance to save someone and I took it, Giorgos. I'll pay her out of my salary if that will make it easier for you."

Papa Michalis interrupted. "It says in the Old Testament, 'he who saves a life, saves the world entire.' And you have, Yannis, you've saved hers. You're a good man."

"I don't know how 'good' he is, Father," Tembelos said sourly. "If it were me, I would have gone with stupid."

* * *

Stathis appointed a successor to Melissa Costas three days later, a slow-moving, ungainly man named Petros Makrakis. He took his time when he introduced himself to Patronas, pausing in midsentence and looking around as if he'd been reading a book and lost his place. Stathis also announced the staff at the station would be cut in half, only Pappas and Ritsos would continue to serve on Spetses, Constantinos and Simonidis to be reassigned to Stathis' own division in Piraeus.

Patronas was sure one of them had betrayed Melissa Costas, called Stathis and told him how Costas had driven Hope Erikson to her apartment and let her take a shower, in flagrant disregard of police protocol; and that the new posting to Piraeus was a reward. However, he didn't know which one of them it was and kept his suspicions to himself. While the move might be good for their careers, he didn't envy them the new assignment. Serving under Stathis? It would be, as Tembelos said, like working for King Herod.

* * *

Patronas hurriedly packed his suitcase and paid the bill for himself and the others at the rooming house. He called Costas before bordering the ferry and changed her starting date, telling her to come to Chios two weeks later than he'd initially said.

"I have to return to Athens and testify at the trial of Hope Erikson and I want to make sure I'll be back on Chios when you arrive, help you with your transition."

Patronas was sure at the very least Hope Erikson would be convicted of two counts of assault. However, the prosecutor in Athens told him he would not push for the maximum sentence in either case, nor would he pursue the charge of murder.

Patronas was questioned at length at the trial, both by the prosecution and the defense, primarily about Hope Erikson's demeanor when he'd met with her at Korydallos Prison.

"Was she of sound mind?" her lawyer asked him at one point.

"No, she was not. In fact, I felt like I was watching her deteriorate right before my eyes. She kept singing and talking nonsense. It was very unsettling."

"A psychotic break?" he offered.

"Yes," Patronas answered. "That was my feeling."

Hope Erikson was duly sentenced to three years for assault, which meant she and the baby would remain together both in the prison in Thebes and after she was released; and her mother-in-law, Sophia, would never gain custody.

"*Dolofonia se vrasmo,*" the prosecutor said at the conclusion of the trial. Her soul was boiling. "Nothing she did was premeditated."

* * *

Costas turned up in Chios on schedule. Sporting a new haircut and a painted face, she waved as she got off the plane.

Tembelos was astounded by the transformation and he continued to stare at her open-mouthed "Well, at least the hair spray's gone," he whispered to Patronas. "But as for the rest, your geisha analogy is holding up nicely. That white skin, those spots of rouge. All she needs is a kimono."

"Give her a chance," Patronas whispered back. "She's trying to find herself."

"Where's she looking? Tokyo?"

After loading up her suitcases, they drove her to her new apartment and helped her get settled. Patronas had found a place near the University of the Aegean in the center of town. On the top floor, it faced the harbor and had come furnished. She was delighted when she saw it and went from room to room, opening all windows and sticking her head out.

She turned back to Patronas. "It's perfect," she said with a grin.

In the days that followed, Costas quickly settled into her new life on Chios, filling in for Patronas at the dig site and subbing for him at the police station on occasion. Patronas' colleagues had looked askance her at first, but they gradually got used to her presence, appreciating how hard she worked and her willingness to undertake any task that was asked of her.

She seemed far calmer than she'd been on Spetses and appeared to have stopped drinking; her eyes were clear in the morning when she came into work, her hands steady. She even joked around and laughed with the others at the station, so much so that even Tembelos came around and chipped in part of his paycheck for her salary, saying from what he'd read, geishas were underpaid.

* * *

After returning to Chios, Patronas often took long, solitary walks in the evening, seeking to regroup. He continued to dwell on the case, specifically the mistakes that he'd made. Papa Michalis had never mentioned Daphne Papadopoulos again and refused to discuss her when Patronas had brought it up. Perhaps he, too, felt guilty about what had happened. Patronas didn't know.

Seeking to cheer him up, Lydia prepared all his favorite foods for dinner one night—*kokkinisto*, beef braised in fresh tomatoes, *dolmadakia*, vine leaves, with *avgolemono*, a sauce made of eggs and lemon. And for dessert, miracle of miracles, fresh *loucoumades*, fried honey balls. The latter had gotten away from her; and they were three times the normal size, as big as oranges and a hundred times more delicious.

After they finished eating, they moved out to the terrace and watched the stars come out. Patronas had been teaching Lydia what he knew of astronomy; and she was an apt pupil, pointing out the various constellations to him. A meteorite went by and they both wished on it. His was simple: may this moment last forever. He had no idea what Lydia wished for.

There was a chill in the air, a hint of winter; and Patronas put his arm around her and drew her close to him, burying his fingers in her tangled hair.

Taking a deep breath, he told her about Dimitra. "She's on her way back to Chios. She's got cancer and she asked me to drive her to her appointments. That's the reason she was calling."

"How bad is it?" Lydia asked.

"She didn't say. All she said was her chemo would last twelve weeks and she might need a course of radiation after it finished."

Lydia listened carefully as he described what Dimitra had said about her prognosis and the doctor's proposed course of treatment; and she kissed him hard after he finished. A long, lingering soulful kiss. He held on to her, afraid Dimitra's resurfacing would cause problems between them.

But Lydia surprised him. "It was good of you to volunteer to drive her to the hospital. Yannis. Chemo's tough. It can be very hard on people."

She continued to talk about what he should do for Dimitra. Special foods and new pajamas, an iPad to distract her during treatment. Patronas listened with growing alarm.

A flaw in Lydia, he believed, this foolish trusting of people, this bottomless well of optimism. She might have started out Greek, but her years in America had ruined her. He'd read once, 'hell was other people,' and so it was in his experience, especially when it came to ex-wives.

Lydia refused to accept this and they'd argued about it more than once. To bolster her case, she'd even quoted Anne Frank, claiming 'people were basically good at heart.' When Patronas pointed out things hadn't gone so well for Anne Frank, Lydia had burst into tears, saying he was a heartless man. Sometimes it was like being married to a child.

"We'll take care of her together," Lydia said. "Kindness is everything."

Patronas looked out at the darkness. He'd been a policeman his entire adult life and, in his opinion, kindness wasn't everything. It wasn't even on the list. Other qualities—greed, fear, lust, to name a few—inevitably ruled the day. Forewarned was forearmed. And forearmed he intended to be with Dimitra.

"When she's coming?" Lydia asked.

"Tomorrow. She'll be flying in from Athens."

"We can work this out, Yannis," Lydia said. "We've got so much. We can afford to be generous. From what you said, she doesn't have long to live."

"You don't know her. Tembelos says she's like Rasputin."

"Kindness is everything," his wife insisted.

"Rasputin," he said again.

* * *

After Lydia fell asleep, Patronas changed into his swimming suit and walked down to the cove. He jumped in, shuddering as he hit the cold water, and swam as fast as he could across the cove. A fierce wind was blowing; and it bent the trees along the shore nearly double and sent pine needles flying, scattering them across the surface of the water.

Laying on his back, Patronas watched the sky, paddling now and then to stay afloat. As he'd told Costas, swimming usually brought him a measure of peace, but tonight it eluded him. Diving deep, he stayed under as long under as his lungs would allow, then broke the surface with a splash, gasping for air.

He heard an owl in the distance, its distinct cry echoing across the cove. It was followed by a rustling in the bushes as the bird's prey sought cover. Like the timid creatures he heard scurrying away, Patronas, too, was afraid. Not, as they were, of the owl, but of the future.

No matter what happened, Dimitra would certainly make her presence felt in his life. He knew her. She was a man-eater, a great white shark, who didn't just bite the hand that fed her, she devoured the person it was attached to. And within hours, she would be arriving on Chios. He could almost see the fin circling him in the water.

She'd never been able to tolerate the happiness of others, was always jealous and did what she could to destroy it. There was no reason to think that she'd changed.

An uncle had given him a conch shell when he was a boy, held it up to his ear and told him to listen. Patronas remembered being transfixed by what he'd heard, the faint call of the sea from deep inside the shell.

Even without it, he could hear the sea now, hear it roaring as it neared the shore, thundering as it bore down upon him. The waves rising higher and then higher still, threatening to drown him, drown his fragile happiness.

About the Author

Leta Serafim is a former journalist who worked at the Washington Post and Los Angeles Times Washington Bureau for many years. In addition to the Greek Island Mystery series, she is the author of a historical novel, To Look on Death No More, based on actual events in Greece during World War II and the children's picture book, *Molly Saw A Bear*.